"Remember what they said about you marrying Dan? Well, I wish you would," Alice pleaded, "I wish you would . . ."

She took Lesley's arm eagerly before she could reply. "If you stayed here it would be all right. I wouldn't be so frightened of the vastness, and the silence in the middle of the night . . . it's as if there's nothing there . . ."

"In the middle of the night, my dear, you'll have Randolph. Just wait till you're married. You won't be frightened any more." For once Lesley was very cold toward her cousin.

Marry Dan? How ridiculous! Lesley was to have been a bride once before—but Alec kept putting off the marriage. And now she was standing in Australia, attending her cousin's wedding, wearing a bridesmaid's dress that was to have been her wedding gown. . . .

NOBODY READS JUST *ONE* LUCY WALKER!

Available from Beagle Books

SWEET AND FARAWAY

Lucy Walker

BEAGLE BOOKS • NEW YORK
An Intext Publisher

This edition published by arrangement with
Crown Publishers, Inc.

First printing: November 1970
Second printing: April 1971
Third printing: April 1972

Printed in the United States of America

BEAGLE BOOKS, INC.
101 Fifth Avenue, New York, NY 10003

CHAPTER ONE

LESLEY WILSON stood at the rails of the coastal ship and watched the solitary figure coming up the jetty from the far shore. Mrs. Lockhart, one of her ship companions, stood on her toes peering into the distance to discern who might be the late-comer.

Lesley began to watch him too.

She had felt embarrassed watching the greeting between her cousin, Alice, and Randolph Baxter. The ship was not properly tied alongside yet and Alice and Randolph could only talk to one another over the side. Lesley sensed unease and anxiety in Alice, and it disturbed her.

So she watched the man coming up the jetty instead.

It was almost as if she were watching Fate make a quiet entry. She didn't know whether it was her mood, or the oddness of the early morning hour; or the fact that the sun had just risen over the rim of the desert, edging the man with black against its fiery red; but there was a hint of something eventful about his coming.

Those on the jetty below turned and looked at him too. He seemed to have an apocryphal importance to them.

Mrs. Lockhart gave a little jump of pleasure.

"Why, it's Dan Baxter!"

"It's Dan," said Randolph. "My brother. . . ."

The men on the wharf lifted their hands in greeting.

"Hiya, Dan!"

"Howya doin', Dan?"

"Where've you been, Dan?"

"Howzit, mate?"

His only answer was a quiet grin. He was dressed like his brother and the jackaroo Bill Daley. They all wore rather tight-fitting drill working trousers and cotton shirts; wide-brimmed slouch hats on the backs of their heads.

Dan Baxter spoke to his brother and then glanced up at the ship's side where Randolph was pointing to his fiancée, just arrived from England. Alice, her face a little white, was looking down.

Dan smiled and raised his hat. "My brother Dan, Alice!"

Alice said, "How do you do?" as she leaned over the ship's side, and Lesley saw her moisten her lips. Dan Baxter's eyes flicked along the faces above the rails. He recognised Mrs. Lockhart.

"What are you doing at sea, Mary? Thought you always went by plane."

He drawled when he spoke.

"I've travelled in her too many times to forsake the old tub altogether, Dan," Mrs. Lockhart said. She put her hand on Lesley's shoulder.

"Alice's cousin," she said. "Lesley Wilson . . . bridesmaid and companion all rolled in one."

Dan took his hat off and swung it round in his hand.

"How do you do?" Lesley said.

"Fine, thank you," said Dan. "How are you?"

Lesley swallowed a little dryly.

"I'm fine too, thank you," she said. She wondered if it sounded silly. Nobody smiled so it must have been the right reply, she thought.

Bill Daley, the jackaroo, half walked and half rolled to the edge of the jetty.

"What about me? Don't I get introduced too?"

"Miss Wilson to you, Bill," Mrs. Lockhart said with a laugh. "See you keep it that way too." She smiled down on Dan. "You'd better take care of Lesley, Dan. The boys might make it tough for her."

"It's a tough country," Dan said. He sounded as if he meant it yet he spoke so softly there was no edge to his words.

Lesley looked at the two brothers. She knew that Randolph, Alice's fiancé, was the younger, but she thought they were equal partners in the big station property which covered a million acres of North-west Australia. Randolph, it seemed, looked after the machinery and sheep, but Dan was a cattle man. Lesley now wished she had listened more intently when Alice and her parents had prattled about Alice's future home. She hadn't listened because she really hadn't cared at the time. She had been nursing her own hurt, which was too deep and too persistent to allow her time to worry about people who lived on the other side of the world. It was only at the last moment and in a desperation of embarrassed and hurt feelings that she had yielded to the persuasions of both her own and Alice's parents to make the journey to Australia as a companion to her cousin. For a month she had been living in a spiritual vacuum. She hadn't given a thought to the Baxters of Coolaroo . . . or to Australia.

She realised she had better begin to care now. It was clear that Alice wasn't the blushing bride she imagined she would be. Something was frightening Alice. Lesley realised she had better look closely at these two men—and their possessions —Alice's whole future depended on them.

Mrs. Lockhart's voice interrupted her thoughts.

"I guess Mrs. Collins stayed out at the station to prepare a decent meal for you," she said. "Mrs. Collins is an elderly cousin—she brought up Dan and Randolph really. She's something of an institution at Coolaroo. You'll both love her."

Lesley felt vaguely comforted on Alice's behalf.

As for herself——

Well, she couldn't care. If only Alec would write more often! Or better still, not at all!

If only she had never met him!

Alec Browning! What was he doing now? It would be night time in England! She shook her head. This was Australia.

She would have to care about Alice. Alice had had a tendency all her life to be first wilful, and then, when repentant, to be clinging and even helpless on occasions. That, of course, was why Alice's parents had wanted Lesley to accompany her cousin to Australia. Lesley's own parents had wanted her to go for different reasons. They just didn't think Alec was good enough and they wanted Lesley to go away and forget him. Easier said than done. Fairly easy to go, when the two families, together with her own good sense, combined to speed her. But not so easy to forget.

The silly things that make one remember with a sudden stab of pain! A Humber Snipe the same vintage as Alec's in Colombo; a letter from him at Fremantle. And always, all the time, a little sagging pain in her chest.

Here at Ninety Mile End an eager bridegroom!

Lesley watched a rope ladder go over the side and the two brothers, Randolph, the prospective bridegroom, first, come up the side of the ship.

She turned delicately away as Randolph put his arms round Alice. Perhaps when Alice felt his warm kiss and the pressure of his arms she would stop looking so disappointed and so frightened.

As for herself? That stab of pain was there again!

She looked at Dan, the other brother. She knew intuitively that one day she would regret not making the most of this moment. Yet she couldn't rise to anything but surface politeness.

He was a little above medium height and his face had the brown burned deep in it. The weather had beaten little fine lines on his forehead and at the corners of his mouth. He wrinkled up his eyes when he turned towards the shore and faced the light. Lesley thought that perhaps this brother looked a little older than he really was.

He shook hands with her thoughtfully, like a surgeon taking his first quick glance at a new patient. There was a certain shyness about him, however, as if it had been necessary for him to take this sharp appraising look—but he regretted having to do it. With the men his manner was less shy, and stronger. More firm.

"Can you beat up Jimmy Walkabout, Mary?" he asked Mrs. Lockhart. "Knowing him, I know there'll be a cup of tea somewhere about."

Jimmy Walkabout was the deck steward and knew everyone in the North-west; and everyone who had ever been there.

"Here he is now," said Mrs. Lockhart. "Anything in the larder, Jimmy?"

"Howdy, Mister Baxter! Well, if it isn't fine seeing you. We don't call in here once in a blue moon but I certainly look around to see who's here from Coolaroo. How's the drought, Boss?"

"Raking awful, Jimmy. Not a drop of rain round Coolaroo. Out at Mars a cloudburst shot through a belt about fifteen hundred yards wide and five miles long. The grass is shooting and the cattle's heading for it. If the barometer stays up we'll muster in a fortnight."

"A muster, *and* a wedding! Say, you do things grand when you really start out there at Coolaroo."

Randolph had turned round now, his arm through Alice's. Lesley noticed the colour had come back into Alice's face. She looked better. It must have been the kiss that had done it—the physical touch!

Lesley had a little stab of pain and noticed Dan's quick surgeon eyes flick away from her. She must have shown her thoughts on her face.

"How you like your girl friend, Mr. Randolph?" Jimmy Walkabout asked. "She's been a great success on board. And the other Miss Wilson too." He beamed on Lesley. "She don't look so serious when she smiles. She sure has got a nice smile."

Everyone laughed and Lesley's smile shone through quite suddenly. She had lovely white shining teeth and a kind and generous mouth. Even Randolph looked at her with interest.

"It was kind of you to come all this way with Alice," he said. He was like Dan, only younger, less mature and less certain. He was terrifically happy to have Alice under his arm, but at the same time was embarrassed by the difficulties of a first greeting in the presence of so many people.

"She'll enjoy it," Mrs. Lockhart said kindly.

Bill Daley had clambered over the side. He stood, hands on his hips, looking down on the girls.

"Toss you which one I have, Randolph, and which is yours."

It was the kind of smart talk Alec Browning had indulged in; that her parents had hated and her own heart had rebelled against. Lesley looked at Bill Daley coldly. She was not going to like him. Not yet, anyway.

"I've got mine right where she's going to stay," Randolph said with a grin. "Under my thumb."

"Nuts," said Bill Daley. "Nobody at Coolaroo has anything under his thumb except Dan. Dan has the whole raking works where he wants them."

He tried to win a smile from Lesley with an arch of his already arched eyebrows. There was something mephistophelian about his too-handsome face. But Lesley's smile had closed down for this session.

"Oh well," Bill shrugged his shoulders. "What chance has a man got when the other fellow is the best man——"

"You know Mrs. Lockhart, Bill?" it was Dan's quiet voice that intervened.

Bill Daley bowed elaborately.

"Indeed and I do, and how are you this fine morning, Mrs. Lockhart? On top of the world?"

"I'm glad I'm not too old for you to take notice of me, Bill. With two such charming ladies in competition, of course, I can hardly hope for the first greeting."

"Madam—your humble and obedient servant!" Bill was all contrition and the elegant manner in which he offered Mrs. Lockhart his arm to escort her along the deck took the edge off Lesley's dislike.

"I think you and Alice had better have breakfast on board," Dan said to Lesley as they moved off in the direction of the steward's pantry. "It'll be hot and unpleasant in the hotel and the sooner we move off, the sooner we'll be home."

"Will it take long to get to Coolaroo?"

"With luck we'll be there by four o'clock this afternoon. There's a fair bit of climbing, you know. We go up into the second table-land. Then there'll be a lunch stop at the Gorge."

"The Gorge?"

Dan smiled.

"A little bit of heaven," he said.

The sunrise had touched the Indian Ocean with pink and amethyst feathers. The sun was shining flat and hot over the desert to the west. A little bit of heaven? Lesley shook her head. It was hardly possible.

As she went to her cabin to put the last minute things in her case she managed a word alone with Alice.

"How do you feel, Alice? Is it going to be all right?" Alice's mouth was still tremulous.

"I think it's all right, Lesley," she whispered. "He looked so different, at first. And that desert——"

"He's very nice," Lesley said consolingly.

Alice looked at her cousin anxiously.

"You think so?"

"Of course I do. If I didn't I'd make you call it off right here before the ship sailed."

Alice looked relieved.

"I expect it is because I haven't seen him for so long. And in England . . . he looked so different."

"Of course he did. He was dressed for the English climate. But it's the same person, you know. And he's nice. Very nice."

CHAPTER TWO

The nicest thing that happened to the Wilson cousins in the coastal town of Ninety Mile End was the meeting with the Macfarlanes.

They had come into the lounge of the hotel rubbing their black curly heads and looked young and crestfallen. They had slept through the arrival of the ship.

When they saw Lesley and Alice they began to precipitate themselves backwards out of the room, but Dan, coming in, grasped them each by a shoulder.

"Come on," Dan said. "Be introduced. These are the girls we've come to take to Coolaroo."

Looking like two bashful schoolboys they allowed Dan to present them.

"Andrew on my right," he said. "And William on my left. Miss Alice Wilson is the golden girl and Miss Lesley Wilson with the dark hair."

They bowed and said "How do you do" in the faintest of Irish brogues. Their manners were courtly and their bows elegant, considering they were in crumpled khaki trousers and gay, equally crumpled tartan shirts, open at the neck.

Lesley said, "How do you do," and couldn't help smiling in return as Andrew's brilliant blue eyes looked beseechingly at her. William was looking steadily and invitingly at Alice. He was a young man who would never have to open his mouth to make love. His eyes did it for him. The colour stole up Alice's pale cheeks.

"You wouldn't be two Irishmen?" Lesley asked.

With a whoop they flung themselves down, Andrew beside Lesley on the settee, and William on the arm of Alice's easy-chair.

"From County Down and no other," said Andrew.

"Where the Mountains of Mourne sweep down to the sea!" said William.

"I learned Gaelic at my mother's breast!" said Andrew.

Dan Baxter had been rolling a cigarette. He looked up with a smile.

"They're a couple of liars," he said. "They were born right here in Ninety Mile End. Their only claim to being Irish is their paternal relative, who was born in Ireland; and Hannans Downs has got more Irishmen working on it than would be found in County Down itself."

"Even the blacks are Irish," Andrew said.

"My father taught them English 'as she is spoke by the Irish'," said William.

"The cockatoos repeat everything they overhear in Irish," said William.

"That would be real parrot talk," Lesley said dryly. There was a shout of laughter and Dan gave her another of his quick, appraising glances. At that moment Randolph came in to say the fleet for Coolaroo was ready.

"*My* girl," he said with emphasis to William and jokingly made to elbow William out of the way.

"And have you got claims on Lesley, Dan?" Andrew asked. "If so, speak now, or for ever hold your peace." He looked mischievously across at Alice and Randolph at his brother. "I'll beat you to her, Bill."

"She's Dan's till after the wedding," said Randolph. "After that it can be ladies' choice."

Lesley wished she didn't feel faintly wearied by this badinage. There was something sweet and naïve about it—but somehow it didn't touch her. She could never, even in a laughing moment, escape the little nagging pain in her heart. If only Alec had been like these boys—like Dan with his quiet calm, the hint of power and decision behind his eyes. Instead of that he was just a no-hoper she had got in the habit of loving.

11

Dan made a gesture towards the door and Lesley followed Alec and Randolph out into the hot road.

The Macfarlanes bowed low, hands over hearts.

"We meet again," Andrew said.

"At Philippi," William said.

"I suppose they mean the wedding?" Lesley asked Dan politely.

"That's what they mean—and the muster. Everyone comes to a celebration."

"How far will they come?"

"Two hundred and ten miles."

"By car?"

"No. By plane. Their own. Two years ago they bought two Anson bombers—one to fly and one for spare parts."

Lesley was surprised. As they stood by one of the cars Dan measured his height beside Lesley. He smiled at her in a friendly way.

"Six inches. Is that enough for a best man over the bridesmaid?"

"I think so," Lesley said.

The fleet for Coolaroo consisted of a heavy Dodge sedan, a Landrover and a big Ford Utility truck: the last almost fantastically splendid in its body-work.

The cars were all loaded up.

"Gear for the wedding," Bill explained.

The girls' luggage was mostly carried in the racks on the hood of the Dodge and in the back of the Landrover. The luggage hold of the Dodge carried the picnic lunch for the overlanding party.

"We look as if we're going out into the desert for ever," Lesley said lightly. Alice gave her a quick, frightened look and turned back to the seaward side of the main street. Lesley thought Alice looked vaguely hunted. She also hoped that Randolph would remember to kiss Alice when he packed her in the Utility. It was wonderful what a kiss at the right moment would do. Again she felt that pang of pain and regret. How often had she longed for Alec to heal a breach with a quick uninvited kiss!

Lesley smiled a little weakly at Dan and took her place in the back seat of the Dodge. Dan had a black boy, resplendent in a sky-blue satin shirt and sombrero, sitting beside him in the front seat. He was called Abe.

At the last moment the Macfarlanes came hastily out of the hotel and flung some parcels on the back seat of the Dodge.

"For Betsy with my love!" said Andrew.

"For Neil . . . with the back of my hand!" said William.

"For Mrs. Collins from us both!" they chanted together.

"Him fella Macfarlane talk plenty like cockatoo," Abe said succinctly, as the car rolled, heavy laden, down the wide unmade street.

"That's just what Miss Wilson said—only more politely," Dan said as he swung the car round a corner and headed for the open plain. There was silence in the car as it ate up the miles of spinifex as they crossed the plain. In the distance the ranges stood against the sky like a blue razorback.

"Ghost gums!" The black boy smiled as he pointed his finger towards a clump of trees.

The day grew hotter.

It seemed hours before the car turned south and Lesley could see they were above the level of the plain they had just crossed. They seemed to be running over level, trackless ground when the car pulled up suddenly.

Bill Daley swung the Landrover round beside them and a minute or two later the Utility came up.

Lesley thought it a strange and uninviting place to stop for lunch.

Dan opened the door for Lesley.

"There's a gorge about forty yards ahead," he said. "See the crack in the ground? It's quite wide when you get up to it—and that clump of green is the top of a cajeput tree growing ninety feet below."

Randolph had taken Alice's arm and walked towards the break in the ground. Lesley heard Alice's exclamation. Then she came up beside them and looked down. There below her was one of the wonders of the earth.

Deep down in the gorge were trees, ferns, red steps running slantwise up the cliff; jasper bars, arching cool caves, strata of shining blue minerals striping the cliff and lying in the bottom of a creek, mirror-still, and the colour of green olives. It was cool and inviting, a magic cavern of water, shade, colour and light.

"Oh!" Astonishment had shocked Lesley out of her dream of herself.

Dan Baxter looked at her with that quick appraising glance that sometimes disturbed the quiet reserve of his face. Then he looked away.

"How did it get there?" asked Alice.

"The underground spring carved out the gorge where it surfaced between the layers of ironstone. It's been thousands of years doing it," Randolph said.

13

"But the colours! The red and blue and green! It shines like Aladdin's cave!"

"That's the North-west; it's all minerals. Those marble bars across the creek are of jasper; the blue is asbestos, the red is ochre from ironstone and laterite. And the green—well, that's just coolness and shade where the ferns and trees grow, plus a bit of copper here and there."

Lesley looked inquiringly at Randolph.

"How many minerals . . .?"

"Hundreds. They mine gold and silver in small shows all around. There's tantalite and uranium, too. The mounted police from Ninety Mile End had to go out two days ago looking for a uranium prospector who's lost out this way somewhere."

"They didn't find him, either," said Dan to Randolph.

"They've asked us to keep a look-out on the way to Coolaroo."

"Has this place got a name?" Alice asked.

"Baxter's Gorge," Randolph said. "Our grandfather found it and was the first white man to go down it."

"It's called after your grandfather?"

"After us all," Dan said quietly. "You're standing on the boundary of Coolaroo Downs."

Leslie remembered snatches of a famous poem:

"A savage place, holy and enchanted . . . five miles meandering."

The black boys had brought the picnic boxes from the car and were carrying them down the steps into the gorge.

"We go down?" Lesley asked.

She began to walk towards the gravelly path leading to the steps. Dan gave her his hand.

"Those tiny pebbles are slippery," he said. At the top step Lesley let go his hand and ran lightly from one to another, down, down, down. The cool sweet fern-smelling air rose to greet her and gently lave her skin.

She looked back and saw Randolph and Alice coming down, Randolph protectingly holding Alice's hand all the way.

Lunch. A fire of sticks between two stones and billy tea. Tinned fruit carried in a vacuum billycan so that it was cold and sweet to the parched palates. Dry biscuits with cold meat and cheese. Conversation about fleeces; the grass shooting at Mars and how soon the cattle would find it; why the hell Dan didn't get rid of the flaming cattle anyway, and where the deuce that prospector had got himself lost.

Alice listened and looked wintry again. Lesley began to

take an interest in the way the men talked together. They seemed to change their personality and a hard streak came through in their voices; their eyes, screwed up and reflective, hid a glint of stubbornness and the will to persist.

Lesley found this interesting. They were quite different from the easy-going, friendly, rather shy men who had taken them from the ship into the hotel at Ninety Mile End. They were men who, in their drawling voices, could talk hard and win the hard way. It chilled Alice but it roused Lesley. Perhaps the few weeks she would stay here until Alice was settled wouldn't be so uninteresting after all.

At last Dan gave the order to break camp.

"With luck we ought to be home by four."

Then began the long, exhausting climb out of the gorge. The black stockman in the gorgeous shirt packed away the lunch things in the back of the Dodge.

"I'll take the Rover," Dan said to Bill. "You take Miss Wilson in the front seat with you, it might be a change for her. Abe can come in the Rover with Joe and me."

Joe was the other black boy who had accompanied Bill.

Lesley felt unexpectedly disappointed. In spite of his tendency to silence she had liked Dan at the wheel. She had felt comfortable and safe. His movements were quiet and easy, yet one defined the ability to move like lightning if necessary.

She didn't really mind Bill Daley. It was the mental effort that would be required all the time to keep up with his sallies.

Lesley wanted to get back to her inner self—to get on with the train of thought she could not resist but which was a whip with which she scourged herself.

Coolaroo homestead was on the upper tableland and stood in a grassy plain; the blue ranges seemed only a few miles nearer. To reach it the cars passed over a small watercourse where the trees stood about in an aged silence that made Lesley feel they had been there for ever and ever. The line of the watercourse could be marked over the flat land by the string of trees that stood on either side.

Beyond the watercourse was another stretch of plain, then a plantation of mulga, a low scrub. Out again on the plain and there beyond stood the homestead, a big, square house with wide verandas all round, two tank-stands like towers, and a host of small buildings and outhouses clustering round the main house.

It all seemed quiet until the cars drove up to the gate of a small tropical garden. Then in the distance the girls could see little black figures hovering round the doorways of some of the lesser houses, a Chinaman outside what was obviously the cook-house and two women in bright, fresh cotton frocks sitting in low-slung canvas chairs on the side cement veranda of the homestead. One of them, an elderly woman with white hair, a gracious manner and a young face, came to the top of the steps to meet the cousins.

"How do you do," she said as she shook hands first with Alice—because Randolph was presenting her and she was so obviously his bride—and then Lesley. "I'm Mrs. Collins, the housekeeper. I hope Dan and Randolph told you about us all."

"Do get out of the way, Con," a petulant voice said from the veranda. "I'm dying to see what Alice looks like."

Lesley wondered if the owner of the voice was an invalid. Alice crossed the veranda and shook hands with a rather big, very lovely woman.

"I'm Betsy," the languid voice said. "I'm another cousin —like Con—only once removed though. Con is about twice removed. We're all related in the North-west and some of us don't really know who to—but that doesn't matter. You're awfully young, aren't you, my dear?"

Alice was obviously relieved by the signs of comfort around her and by Betsy's apparent, though rather untidy, fashionableness. Betsy, Lesley thought, was like an over-bloomed rose.

"I'm twenty-five," Alice said. "Perhaps I look younger than I ought—for station life."

"Nonsense, child. You've got to be young. Otherwise the life will kill you." This seemed to be the opposite of what she had been about to say in the first place. Her voice was languid though not unpleasant. Her manner was tired but not unfriendly. She looked around Alice at Lesley.

"You're a cousin—or something—too, aren't you? How on earth would the human race go on without cousins? And fancy coming all this way to see one married!"

Lesley shook hands. She had never met anyone like Betsy before. She wondered what was the rest of her name and why she and Alice had not heard of her before.

Randolph came over now and bending down over the chair kissed Betsy on the cheek.

"Well, old girl!" he said. "How did you get here, and what have you done with Brian?"

"He flew me in last night, two hours after you left for Ninety Mile End. We've had a row, so he's gone to Melbourne to buy for the stud and I'm going to stay here."

"Good for you. You can look after Alice for me."

"Look after nobody. Somebody's going to look after me. I'm *tired*."

Dan stepped up on to the veranda and stood looking down at Betsy with a mild grin.

"Was there ever a time when you weren't tired, Betsy?"

"I'm never tired looking at you, Dan. You make me feel the world's not full of yokels after all."

He bent down and kissed her on the cheek as Randolph had done. When he straightened up he turned to Lesley.

"This is Betsy Baxter," he said. "She is married to a cousin who has a station farther north."

Lesley smiled politely again. Dan looked away from her to Betsy.

"Jimmy Walkabout says she doesn't look so serious when she smiles," he said. "And she did smile once—very early this morning."

Mrs. Collins came up and took Lesley's hand case from her.

"Don't do it too often in this climate," she said. "It gives you wrinkles round the mouth. That's what's wrong with Dan—it's his smile——".

Lesley found herself looking into Dan's face and he into hers. This discussion about the relative merits of their smiles had caught them each wondering about the other. Simultaneously they broke into laughter. Lesley was suddenly transformed into a rather young and lovely English girl with a smile like sunshine. Then it became self-conscious and a little wistful. She turned quickly to Mrs. Collins.

"I'll carry that—you mustn't trouble. It's so light really."

"Nonsense. Come along and have a wash up while I make the tea. Randolph will look after Alice, I'm sure."

Lesley followed Mrs. Collins down a passage, through the house on to a veranda on the other side. From this was a short covered way leading to an annexe—a cement brick building and evidently much newer than the old homestead.

"You've got a room each until the wedding guests arrive," Mrs. Collins said. "Then you'll have to share. Will you mind?"

"Not in the least," Lesley said. "Are you expecting many for the wedding?"

"About thirty. Not counting those who will fly in and camp out in the mulga."

"Do many fly?"

"Nearly all of them. They've mostly got planes. Not Dan and Randolph though—they were both naval men in the war.

17

The others all learned their sky tricks from being in the Air Force or having older brothers in it, like the Macfarlanes. The Air Force was quite the fashion in the North-west during the war. Bill Daley is a pilot and he's always bothering Dan and Randolph to buy a Dove or Moth plane."

" It would make a difference to the isolation, wouldn't it?"

" That's what the boys like about Coolaroo. Alice might get Randolph to weaken, however. We must wait and see."

Lesley didn't know much about Alice's persuasive qualities. She knew that Alice often got her own way when she herself could take the initiative. How she would fare persuading a husband, Lesley couldn't guess. Randolph, however, looked easy-going and very easily pleased himself. Lesley felt rather tenderly towards his boyish pleasure, half masked by shyness, in bringing Alice to the station. He would be kind to Alice, that was clear. There was no hardness in him.

Dan now. He was another cup of tea altogether. There was a core of firmness in Dan. If it had been he whom Alice had crossed the world to marry there mightn't have been such a good chance of her getting her own way.

On the other hand, was it good for Alice to get her own way?

The room to which Mrs. Collins took Lesley was a large, square, cool room. The annexe, she thought, was decidedly cooler than the inside of the house.

" I'm afraid it's hot at night time," Mrs. Collins said. " The wooden part of the old homestead is hot in the daytime but cools down quickly. Everyone sleeps out on the verandas. We thought you might not be used to it and would wait and see which you would prefer."

When Lesley had glanced round the room she turned to Mrs. Collins with a smile.

" I think all this brightness must be your doing," she said. " I can't believe the brothers would have had much to do with those chintzes and muslins."

Long sheer muslin curtains hung from the double windows, and all the chairs, including two small easy-chairs, were neatly covered in pretty pastel chintz.

" We took the patterns from English magazines," Mrs. Collins said. " We thought it would make Alice feel more at home. And this is to be her sitting-room when they come back from the honeymoon. The next room is the bedroom and it leads on to a cement veranda facing south. It will be quite cut off from the rest of the house so they will be private."

Mrs. Collins looked at Lesley with a conspiratorial smile. " Would you like to see it?"

"I would—but is it a surprise for Alice? Should I wait till she has seen it?"

"No. Because we need your advice. You must tell me what I can do to add to its comfort while they are away. Unfortunately it will have to be used by the wedding guests."

Mrs. Collins had walked to the door and now led the way down the short passage. Through the open door at the end of it Lesley could see the patch of mulga across the plain. Beyond it were the trees along the watercourse.

When the bedroom door was opened Lesley thought the whole effect was charming. The whole room had been done in matching English chintzes and on the floor, which was wall-to-wall covered by a linoleum, was a dark pink carpet.

Lesley felt the room had only one disadvantage. It looked, and all the furniture in it, so painfully new. It didn't look lived in. Knowing Alice, Lesley felt the stiffness of the room could be broken by putting about a few personal possessions.

At the foot of the two pretty beds were long, double windows opening out on to the veranda. This was wire-netted against mosquitoes and flies and also contained two brand-new unslept-in beds.

Lesley suddenly thought of the long, long drive from Ninety Mile End.

"However did you get all this stuff here?" she asked.

"By ship, by truck and by plane. Randolph has been working on it for a year. In fact he hasn't had his mind on anything else. Dan has done all the work on the run; and they all helped make the bricks."

"Make the bricks?"

"Cement bricks. Yes, they built this annexe. Randolph and Dan, and young Neil, Betsy's boy—whenever he could get across from Alexander. In fact they've all become infected with building mania. Dan is going to build himself a house on the other side of the mulga. He's got the concrete mixing machine down there now, and young Neil's been at it all day."

"Neil is here now? Neil Baxter. Is that right?"

"Yes. They're all Baxters. Betsy was a Baxter before she married too . . . she married a distant cousin."

Mrs. Collins now pointed out the way to the shower room. It was under one of the big tank-stands.

"Mind that hot water tap," she said. "The water is sun-heated through those coils passing round the tank. It's nearly boiling in the middle of the day."

"I think I'd like a cold shower," Lesley said with a smile. It was intolerably hot.

When Mrs. Collins had gone away she took off her dress

and lay down for a moment on her bed. Where was Alice? Was Randolph making her happy?

Lesley felt tired to the point of extreme exhaustion. She had been up since before dawn.

Her eyelids dropped over her eyes. She thought she would rest . . . for just a few minutes . . .

CHAPTER THREE

There was mounting excitement at Coolaroo as the wedding day drew near. A plane had come in off the regular run to bring an entire load of fresh vegetables, salads and fruits; of turkeys, chickens and crayfish tails, all of which were placed without delay in the deep freeze off the engine room.

Nothing was too much trouble for Randolph. Alice might have been not only his bride but his queen. The only drawback about his enthusiasm was that he spent so much time on preparations, on organising the station and the neighbours, that he had only time for the shortest of sessions alone with Alice when he came in off the run or from the wireless transceiver set where the whole North-west was ringing with the daily doings of the Coolaroo wedding.

All of this stirred Lesley to interest but left Alice puzzled and faintly discontented that she saw so little of Randolph. Lesley rightly guessed that when Alice was with her fiancé her misgivings were allayed. When he was away from her the strangeness of the life, the vastness of the distances, and the extraordinary interchange of daily conversations with people hundreds and hundreds of miles apart—as if they were next-door neighbours—intimidated her.

" But they are next-door neighbours," Bill Daley said. " Joe Brennan from Witchery now—he's only a hundred and thirty-seven miles away. And the Macfarlanes——"

" Alice thinks they ought to sound like a hundred and thirty-seven miles away . . ." Betsy said in her drawling languid voice. " On the wireless they sound as if they're in the next room."

" I don't think so at all," Alice said. " It's just that it's all so *odd*."

Betsy looked at her across the veranda with lovely, sleepy cat's eyes. There was a bored scepticism in her manner towards Alice. It was clear, even to Lesley, that Betsy had no faith in Alice making a success of managing a station homestead.

"Good job Con's always around," Betsy said once. "What the deuce would happen to Coolaroo without Con—I don't know."

Neil, her twelve-year-old son, had intervened on this one.

"I think Dan runs Coolaroo. Of course I know Randolph is supposed to run his share of it too. And he talks more than Dan does. But underneath it's Dan who really does the thinking."

"You're too perspicacious for a child, Neil—" Betsy said.

"Perspi . . . what?" said Neil.

"Go and look it up in a dictionary," Dan said. "That's the best way you'll educate yourself."

"Making bricks is an education. You said so," said Neil.

"That's because I was making use of you, my boy. I had to have a rational excuse."

"Is that where you keep sneaking off to, Dan? Building your own house? What for? Alice and Randolph won't need the homestead as well as the annexe."

"He might get married himself," said Neil. "I think he ought to marry Lesley. Then she wouldn't have to go all that way back to England and it would save a lot of trouble if they both got married at once."

Nobody said anything for a few minutes. Lesley went on idly gazing out over the plain. She hardly heard what the boy was saying. Dan rolled himself a cigarette and had arrived at the licking stage before he vouchsafed an answer.

"Maybe Lesley's not the marrying kind either . . ." he said softly. "And that's something you don't pry into, boy. Never ask a woman her politics, the state of her bank account or her matrimonial intentions. It's bad manners."

Lesley went on with her faintly wistful day-dreaming, but Betsy was watching her profile.

"Nothing clicks there——" she thought. "Well, she's the only woman in the North-west who is *not* setting her hat for Dan. Must be a love affair in her own country."

"How long are you staying, Lesley?" she asked. She sounded only half interested, but in reality her ears were sharply pricked for the faintest edge of feeling that Lesley might show in her answer.

"I have an option on two ships," Lesley replied. "The first leaves Fremantle about a fortnight after the wedding and about the time Alice and Randolph are due back from Adelaide. The second goes a fortnight later. It really depends on whether Alice would like me here when she returns or not. I haven't pressed her yet."

"It's a long way to come for so short a time," Betsy said. "You'd better persuade her into staying for the Alexander River races anyway, Dan."

"I hope she won't need persuading," Dan said. "We all want Lesley to stay. Specially Alice, I think."

This, too, was said without the ease with which Dan usually spoke. Then he, too, had noticed how doubtful Alice seemed about settling down! Lesley reflected that it would matter a great deal to all their comfort if Alice was happy. They all had to live so close together!

Lesley later asked Alice about this.

They were in their room changing into fresh, pretty cotton frocks for the evening meal.

"You'll be glad of Mrs. Collins, won't you, Alice? She knows the ropes of managing the homestead end of the station. And she'd be company for you during the day. I believe the men sometimes stay away days at a time when they're outback on the run."

"Oh, yes. I'd hate Mrs. Collins to go away," Alice said. She stopped parting her hair in the middle and looked at Lesley through the mirror.

"You don't think she would go?" she asked. There was an edge of panic in her voice. "I wouldn't understand all those black people—and the way the food is got out of the storehouse every day. And I couldn't bear to be alone."

Lesley tried her soothing tactics.

"I think she is more likely to be afraid you wouldn't want her than that she is likely to go. After all, this has always been her home. She brought up the two boys."

"But Dan's building a house. . . . Perhaps he means to take her there."

"Nonsense. Dan will get married too. And it's Randolph Mrs. Collins loves. She would never leave him unless you drove her away."

Alice moistened her lips and went on combing and parting her hair.

"I'd hate Betsy to stay," she said at last. "She's nice—but, oh, that laziness! And the sort of feline way she watches me . . ."

"Betsy's all right," Lesley said lightly. "She's just different from anyone we've ever known. She *is* lazy and that's all that is wrong with her. But she's very lovely—and quite often amusing."

Alice put down her comb and picked up her dress from the bed.

"You know, I thought she was an invalid at first."

Lesley laughed.

"So did I. And I was too nervous to ask what was the matter with her. I got quite a shock on the first night when she walked into dinner—as spry as any of us. But, let's not talk about her unkindly. I think she is rather kind underneath that tired and faintly feline manner. Get round the right side of her, Alice. She'll probably be a wonderful friend. As some kind of a relation she most likely feels she has a prior claim to your affections. So give her some. You never can tell, you might get lots back in return."

"Cast your bread on the waters . . . sort of thing. . . ."

The girls had their dresses on now. Alice turned impulsively to Lesley.

"You know what young Neil said about marrying Dan? I wish you would, Lesley. . . , Oh, I wish you would."

She took Lesley's arm eagerly.

"If you stayed here it would be all right. I wouldn't be so frightened of the vastness. That black, black sky at night and the silence!" She dropped Lesley's arm and lifted her hands to her face.

"The silence . . . in the middle of the night . . . it's like . . . as if there's nothing . . ."

"In the middle of the night, my dear, you'll have Randolph. Just wait till you're married. You won't be frightened any more."

For once Lesley's manner was faintly cold with Alice.

Marry Dan? Well, upon my word! Under her breath Lesley gave a short laugh. Then she thought of Dan. She had a sudden quick mental picture of him standing on the veranda, his slouch hat pushed back on his head, the inevitable cigarette being rolled between his fingers, his face lifted up quickly and his white teeth flashing in the brown of his face as he said:

"A kingdom? A man owns a kingdom when he runs cattle in the North-west. He is monarch of all he surveys— and it's not a legend."

There had been that quick challenging look in his eyes and then the quiet reserve had closed over his face. Yet, for one moment he had looked like a king. The way he stood, his feet a little apart, his body exactly balanced between them; a disregard for the things that didn't matter. There had been a small whip-like kind of a smile flick across his face and he had turned and walked down the steps from the veranda. The cattle king had gone out to his horse.

The mental picture faded but Lesley felt a sudden spasm of her heart.

How puny Alec would seem beside him. Alec! With his conquest of one small office square in Kensington High Street . . . and this man! Monarch, indeed, of all he surveyed. A million acres!

Lesley shook her head as if she had had an unexpected dream and let her hand rest on Alice's arm.

"If you want me to stay until you come back from Adelaide I'll do that," she said. "But not any longer. I've got to get back to my job. They mightn't hold it open for me too long."

"Your job? Off-sider to that little beast of an Alec Browning? I don't want to hurt you, Lesley . . . but I hope he's got someone else by the time you do get back. It's the only way to shake you off him."

Lesley felt faintly annoyed with Alice's selfishness, but, strangely, the words didn't scarify that old wound as they had so often done before. In fact she didn't feel very hurt at all.

Alice had no trouble with her love affairs, only with her surroundings.

Two days before the wedding people began to arrive.

The first was a Utility truck loaded to the last top inch with camping gear, water-bags hanging from the bumpers and axles—the whole covered with a thick brown layer of dried, caked mud.

Randolph came riding in from the stockyards down by the mulga and Bill Daley galloped across the plain to meet the truck. The driver was a pearler from Broome with his first mate and his wife.

"Passing this way . . ." he said. "So I had to be in on it. When's the wedding and where's the bride?"

The truck came on across the plain to the gate of the tropical garden around the homestead. Randolph had gone out and there was much back slapping and shouting of greetings.

"Look who's here," Randolph said, leading the party, dust-laden and rolling in their gaits, to the veranda.

"Well, if it's not Bill Halidane himself," drawled Betsy, without getting up from her chair. "Couldn't be a wedding without you, Bill."

"There's hardly one he's missed," his wife said, sitting down quickly in one of the low-slung chairs. "My hat, it's hot!"

The men were led inside and Dan came round the veranda from the cook-house direction. He shook hands with Mrs. Halidane warmly. She was a plump woman, fortyish, with good-nature written large all over her face.

"Where did you come through the mud?" he asked.

"Round by Mars," she said. "It's grand out there, Dan, and there's cattle already coming down from the hills. You'll have a grand muster if the barometer keeps up."

That was enough for Dan. He went to the hall door and tapped the barometer hanging on the wall inside.

"All right so far," he said with a grin. "A downpour all over Coolaroo and the ranges would disperse the brutes everywhere. God knows we want rain—but let's muster at Mars first!"

"What on earth did you go round Mars way for?" Betsy asked.

"The prospector," Mrs. Halidane said. "They haven't found a trace of him. Everyone going through Ninety Mile End is deflected a little to get as much ground covered as possible."

"Sergeant Holland is due through here anytime," Betsy said with a yawn. "I hope they don't bring him in dead. That would spoil the wedding."

Mrs. Halidane was looking at Lesley curiously. In their quick exchange of news the Coolaroo people had not yet introduced Lesley.

"This is Lesley Wilson," Betsy said. "And don't look at her quite so earnestly. She is *not* the bride."

"She's pretty enough," Mrs. Halidane said. "How do you do, Miss Wilson? How do you like the North?"

"She's much too well-mannered to make any adverse comments," Betsy said. "It's more instructive to watch her face."

Lesley looked at Betsy with some surprise. She didn't know Betsy took so much interest in her.

"My face?" she said. "I hope it registers my gratitude for all your hospitality. I've never met its equal. I think the way Dan refrains from riding out and around his beloved run in order to see that Alice has the best possible wedding and that I want for nothing . . . is chivalry itself. I know his heart is on the run and he would really like to go out to Mars and see how much the cattle are rallying to the feed."

Dan looked at Lesley with interest.

"I'm afraid the wedding and the ladies would take precedence over cattle any time," he said. "But that was a nice speech, Lesley."

Lesley was aware now that Betsy was watching her with a faintly ironical smile. She hoped she didn't think that she, Lesley, was making pretty speeches to Dan in order to make an impression on him. The colour crept up her cheek.

"Have you come far, Mrs. Halidane?" she asked politely.

"Five hundred miles. One of the luggers got blown ashore in that blow that gave Dan his rainfall out at Mars. Bill had to come down to see if it could be salvaged."

Mrs. Collins now appeared. She walked happily over towards her guests.

"What luck!" she said with real pleasure. "We didn't count on you and Bill, Janet."

Tea and traymobiles laden with food appeared in Mrs. Collins's wake.

"Hallo, Belle. How are you?" Mrs. Halidane asked the lubra with a smile. Belle giggled self-consciously.

"I plenty good, Mis' Hald'un. You come down for weddin'. Plenty food everywhere. You stay long time?"

"Till the wedding's over, Belle. Where's the best place to camp, Dan? In the mulga, I suppose?"

"Bill and Ed can camp," Dan said quietly. "I expect Con will find a bed in the homestead for you."

"Of course," Mrs. Collins said. "You come in with me, Janet. Then we can really talk."

"What's the news, anyway?"

"The chief news is that the drought's breaking, Dan. Thunderstorms like you got out at Mars are turning into real downpours up in the Kimberleys. It's two years since there was water in the Roberts River and it's flowing freely."

"It's three years since we had any here in Coolaroo stream," Mrs. Collins said. "We want it badly—but please God it will hold off until Dan gets the round-up at Mars over. Then please God it will come in torrents!"

Dan said "Amen!" and Betsy yawned.

There was a sudden silence and everyone cocked an ear as if listening. Dan went to the edge of the veranda and peered out into the eastern sky.

"There she comes," he said at last. "Bet it's the Brennans."

A speck in the sky became a hum like a bee and a minute later a plane could be seen coming in low towards the homestead. Randolph and his two guests came round the side of the garden and Bill Daley came clumping through the house.

"Where is Alice?" Mrs. Collins asked Lesley gently.

"She was lying down. I thought I'd leave her there for a while."

"A good idea. Supposing I go and see how she is? I'll take her a cup of tea."

"That's very kind of you. Perhaps I should go. You would like to see your friends arrive . . ."

"I'll see them all right," Mrs. Collins said, getting up with a smile. " I never miss the fun. But I think I'll take Alice a cup of tea all the same."

She poured some tea and disappeared into the house.

Mrs. Halidane was standing now and looking out from under the eaves of the veranda. The plane was very low and came down circling the homestead. It showed two heads-in the cockpit and the shadow of others under the glassed dome. The pilot leaned out, waving a gloved hand.

" The Brennans, hurray!" said Bill Daley. " Now it really looks like a wedding."

" Take out the small 'Ute', will you, Bill?" Dan said. " Don't run her down the paddock till he's landed."

" You're telling me," said Bill. " I've landed in those paddocks with trucks and motor bicycles and even horses dancing a fandango all over the raking place!"

He disappeared in the direction of the garages and at the same time the plane came down and landed with a few bumpety jumps down the far end of the paddock. It was half a mile away. A minute later the " Ute " sped out of the garages and with a roar of the exhaust it went to meet the plane taxi-ing nearer the homestead.

On the veranda, the mounting excitement was enough to bring even Betsy up out of her chair. She pushed back a strand of hair and leaned nonchalantly against the veranda post, long jade green cigarette holder in her hand.

" Here they all come," she said. " Now will begin the fight for Dan. With everyone knowing what everyone's up to. Except Dan."

Lesley looked at Betsy curiously. She couldn't help admiring her attractiveness. In spite of her rather big figure she was very lovely in an ungroomed, wispy kind of a way.

" Whatever do you mean?" Lesley asked.

" Well, he is the cattle king, you know. And deuced attractive too, if you ask me," Betsy drawled. Then she turned her tired yellow-green eyes on Lesley. " Don't you think so?"

" Yes, I do," Lesley said frankly. " He's one of the nicest persons I've ever met."

" You say that too darned coldly, my girl. You wait till you see Hannah and Mary Brennan dance round Dan . . ."

" Well, why not?" Lesley said. " If they like him, and he likes them."

" Why not, indeed," Betsy said languidly as she went back to her chair.

Mrs. Collins came back on the veranda.

"Alice is dressing now," she said. "I do hope she likes the Brennan girls. They're noisy but great fun."

"You find everybody great fun, Con," Betsy said. "For my part I find them slightly kittenish."

Lesley wouldn't have summed them up this way. Mary Brennan was dark-haired and petite. She had a small mouth and very red lips and an olive, suntanned skin. Hannah was taller and browner and not quite so pretty but was excitable and a little noisy.

"Hallo, everyone. Where's the bride?" Everyone arrived at the same time. The Brennans, mother, son and two daughters. Randolph beaming joyfully, Bill Daley shouting greetings; Dan smiling benignly on everyone as they trooped up the garden path and thundered on to the veranda.

The Brennans looked at Lesley curiously and with pleasure.

"I'm not Alice," Lesley said hastily. "I'm just the cousin. Alice will be here in a minute."

"Just the cousin!" Hannah Brennan said with emphasis. "I've always found cousins a positive menace. And if you're going to hang on Dan's arm just because you're the cousin, as well as bridesmaid, you're more than a menace."

There was laughter all round and Dan smiled reassuringly at Hannah.

"It's only for a little while, old girl. Lesley's very decorative too. I'd rather spend my time looking at her than having her under my arm where I can't see her."

"That's the speech of the season, Dan," Mrs. Brennan said, coming up and kissing him warmly on the cheek. "Goodness knows what's in store for us when you toast the bridesmaid's health. You do do that, don't you?"

Alice had come out on to the veranda and everyone turned to her. She looked very pretty and fresh in her gay cotton dress. Lesley noticed the quick, anxious look she gave Randolph and then the reassurance that settled on her pretty, dainty features. Randolph crossed the veranda to her side and put his arm along her shoulder.

"Here she is," he said proudly. "The future Mrs. Baxter."

Looking at his happy-go-lucky, good-natured face Lesley thought Alice was very lucky. If only this all weren't in a strange country. How very happy Alice would be.

More and more people came as the day and next day passed. The homestead was overflowing and Lesley gave up all attempt to remember who was everyone, what name belonged to what person, and how many hundreds of miles they had travelled by car, Utility truck, and plane to get here.

Most of the men camped under the trees along the watercourse. The verandas were over-flowing with canvas stretcher beds produced from the store-house. Food was prepared in vast quantities not only by the Chinese cook and his cohorts in the cook-house but by Mrs. Collins, Belle and Lesley in the pantry of the homestead.

Corks popped, glasses tumbled off the verandas and were broken and laughter rang out across the garden.

Randolph was here, there and everywhere, the born host. Everyone was being looked after and every now and again a stockman or a black boy was posted to watch for the Macfarlanes who were bringing the minister with them.

Down in the little barn which stood beside consecrated ground where Baxters lay in their last beds alongside the wives and children of stockmen long gone, a white-covered altar had been set up and dishes of water placed ready to receive, at the last minute, the magnolias from the tropical garden.

In Lesley and Alice's room the wedding-dress hung.

Very late on Saturday night, after Alice had fallen asleep from sheer exhaustion of talking to too many strange people, Lesley unpacked her own pretty pink and white frock. As she lifted it out of its tissue papers there came a faint scratching at the door.

Lesley got up from her knees and opened the door. It was Mrs. Collins, the last to go to bed.

" May I come in a minute? I won't wake Alice," she whispered. When she saw Lesley's frock, still folded, a smile lit up her kind, homely features.

" There it is," she said. " That is what I wanted to ask you about. I wanted to know if I could help you with your frock. So far we have all been wrapped up in Alice's pretty clothes."

Lesley invited the older woman to sit down on the end of her bed.

" Alice is the bride," she said. " And I'm so glad everyone is being so nice to her."

" She will be happy!" Mrs. Collins said. Then she looked up anxiously at Lesley. " It is only the strangeness of everything that makes her nervous. Randolph adores her. He will give her everything. He will make her happy. He is so very happy himself—it will be infectious."

Mrs. Collins was faintly defensive.

Lesley sat down on the bed beside her and gave her hand the tiniest pat.

" She'll be happy," she said. " I know Alice. And I love your Randolph myself. Just as you say—he is so happy. No one could be with him for long without being happy too."

Tears suddenly sprang into Mrs. Collins's eyes.

"They are fine boys," she said. "Fine men, now."

"I know. And it's your doing. You feel proud of them and quite rightly."

Mrs. Collins recovered her composure.

"May I see your dress?"

Lesley stood up and shook out the lovely soft chiffon pleats.

"Oh, how lovely. That could be a bride's frock too. Lesley. . . ." Mrs. Collins leaned forward impulsively. "Stay a little while. Don't go back to England yet. I need you . . . while Alice and Randolph are away."

Then she caught sight of Lesley's face. In the subdued light Lesley's face was white and strained. She stood looking down at the lovely dress. Like a bride's dress, Mrs. Collins had said. It *had* been made as a bride's dress . . . then the wedding had been put off, then put off again. Alec had to go away. Then he had to go away again. In the end Lesley's pride, together with Alice's departure for Australia and their combined parents conspiring together, had managed to get Lesley, and her lovely dress, out of England and out of Alec's toils.

The dress had been shortened, an extra layer of pleated chiffon and a rose-pink velvet sash added—a bride's dress had become a bridesmaid's frock.

Mrs. Collins could not guess Lesley's thoughts but she knew she had touched on something old, unhappy and far away when she had made her remark about the dress.

"Lesley, my dear. Wear that lovely big shady hat with it. The one we put together with Betsy's help the other day. And Dan will have a gift for you—and I have one. Altogether you will look lovely, my dear. . . ."

She looked as if she would like to have gone on and say something more. Perhaps good taste forbade it. Or was it the whiteness of Lesley's face?

CHAPTER FOUR

On Alice's wedding day the gods were kind to the little world of Coolaroo Downs. Lesley was first of the cousins out of bed.

"It's cooler," she said. "The flowers will stay fresh after all."

Yesterday, she and Alice had been given all that the tropical garden would yield in the way of flowers and shrubs. The garden was kept perpetually wet and fragrant with water pumped up from the artesian basins hundreds of feet below the ground level. The result of this was a corner of abundance in the desert—creepers, ferns, magnolias and orchids.

Lesley came back from the shower-house, glowing.

"Oh, Alice, you should see the garden—and the paths. They've been up all night. They've got the gayest canvas roofs to the rotary clothes hoists and there's bunting and decorations everywhere. It's like a fairyland."

"Am I supposed to look at it, do you think?" Alice asked.

"Have just a little peep. It will make you feel so happy."

Alice tiptoed around the veranda corner with Lesley. Her eyes lit up when she saw the gaiety of the scene all around.

"They never said a word . . ." she said.

"That's your Randolph for you. Now you know why he's been so busy."

"He is a pet."

"They're all pets in a way . . ." Lesley said musingly as they went back to their room. "Betsy's the strangest pet of them all. I didn't think she approved of us overmuch but look at that heavenly hat!"

Betsy was not all idleness. She had a flair for hats and their decoration and she had brought out a lovely broad-brimmed leghorn straw hat and trimmed it for Lesley. Soft blue bows, sky and delphinium blue, swathed the crown. When Lesley put on the hat her eyes reflected the blue till they, too, were like delphiniums.

Alice had her breakfast brought to her and only when everyone else had been to the shower-house and had disappeared each to his own dressing-room was she allowed to take her bath.

The lovely wedding-gown of net and tulle was taken down from its hanger and Mrs. Collins and Lesley together slipped it over Alice's head.

"Your hair is as fair and soft as a child's," cousin Con said tenderly. Truly Alice looked a lovely picture. The colour had risen in her cheeks.

"I wish I could see Randolph . . . just for a minute. . . ."

"You shall. All in good time. He's polished up like a guard's officer and much more nervous than you are, Alice."

Mrs. Collins looked at the girl tenderly.

"I've never seen anyone more happy than he is, Alice," she said. "I've got to thank you for that——"

Mr. Brennan, who was to act as the giver-away, came to the door. He patted Alice's hand as she placed it on his arm.

"It's proud I am myself," he said. "Are you ready, my dear?"

Alice craned her neck for sight of Randolph.

"Randolph will be down at the little church," Lesley whispered. "Smile, Alice! You look so *lovely.*"

Alice took courage from Mr. Brennan's kindliness and the little procession moved out of the front entrance of the homestead between a line of smiling stockmen to the little frame barn down by the dry river-bed.

When Lesley took Dan's arm he looked at her quickly and then away again as if he was shy of looking too closely at her face with its frame of dark hair and the big hat.

There was a complete silence between them as if neither could find the right word to say. Then Dan gently touched Lesley's hand where it rested on his arm.

Inside the barn Randolph was waiting with Joe Brennan. He turned round as Alice entered. His hair was plastered down to perfection and as Mrs. Collins had said, everything about him was shining. He turned back to the little altar and settled his shoulders. Lesley thought she was never again likely to see happiness and pride sticking out like a pair of wings from a man's back.

The barn was hung with baskets of trailing tropical creepers; great stone pickle jars, painted all colours of the rainbow, stood in groups bearing the branches of gum trees and mulga. A wire run underground from the engine room provided the energy to move the punkah which the ingenuity of Randolph and Bill Daley had erected for the occasion.

Betsy, lavish with graciousness, stood with Mrs. Collins to receive the wedding party as it returned from the ceremony. The Brennan girls and Christine Macintosh stood around her like a cloud of youth and beauty.

When Randolph reached the steps he stopped, lifted Alice up in his arms and mounted them thus.

Dan looked hesitatingly at Lesley, then, taking her hand off his arm, he held it high as she preceded him on to the veranda.

"That's the spirit, Dan," someone shouted from the garden. There was a laugh all round at his rather old-world courtesy and yet there was a certain pride in their laughter.

"That's the way to do it, Dan. You show 'em how—and how!"

"When did you do all these decorations, Dan?" Lesley asked.

"When you were all asleep," he said with a smile. "You like them?"

"Oh, yes. Particularly the flowers and the little green

trees around the veranda. You must have been growing them in secret for a long time."

"Randolph has—ever since he came back from England. He started planning his wedding right away."

"In England they'd be grown in a hothouse, but here——"

"It was a cool house," Dan said. "Under the tank-stand —the one where the shower-house isn't."

They found themselves surrounded by relatives and friends who, having kissed the bride, now felt it right and proper they should kiss the bridesmaid and best man.

All was laughter and rejoicing. As Lesley threaded her way through several generations of Baxter's to Alice's side, she noticed Dan and Mrs. Collins exchange a glance. Dan went to Alice and took a long-stemmed flower from her sheaf of gladioli; then, putting on his hat he walked down the garden path with Mrs. Collins. They walked back towards the barn and its miniature graveyard beside it. Intuitively, Lesley knew he had gone to put Alice's flower on the grave of his parents. Her eyes smarted with unshed tears for a minute.

"They are *good*," she thought. "So sterling!"

She watched Hannah Brennan waiting for Dan to come back. Hannah had a cool drink in either hand and she stood on tiptoes to see over the heads of the others.

But it was Mary Brennan who was first. She had been with those on the path below the veranda and had darted towards the gate with a drink for both Dan and Mrs. Collins. When Dan took his glass from her she reached up and kissed him. Dan smiled and patted her shoulder.

Alice did not need Lesley now. She seemed free of all her inhibitions as she clung laughing and blushing to Randolph's arm.

Hannah turned away with a petulant exclamation and would not rally to the bantering she got from the young men.

"Better luck next time, Han. You need salt to catch Dan."

"How's it going, Lesley?" It was Bill Daley leaning over her shoulder.

"Oh, lovely! It's all so gay—and colourful. And Alice looks so happy!"

"So does the bridesmaid!"

Lesley smiled back at Bill. From the edge of the veranda Dan noticed how sunny her face was when it broke out in that unexpected smile.

Andy and William Macfarlane descended on Lesley together.

" There's only one person looks as beautiful as the bride
. . ." began Andy.

" There's only one person has the same charm . . ."

" The same poise . . ."

" The same sweet welcoming smile for Macfarlane and
Macfarlane."

Over their shoulders Lesley could see the baleful looks of
the North-west girls. They liked Lesley—but they didn't like
her monopolising their young men. Next to Dan Baxter the
Macfarlanes were the popular partners of the North. Betsy,
smoking from her long jade green holder, noticed the uncertain look Lesley shot in the girls' direction.

" Make hay while the sun shines, my dear," she said as
she passed. " After all, it won't be long before you're back
in England."

Betsy sipped champagne and watched all through her
sleepy cat's eyes.

When Alice and Randolph came out on the veranda—Alice
now dressed in a pretty silk shantung frock and a little
close-fitting hat, there was a shout of:

" To horse!"

Those who had mounts, including all the stockmen, and
Dan, made for the hitching rails where saddled horses stood
in a row. Bill Daley brought up the Dodge and hoisted into
it the hand luggage and made room in the front seat for Joe
Brennan.

The whole—the Dodge, surrounded by galloping, shouting
horsemen, yelping dogs and cracking stock-whips, moved
lustily down the paddock where the Brennans' plane stood
gleaming in the sun.

Joe Brennan was flying the couple to the coast, where they
would take the mail plane to Darwin, then a plane south to
Adelaide.

Alice had clung a minute to Lesley.

" Be here when I come back. Promise? Promise?"

Then everyone turned their backs on food, flowers and
tables. Each found a place in the shade and within the hour
silence reigned over Coolaroo Downs. The wedding was over
—the sun was still above the western plain, but the wedding
guests slept.

CHAPTER FIVE

The next day or two following the wedding the house guests settled down to enjoying being with one another. They sat and lounged about for the first day, the men yarning and the girls whispering to the accompaniment of trills of laughter on the annexe veranda or on the east side away from the male gallery on the front veranda.

Christine Macintosh, the Macfarlanes' cousin, had just come from Sydney and was an authority on hair-do's, the latest colour in nail varnishes, the proper length from the ground of the newest fashions. She urged them to let her cut and curl their hair to the new short length.

The Brennan girls were eager but tremulous and it was little Mary who first took the plunge.

Amidst laughter they gathered together to watch Christine shear away Mary's dark locks. Then followed a shampoo and a setting of the short curls with bobby pins.

When Mary emerged finally with a cheeky gipsy cut and her pretty starry face greatly enhanced by the fashionableness of her hair-do there was a rush for Christine to do likewise to the others.

Lesley was only a year or two older than these girls, but somehow she could not quite join in with the fun on the annexe veranda. Instead, she spent the morning putting away Alice's clothes and tidying up the rooms. Outside the window she could hear the laughter and every now and again someone would pop a head in.

"Lesley, Christine says everyone in Sydney is wearing a dark tan make-up. Is that right? Is that the latest fashion in London?"

"Well, not too dark in London," Lesley said. "Don't forget English girls haven't your tanned skins."

"Lesley, this magazine says sheath skirts are all the fashion and all the pictures in this other show lovely full flimsy skirts. What are they wearing in London?"

Thus, though she was not in the fun, she was not exactly out of it.

For lunch they all ate large quantities of the left-over cold turkey and ham and chicken and lamb. More tins of fruit were opened; and lashings of tinned cream were poured over mayonnaise dressings and the dessert.

Afterwards everyone went to sleep again.

That evening Lesley received her first lesson in domestic cricket. The men played a kind of French cricket wherein anyone getting the ball can try to bowl the batsman. The ball was a soft rubber one and the speed and dexterity with which they made passes to one another; with which they feinted then threw; and with which the batsman turned, twisted and had eyes all round him, was a revelation.

"Come on, England," Bill called to Lesley. "You're in!"

With a laugh she took the bat and hugged it close to her legs as she had seen the others do. The game was purely defensive and her legs were the only stumps. She saw the ball thrown to a stockman and swung round to defend herself from him; an instant later the ball was thrown from the other side with the speed of lightning and touched her ankle. She was out.

She looked at Dan indignantly.

"But you didn't have the ball," she said. "He did!" she pointed to the stockman. "I believe you've got two balls."

There was a shout of laughter.

"That's the game," Dan said. "You only thought Walsh had the ball. The swiftness of the hand deceives the eye in this game. Bill made to throw him the ball and Walsh made as if to catch it. That was to deceive you. I had it all the time."

The other girls went in one by one but fared no better. Years of practice and speed had made a wizard of the game for the men.

"Do you ever play real cricket?" Lesley asked.

"Too right," Andy Macfarlane said. "The annual North-west cricket match is the match of the season."

"We can't play it here in this weather very often," Bill said as he came over to the veranda for a drink. "Too far to run in the heat. Hence this French cricket game we play. But it's wonderful training for the other game."

Quite often Lesley didn't see the ball at all—it moved with such flashing speed.

On the second day Dan and some of his men went rather half-heartedly back to the real work of running a station.

"Got to see the troughs have fresh water out on the run," he said ruefully. "Can't have Randolph coming back and finding his fifteen thousand sheep dead of thirst."

"Can we come too, Dan?" This was a chorus from the girls.

"Haven't got enough horses."

"Oh, yes, you have. You just don't want us." There was a chorus of laughter as those who wanted to go out on the run made for the stables.

Bill Daley teased and rallied them; the stockmen were belligerent but ended up by lending their second mounts. Lesley did not go although she hoped she would have an opportunity of going out on the run before she returned to England.

She could ride a little but somehow she could not make the dash in jeans these girls did—mounting strange horses almost on the run—riding with the long stirrup and not bothering to adapt the girth. She thought she would wait until there was a time to think and not race. Instead she spent the day showing Betsy a knitting pattern from one of the many magazines the girls had left strewn around.

"Can't see how you can work those things out," Betsy drawled. "Beyond me. I'll only make a mess of it."

"A knitting pattern is the best known form of an intelligence test," Lesley said lightly. "So you'd better qualify, Betsy. It won't do to pretend you can't do what the average woman can do—if she tries."

"How frightful," said Betsy. "I've been going round all my life saying I can't understand them and now you tell me I've been labelling myself a moron."

"You can redeem yourself with this one. It's easy—and look—very pretty."

Betsy leaned forward and actually showed interest in the piece of dainty primrose yellow knitting Lesley held in her hand.

"Mm! . . ." she said. "My colour too." She looked at Lesley out of her hazel sleepy eyes. "You wouldn't be trying to reform me, would you, Lesley?"

"Not willingly," Lesley laughed. "It might be a waste of life to spend it sitting there—but it's very decorative. Who would really want to change you, Betsy?"

"Alice," Betsy said. "Alice and I would drive one another mad."

Lesley decided to say nothing and instead bent her head over the pattern.

"Two purl, two plain, slip one, purl one, plain one . . ." she said, knitting and reading at the same time.

"The parting down your hair is always so straight, Lesley. However do you get it that way? My hair now—it's all over the place——"

Lesley looked up and caught Betsy's calculating eye. There

wasn't any detail that Betsy really missed about anybody. Yet there was no real unkindness.

That evening Dan stopped by Lesley's chair on the veranda as he came in from the paddocks. Betsy was asleep again and Mrs. Collins was herself wrapped in crochet patterns with Mrs. Brennan.

"Well, how are you doing, mate?" he asked. He stood looking down at her. "Not tired of Coolaroo yet?"

There was something heart-warming in the way he called her "mate". Lesley rather liked it. She liked the quiet authority with which he threw off his young admirers when he had had enough of their fun. Like a big shaggy dog shaking off the puppies when he was tired of their playing all over him, and then stalking away benign but indifferent.

"I'm not tired of Coolaroo," Lesley said. "I like it. I'm beginning to count the days rather reluctantly."

"Don't do that," Dan said. "We're not going to let you leave on the *Oronsay,* you know. I wanted to ask you about that—if I could alter your bookings. I can do it through the Bank."

Lesley took in a breath.

"That's very kind of you. But why not the *Oronsay?*"

"You promised Alice to wait for her. Remember?" He sat down in an easy chair beside her and began to roll a cigarette. "She'll be away longer than that fortnight they talked about. Or I'm a Dutchman."

"What makes you think that?"

"I don't think it. I know it. Joe Brennan didn't come back—you probably noticed that omission. That means he's gone with them. Well, to be honest, he did go with them. Once Joe starts showing people the high spots there's no saying when they'll decide to go back to work."

He smiled rather wryly at Lesley.

"That means fifteen thousand sheep on my hands—right in the middle of a cattle muster."

"Fifteen thousand and one," Lesley said with a little laugh. "I feel rather sheepish being left on your hands too."

"Don't you think that. I want you. I'd like to be certain Alice would come back to find you here. I think it would make a difference to Randolph—to their whole life together. And no end of difference to Con to have you here to help them settle down."

Lesley drew in the corners of her mouth. He hadn't said anything about it making a difference to Alice as a person—only as a wife. Didn't he care whether Alice was happy except as it affected Randolph and Mrs. Collins—even himself?

"How do you really know Joe Brennan has gone with them?"

"The six o'clock session," Dan said, nodding his head in the direction of the office door which opened out on to the side veranda. An extension had been made to the office to house the transceiver set. "Randolph came through on it and told the whole North-west what a whale of a time they were all having. Joe is taking them to Adelaide himself."

"I hope Randolph and Joe weren't having such a whale of a time they forgot to ask Alice if she minded a three-cornered honeymoon."

Dan was silent a minute.

"I think Joe might be good for Alice," he said at length and slowly as if he was thinking out every word before he uttered it. "He's a crowd in himself. Alice will get to know more of the North-west by knowing Joe than by living at Coolaroo six months——"

Lesley was beginning to feel the back of her neck prickly with annoyance. She suspected that Dan was telling her, in his own fashion, that he knew quite well that Alice wasn't as happy as she might be about Coolaroo.

"But she will live at Coolaroo—perhaps for ever——"

Dan looked at Lesley quizzically.

"We rather like it, you know," he said. "We'd like it better if you stayed a little longer——"

There was just that touch of authority in Dan's voice that made Lesley suspect him. Was he arranging everybody's life to suit Coolaroo? Funny how these quiet men so often got their own way. And funny how the very thought of having her own life ordered roused a feeling of rebellion in her. Her life had been ordered by other people in the past. Now she wanted to be left alone—to decide for herself whether to come or go—stay or depart.

"Would you like a cool drink, Lesley? Supposing you let me mix you a Coolaroo special?"

"I like lemon and passion-fruit in it," Lesley said with a smile.

Betsy's voice came from the end of the veranda.

"Me too, Dan. Don't see what you two have got to talk about so long. Mighty cosy of you down that end of the veranda, and never raising your voices once so I could hear. You weren't making clandestine proposals by any chance, Dan?"

Lesley focused her attention on a flight of white cockatoos

making for the mulga. She didn't know whether it was the after effects of the wedding or not, but quite suddenly she didn't think these Baxters were so good and so kind and so sterling after all.

" I was proposing Lesley misses the *Oronsay* and stays with us longer," Dan said.

" You've got to have a special permit to stay on Coolaroo," Betsy drawled. " Every time I begin to outstay my welcome you boys make it clear that Brian and Alexander Station are my provinces, not the Baxters and Coolaroo."

If Betsy had expected a denial from Dan she was disappointed. He stood up.

" I'll get those drinks," he said. With that he went inside.

" Callous brute," said Betsy sulkily. " He never cares how people *feel*. Only what they *do*."

Lesley remained silent. She felt vaguely depressed about the news of Alice and Randolph. She knew Alice had been longing for a period to be with Randolph alone. She wanted reassurance that her love for him was greater than her fear of the vast spaces of Australia.

" Do you suppose men like Dan have any emotional life at all?" Betsy asked unexpectedly. " Is it just the women who do the ' feeling ' while the men get on with the business of bringing in the bacon?"

" I don't know," said Lesley. " After all, we're supposed to be inexplicable to them. They might as well have some reserves from us."

" But in your experience . . ." Betsy persisted.

" My experience has been very limited, I'm afraid," Lesley said. As she sipped the cool drink Dan brought her she allowed herself a quiet smile. Betsy had a certain quality of shrewdness—but she wasn't so shrewd as all that. She wasn't going to violate Lesley's reserves that way; not yet, anyway.

The next day Dan rode out to a cattle camp towards the ranges. The Macfarlanes went with him on borrowed horses, and Neil, a slouch hat and horse reserved for his use when he visited Coolaroo, frisked about excitedly at being allowed to accompany the men. There were several stockmen, two of whom went on motor bicycles.

The Halidanes bade a reluctant farewell and were the first of the house party to strike camp. Mrs. Brennan threatened that they must borrow the big Utility and drive into Ninety Mile End and find if they could get out to Witchery by getting the mail plane to alter its course. No one would hear of this.

"Dan needs us for the muster," Andy Macfarlane said. "And we need you for the fun."

"Nobody can go till we go," William Macfarlane said. "And we're not going till we're driven off with a gun."

This decision was received with delight by all. Lesley said nothing but Andy made her a posy of the purple hibiscus, and William brought in a baby cockatoo from the mulga.

"They mean it all kindly," Mrs. Collins said. "Just give them a few smiles—that's all they want, Lesley."

Lesley did smile at them and the brothers went off yodelling with joy.

"How do you manage to do it, Lesley?" Mary Brennan asked. "We all smile on the Macfarlanes—and they don't take an atom of notice."

"Macfarlanes, my foot!" said Betsy from the depths of her chair. "It's Dan you're all dancing a fandango round."

"That's only because Andy and William won't take any notice of us," Hannah said, with a toss of her head.

Betsy slewed her cat's eyes round to see how Lesley took that. It was quite clear to all that Hannah could have William's heart for the stooping and his antics were only a defence against laughter at his lovelornness over Hannah Brennan.

Mrs. Collins followed Lesley to her room when she went to put her hibiscus in a bowl of water.

"So soon to droop," she said sadly. "It is a pity to pick them. When night comes they fold up and die."

"They do that on the trees," Mrs. Collins said. "If you put them near the light they will stay open longer."

Mrs. Collins picked up the cocky Lesley had put on the rail at the end of her bed.

"This little fellow won't die for a hundred and fifty years," she said. "They're little wretches for stealing the almonds—and one's heart."

She cuddled the tiny little bird in her hand and tickled his poll. The cocky nestled against her.

"He's a darling," Lesley said. "Will you look after him when I go home? I don't suppose they would let me take a cockatoo on the ship."

"Don't go home then, my dear. Stay with us, Lesley." She went on tickling the cocky's poll. "This little fellow will take to you like a mother, then you won't be able to go."

Lesley laughed.

"I've got a mother of my own, you know. And a father. And sundry other people I belong to in England."

They sat on the bed, Mrs. Collins holding the cocky and them both doing their share of tickling him.

" Is it the sundry others that matter?"

She was quick to note the little hard, hurt light that came into Lesley's eyes.

" Please don't think I'm curious. It's just that I overheard Dan speaking to you on the veranda yesterday. I had opened the windows to let in the air. He asked you to stay—and you didn't seem very enthusiastic. . . ." Mrs. Collins paused and then when Lesley said nothing she went on hurriedly: " Dan likes you, my dear. I know he sounded as if he wanted you to stay—just for Coolaroo's sake. But he's very shy—he wouldn't know how to tell you he would like you to stay for your own sake. Because we like having you. Visitors are a tonic to us."

Lesley felt the colour stealing up her cheek.

She took the cocky from Mrs. Collins and let it nestle against her face. " Alice will be all right, you know, if Randolph remembers, in his general joy for living, that she wants a little of his time to herself."

" I wasn't thinking of Alice only," Mrs. Collins said gently, " though I'm quite prepared to do that, too. You see, I love my boys. They are my whole life. I'd do anything to help them to real happiness. As for Randolph. . . ."

She stopped and when she started again there was the faintest break in her voice.

" You could go the length and breadth of the world and not find anyone more generous—so happy—so——" She stopped altogether. She bent her head as she put out her hand to the cocky.

Lesley was puzzled. Why had Mrs. Collins found it necessary to come and say this? Randolph was so obviously all these things.

" I know," Lesley said kindly. " I love him, too. Alice loves him and all she needs is a little help and understanding in adjusting herself to a new country and a new way of life."

" She will be all right if she understands the credit side of things," Mrs. Collins said. " She is a Baxter. That means a lot in Australia. You see, the Baxters are very clannish. All pastoralists' families are somewhat like that. It's like your aristocracy—they marry one another. Randolph has brought a girl from over the sea—and that's a good thing. But it is also an unusual thing. Everyone will be watching to see how it turns out and though everyone loves Randolph they will do a little sly smiling behind their hands if it doesn't. No one would want to harm his happiness, but they are a little—a little intrigued—that a Baxter hasn't married a Baxter. Do you see, Lesley?"

"Yes, I think I do see," Lesley said quietly. She could not possibly be angry with this kind, pleasant, Baxter-loving woman and yet something in her wanted to be angry. In spite of their apparent guilelessness these people were very shrewd. They had summed up Alice and they knew their countrymen. They were going—in their quiet not-so-guileless way—to see that Alice didn't let Randolph down. Well, not Randolph, so much, as a *Baxter*! And that nice quiet guileless man out there—Dan Baxter—was calling the tune.

Mrs. Collins got up and went to the door.

"Think about staying a little longer, will you, Lesley? We love visitors—here in the North-west. And Dan wishes it."

Dan wishes it!

Lesley did not so much feel angry as flabbergasted. She also felt like shaking Alice. If only Alice wouldn't show her feelings so!

She put the cocky on the bottom rail of her bed. She kissed his little beak tenderly.

"We've only got each other, cocky," she said. "Those Baxters have all got one another. It must be like living in a stronghold of affection—and loyalty."

Having thought that, Lesley could no longer feel angry with them.

CHAPTER SIX

After lunch the next day Lesley took her siesta on the veranda in company with Mrs. Brennan, who made no apologies about putting her handkerchief over her face and letting it blow gently in and out to her ample breathing.

"It muffles the snores," Mrs. Collins whispered to Lesley. "Not that she snores very loudly at all, but Betsy objects."

"How does Betsy know?" Lesley whispered back. "She's always asleep herself."

"Only with one eye." Mrs. Collins gave Lesley a conspiratorial smile.

Lesley dozed a little. Anything, she thought, is better than lying in this bath of ennui. She understood why all the younger people had gone out on the run. They were too young to want to sleep their lives away. And wasn't she still young herself? Yes, young—but a "visitor"—someone to be cotton-woolled—to be *with* but not *of* these North-west people. Wherever she turned Lesley found kindness and hospitality, but also barriers. She got up and stole down to the tank-stand to take a shower. When she came out she found Bill Daley sitting on the rail of the other tank-stand.

"Put your towel on your head and run for it," he advised. "You'll get sunstroke standing there. There's some tea on the boil in the pantry. Pour yourself a cup. I'll be with you in a minute."

She did not run to the house. She walked there thoughtfully.

In the pantry she found a kettle boiling on a primus and teapot and cups set on the table beside it. She made the tea and was still in a dilemma as what next to do when Bill Daley came in, his towel loosely over his arm, his showered body big and shining and vibrant with life. Lesley thought she herself must look as if she had shrunk when standing beside him.

He took the teapot out of her hands and poured the tea.

"One for you, and one for me," he said. "I'm taking you out to the stockyards in ten minutes."

"I haven't riding clothes," Lesley said. "And I haven't plucked up the courage to borrow jeans from somebody yet."

"We're going in the jeep—beg pardon—Landrover. We got in the habit of calling 'em jeeps in the war."

"Is this an invitation or a command?"

"Both." He sipped his tea and grinned at her. "You want to go, don't you? What are you going to tell them back home in England about a sheep and cattle station? A place where they have weddings on verandas, and otherwise sleep?"

"I would like to see the run—I admit that. And thank you for asking me. I'm coming."

"Good for you. Put on a hat and come out to the garages behind the cook-house. Bring a scarf for your neck; the sun can burn it too, you know."

Lesley had spoken the truth. She would like to go on the run; she would like to try driving a Landrover over trackless paddocks; she would like to see where Dan and Neil and the girls had gone and what sort of work they did when they went off booted and slouch-hatted, with stock-whips under their arms and string tied round their trouser legs—the girls in blue denim jeans.

"Betsy's skin stays beautifully soft," Lesley said later, when rollicking over the plain and Bill admonished her for a second time about keeping her hat on.

"She never goes out in the sun," he answered. "She beats

a one-way track between the bedroom, the pantry, the veranda and—after dark—the washhouse."

" Won't she be interested in the muster?"

" Not our Betsy. No heat and flies and sunburn for Betsy. She'll just stay at home and keep cool. Do you know what? When she was a girl she won every junior hack event in the Royal Show down south. Every event she ever entered for."

" And she's given up riding altogether?" Lesley asked incredulously.

" Brian—that's her husband—he gave it up for her. He likes Betsy the way she is now. Downy and soft and curled up like a favourite cat."

Lesley said " Oh!" How aptly Bill had described Betsy. Even though he, as a jackaroo, had equal social status as the family, she didn't like discussing Betsy in too great a detail with him. She wasn't sure he mightn't say something not altogether in good taste.

They were now driving very fast, out towards the broken hills along a line beside the bank of the dried-out water-course.

Suddenly, and pointlessly, Bill pulled up. There was nothing around them but a waste of brown land and burnt ends of grass.

" How do you like the view . . . Lesley?"

" I'm not really interested in the view. I was wondering which I disliked the most—your speed, or your lack of it. Do we have to stop here?"

" You're not impressed by the view?"

" I'm much more concerned about my likelihood of dying of thirst if I get out and walk."

" Nonsense. Dan Baxter wouldn't let you die of thirst. He's probably looking at us this very minute through his spy-glass. What does he see, you ask? Why, through a tiny circle he sees a beautiful picture of a beautiful lady sitting in a jeep. She has a man beside her and is looking into his face. Two profiles! One turned left and one turned right. Man . . . mmm! The girl's profile's not too bad, either; and blow me down if the man's profile doesn't belong to that raking jackaroo. Bill Daley first and last with the ladies—as usual!"

Lesley wished she found this amusing, but she didn't. Bill Daley was leaning over her as he drew his little word picture and she had a panicky moment when she thought he might bend down another two inches and kiss her; and that Dan Baxter could see it all.

" You don't suppose Dan Baxter would let you walk home,

do you?" he asked, with his eyebrows cocked so high they nearly touched the hair-line. "He's very chivalrous, is Dan. You watch him cut me out as soon as we get within coo-ee. Employer's rights. Baxters first and the jackaroo can have what's left."

Lesley bit her lip. Only the bitterness inherent in Bill's words stopped her from feeling angry. It was true that Bill paid a great deal of attention to the girls but immediately Dan put in an appearance they were off after him with a shriek of giggles. Yet Dan did nothing at all to deflect all this feminine attention to himself.

Bill Daley glanced at her quickly and was evidently moved by her expression. He sighed philosophically.

"I'm only teasing," he said. "Dan Baxter's far more interested in those young colts they're bringing in this afternoon. He wouldn't care if there was an army of jeeps advancing over the plain. You can do what you like, Lesley. He wouldn't care. He's never looked at any woman. That's half his attraction."

He started up the engine and in another ten minutes they were in the mesa country.

"Men, dogs and horses in sight," Bill said cheerfully. "Feel okay now?"

He accelerated and shot the jeep forward at a hilarious gallop. His passenger had to steady herself by clutching his arm and it was thus they came to a standstill and all but fell out at the feet of Dan Baxter and his stockmen.

Dan said, "Oh, it's you, Lesley!" There was an element of surprise in his voice which relieved Lesley. Then he hadn't been watching her progress from the homestead through his spy-glass!

He looked from Lesley to Bill, and flicked his boots with his stock-whip. Then without another word he turned his horse towards the black stockman, Abe, who was at the head of a string of horses.

"That lot can go," he said. Lesley was surprised at the almost metallic sound of his words as he gave the command. In a minute the horses released were streaming for the hills, stock-whips were cracking and dogs barking to help them on their way.

Neil came riding over to Lesley.

"What are you doing here?" he asked. "Did Bill forget to tell you the sun will frizzle your skin up?"

"He reminded me," Lesley said, with a faintly forlorn air that stirred even the young heart of Neil.

"We aren't a bit nice to you, are we? We're really awfully glad you've come—only—well—it won't be too much for you, will it, Lesley? Apart from the sun, there's the flies, you know. They're the biting kind."

Lesley smiled at the boy. He had a quaint and grown-up charm.

"I'm all right, Neil," she said. "I'm stronger than you think."

Bill Daley had leapt out of the driver's seat the minute they had stopped. He had gone over to the stockyards and was already mounted to the top rail and looking over the colts in the yard.

"That jeep's a rotten way to travel over the plain," said Neil. "Aren't you nearly dead?"

"I'm a bit sore underneath, Neil. I think I'll get out and stretch myself."

"Oh please do. Would you like some billy tea?"

Lesley was out standing on the sandy space that stretched like a race all round the stockyards.

"I'd love some. Shall I come with you?"

Neil was off his horse and hitched it to the corner post nearest home.

"Yes. Please do. You can hold the mugs while I pour. The girls are round the other wing of that mob of cattle the men have rounded up. You can see them raising the dust like nobody's business about half a mile over there."

He pointed to a dusty bowl of activity beyond the stockyards and in a hollow between the broken hills.

Lesley felt grateful to young Neil, not only for his courteous manners but for just being there. In her embarrassment she was glad to cling to anyone.

Dan had swung off his horse on to the rails beside Bill Daley and was pointing out some points for the other to notice. Presently he jumped down and came towards Neil and Lesley. He flashed that quick penetrating look of his towards Lesley. The stern appraising look gave way to a half smile.

"You were rather brave, weren't you?" he said. "It's not much fun in the heat at this hour of the day."

Lesley wanted to ask what qualities the Brennan girls had that he so respected and yet which he thought she herself was lacking. How could he know what she could stand up to and what would be too much for her? Was he judging her by Betsy's standards? Or by Alice's?

She bit her lip and turned away as if to ask Neil for more

47

tea. After all, how could he know? Betsy was lazy and sun shy. Alice was just plain frightened. How should he know in what way she, Lesley, differed.

"Do you know anything worse than sitting about doing nothing? Especially in the heat?" she asked lightly.

"We must think of something to entertain you," he said in a slow thoughtful drawl. Lesley realised he had not meant to hurt her. There was nothing in Dan Baxter that would hurt anyone—any living thing. His annoyance at her appearance and his perfunctory greeting had probably been as much for Bill as for herself.

"It was really curiosity that brought me," she said, making conversation to overcome the awkwardness she had felt. "I'll have to tell them something about station life when I get back home, you know."

"Yes. It was thoughtless of us not to have arranged something," Dan said slowly. "However, now that you're here I'll point out one or two things. Those horses, and the colts we've kept, have been brought in from a round-up and camp out at Mars. The horses will find their way back because of the feed. Ordinarily we wouldn't let them go. The cattle through there have been rounded up in this hilly section of the run to save time when we muster on Monday. They came down for water, and the men—with Mary and Hannah—have rounded them up and will yard them. It's just a little bit of Monday's work being done in advance."

"I see." Lesley stood beside Dan as he pointed to the distance. She noticed the firm line of his jaw and when close to him like this, with the sun and light pouring on to him, she could see the faint sprinkling of freckles under the deep burn of his skin. She could count the three lines of wrinkles round his mouth and noticed the polished whiteness of his teeth. She had a silly moment when she wanted to ask him how many times a day he cleaned his teeth.

He turned to her and caught the foolish look in her eyes.

"You weren't even listening to me," he said with a smile.

"I was. Shall I repeat it after you?"

"No, you'll get in that Landrover and go home, young lady. That wind burns worse than the sun."

Without waiting for her reply he moved over to his horse and swung up in the saddle.

"Joe!" Dan's voice was sudden and effective. The stockman, riding a glorious stallion, propped back, wheeled his horse on his back legs and trotted amicably towards Dan. There was a minute's silence.

"Joe, how about you driving Miss Wilson home? I want

48

Bill, now he's here, and the sun will be too much for Miss Wilson."

The stockman looked half pleased, half doubtful. His eyes looked longingly towards the Landrover and one could guess he didn't often have the opportunity to drive it. On the other hand he had an anxious moment about his horse.

"Bill Daley will take Wildfire home, Joe," Dan said quietly.

"Okay, Boss!"

Dan turned his horse.

Lesley felt like a scolded schoolgirl as she went back to the car. They must all be cursing her under their breaths. In some inexplicable way her coming had spoilt the afternoon's fun. Bill Daley, however, seemed all high spirits and enjoyment. Already he was in Wildfire's saddle.

A dog that had been watching him, tongue lolling and ears pricked, knew to the split second when Bill was ready. He was away like a brown streak through the boulders and mesas. Wildfire, heels flying and sparks striking from the ironstone rocks, was after him at breakneck speed. Lesley rose in her seat to watch him. Whatever else anyone thought of Bill Daley they had only admiration for him as a horseman. Every eye was on him as he galloped off.

Dan rode over to the Landrover as Joe started it up. He touched his hat with his stock-whip and then turned back to the yards. Joe cut off the engine and sat, his arms resting on the steering wheel, gazing over the ranges.

"Blow me down," he said pointing to a fine pencil of smoke. The pencil broke up and became a series of smoke puffs, then a snaky line. Then once again a fine straight line pointing to heaven.

"Blacks having smoke talk," Joe said. He stood up in the Landrover.

"Hey, Boss! Watcha make of that?" He pointed to the smoke. Dan sat his horse, his hat pulled down over his eyes to shade them from the light. Lesley thought how easily he sat in the saddle, as if he had been born in it; his feet long in the stirrups and his back curved a little so as to make him look welded in the saddle.

"What's it about, Abe?" Dan asked the black man.

"They'm come longa way, that fella. They'm sit down plenty tired. Mine tink it that Sergeant Holland found white fella prospector."

"That's about it," said Dan. He turned back to the Landrover.

"Will you tell Mrs. Collins, Lesley? They will probably

have picked up the smoke talk at the homestead anyway and it might be necessary to get a message through to the Flying Doctor at Port Hedland."

"Yes, of course," Lesley said. "What will they do?"

"Send out a scout plane—or even the Flying Doctor—to see if they can make a landing. They'll be all right if they're out of the hilly country."

Once again he saluted with his stock-whip to the rim of his hat and rode away.

CHAPTER SEVEN

The hot weather had settled down again on Coolaroo so on that evening there was no French cricket. The men pushed the piano to the open doorway of the drawing-room and veranda and Betsy, emerging from her hibernation, and dressed—or rather enveloped—in a soft crushed pink cloud of chiffon, sat at the piano, her long golden liquid fingers wandering up and down the keys in every known melody, popular and classical.

The inhabitants of Coolaroo lay or sat about the veranda in voluptuous enjoyment of the purple star-still night. Down by the humpies a stockman with a concertina was picking up the melodies as Betsy played them and the blacks were singing their shrill version of them. Outside the cook-house the Chinese sat in silence, the golden glow from his smoking the only evidence that anyone was about. On the veranda the girls had told gossipy stories and the men had yarned.

Now all were full of languor. The only music was Betsy's.

Lesley turned her head and watched the long, rhythmic stroking of those keys. Betsy played sentiment but without too much sentimentality.

Lesley wished she could get rid of the pain that was in her chest again. Funny how the wedding and the strangeness of events had driven it away for a few days. Now it was back again—a spiteful enemy that had only given her relief in order that its sting might be all the more effective when it returned.

Andy Macfarlane sat on the steps of the veranda, his back to a post, his left hand within touching distance of Lesley's feet. His brother lay on a rug beside Hannah. Hannah's head was appreciably near Dan's feet. Mary stood draped over the piano, her gaze sometimes resting on Dan's head, sometimes dreaming over the dark shadows of the garden;

sometimes resting thoughtfully on Andy Macfarlane's hand where it strayed, playing with a rectangle of matches ever creeping nearer and nearer Lesley's feet.

Lesley was quite sure that she did not love Alec any more. It was true—just as her parents had said—a break away from her own country would work the miracle of a change of heart with a change of places. She never wanted to see him again. She would like to get a job somewhere else. But that wasn't so easy in England. Not a job so well paid and with so much individual freedom. But she had never been free from the tyranny of Alec and his occasional bursts of love and attention. The tyranny of the heart was the worst tyranny of all, surely.

Now there remained this pain in the chest.

Betsy's hands dropped from the keys. She sat still, drooping a little as she looked at the piano. Then she looked round.

"Are you all asleep?" she asked at length. "And who's holding hands with whom?"

Hannah tossed her head. Mary stirred restlessly from above the piano. William Macfarlane put out a quick hand and caught Hannah's ankle and she squealed. Andy looked up quizzically in Lesley's face.

"I'm all for holding hands with Lesley if she'll come for a walk with me. How about the mulga, Lesley? Walk that far? Promise not to kiss you more than three times coming and going."

The spell was broken.

Bill Daley came up the cement path knocking out his pipe on the back of his hand.

"That's my territory, Andy," he said. He put one foot on the veranda step and frowned down on the young man. "When Lesley goes walking in the moonlight she goes walking with me."

"That leaves only William and Dan to make me an offer," Betsy said, with a yawn. "What it is to be popular! Who are you going with, Lesley?"

Betsy had left the piano-stool and was sitting in her favourite chair.

"I haven't invited Lesley yet," said Neil, suddenly coming to life from the end of the veranda. "Why leave me out. I'm one of the men, too, aren't I, Lesley?"

"You certainly are," Lesley said with a laugh. "And quite the most charming of them, Neil. I would like very much to be taken for a walk by you."

She stood up and smoothed down her skirts.

"Right," said Dan. "Get the big torch, young Neil.

We'll take Lesley down and show her the new house. You fellers are so hell-bent on visiting the mulga—you take the girls."

"No mention of me, of course," said Betsy.

"You're coming with us," said Dan. "Get those slippers off your feet, old girl, and put on a decent pair of shoes."

"I'll put the kettle on and tune into Port Hedland," Betsy said languidly. "I'd rather have the news come to me than go walking out in search of it."

"What news can you find down by the new house?" Neil asked, bewildered.

"You'll probably make it yourself, Neil. Only you're far to young to understand *that*."

Lesley bit her lip. She felt as if she would like to throw something at Betsy. Why was Betsy always making innuendoes?

Dan came to the edge of the veranda and took Lesley's arm. He looked down at her feet.

"How are your shoes? Even with the torch one doesn't see very well."

Hannah Brennan screwed herself round on the rug and looked at Lesley's shoes.

"They're very much all right," she said coolly. "Not too low to be dull and not too high to be silly. London fashions, I suppose, Lesley."

Poor Hannah. Lesley, who had not tried, had won the affection of those whom Hannah so eagerly sought herself. Dan Baxter and Andy Macfarlane! Dan had not given his heart, of course—but he was giving his attention. Andy Macfarlane was making a goat of himself over the English girl. He was too young for her, anyway. As for Bill Daley! Well, Hannah gave Lesley sufficient credit not to be taken in by Bill's antics.

Hannah wasn't sure whether Lesley's lack of interest in the menfolk wasn't also an oblique insult to the girls. After all, there wasn't a female north of the leper line who wouldn't give her heart to Dan Baxter with a rush if she thought she had half a chance of his noticing it.

As for Andy Macfarlane! Hannah's eyes filled with tears because the night in all its solemn starlight beauty had filled her with melancholy too.

"Damn shoes," she said, humping up. "Who wants to walk in the mulga anyway!"

Hannah ran inside, almost colliding with Mrs. Collins, who had come to the door to announce supper.

"What is the matter with Hannah?" she asked, puzzled.

52

There was a minute's awkward silence then Mary followed her sister.

"Perhaps she has a headache," Mary said. "After all, she did all the wing work mustering to-day."

"Now Mary's gone," said William, raising himself on his elbows and gazing after the girls with exaggerated sorrow in his voice. "What's the matter with Mary?"

Mrs. Collins stopped and turned to watch the girls disappearing down the long passage.

"Has someone been teasing them?" she asked.

"Yes. Lesley has," Betsy said, and at the same time stretched her arms high over her head. "What's for supper, Con dear? Dan and Lesley—not to forget Neil—won't be in for theirs. We can have the lot between us."

Once again Lesley longed to have something to throw at Betsy. Bill Daley came to the rescue.

"You stick to your own rations, Betsy," he said. "Soon you won't be able to get up off that chair. I guess Brian will have something to say if we let you get too fat and too lazy."

"Brian likes me this way," Betsy said in her most sultry manner and there wasn't anyone there who didn't believe her.

Neil had come back now with the big torch and Dan led the way down the garden path.

"You look after them, young Neil," said Andy in a voice of resignation. "They won't be looking which way they're going themselves. They'll be stargazing."

Dan gave a half laugh as he guided Lesley through the small garden gate and they went out into the paddock.

"You don't mind all that teasing, do you?" Lesley asked. Dan gave a good-humoured chuckle.

"It's their way of not being bored," he said. "As for the stargazing—well, just stop and look!"

The plain sloped away from them down to the dried-out bed of the watercourse half a mile away. Beyond the thin line of trees was a great moon-white stretch of plain before the dark ridge of the ranges raised dark patches along the sky-line. Low to the south, the Southern Cross hung like a brilliant jewel on dark velvet.

They stood in silence, Lesley's arm along Neil's shoulder, her left hand linked in Dan's arm. The immensity of this timeless land hung over her, reminding her of vastness and timelessness as one could never conceive them in the country she had come from. Something in her went out to meet the night. She stood quite still and let it lave around her. Then

Dan flashed on his torch and began to lead the way down the slope to the place where he was building his house near the bed of the creek.

They walked on in silence for a few minutes.

"This is a big house," Neil volunteered. "Dan and me's going to live in it by ourselves."

"Someone to cook and scrub for us, young 'un."

"Well, if you don't get married it will have to be one of the lubras."

"Heaven preserve us," said Dan. "I'd rather get married."

"Why are you going to live with Dan, Neil?" Lesley asked. "Haven't you a home of your own? What about Alexander?"

"That's Dad and Mum's. I'd rather stay with Dan."

"You wait till I take the stick to you, young Neil. That'll change your mind," Dan said.

"I live here half the time, anyway," said Neil. "I might as well stay altogether."

"When Betsy gets bored with Alexander she comes back to Coolaroo," Dan said to Lesley. "Then when she gets homesick she goes back to Alexander. That way she and Brian keep in love with one another."

"Here it is," said Neil. "Look at the foundation stones. That's so the house won't get swept away if ever the Coolaroo floods."

Lesley was looking at the great black blocks of foundation stone but thinking of Dan's remark about Betsy and Brian staying in love. What did Dan Baxter know of love? According to hearsay everyone fell in love with Dan but he loved nobody. At least, not beyond the terms of friendship, or kinship.

"That stone is lava—volcanic. We blasted it out a couple of years ago and brought it out of the mesa country by truck. In the horse and buggy age they had to build their houses of wood and galvanised iron because they couldn't transport stone or material for concrete."

Dan was speaking as softly as the night as it hung around in its velvet silence.

"That's why the first homestead at Coolaroo is wooden and the new part concrete," Neil volunteered.

Lesley said nothing but stood and looked at the black lines of the house's foundations in a moon-swept gap between the straggly trees.

"Do you like it, Lesley?" Neil asked anxiously.

"Of course I do, Neil. But I can't really see it, you know. I was wondering why you worried about it being flooded away. Is there ever any water in the creek?"

Dan gave a laugh.

"You'll see it in a week or two with luck. The cloudbursts over Mars are the first of the seasonal rains. I hope there'll be more—but not before we've mustered the cattle that will come down for the feed round Mars. We've had three years' drought—we're due for rain in the Coolaroo."

They turned back towards the homestead. On a little rise they looked back towards the place where Dan was building his house.

"You can see the plan better from here," he said. "Veranda all round, of course. Passage straight through and an annexe for the cook-house instead of having to go a hundred yards down the paddock."

"Why are you building a house, Dan?" Lesley asked. "Are you going to leave Coolaroo homestead to Alice and Randolph?"

"I think it's a good idea," Dan said.

"What about Mrs. Collins? Are you going to take her or are you going to leave her to Alice?"

There was a little silence. When Dan spoke his voice was back in the tones of the afternoon. He wasn't the kindly host but the ruler of this little world.

"Con is not an article of furniture who can be moved from one place to another, you know."

Another silence. Then Dan continued:

"I know you care for Alice and worry about her, Lesley— but don't you think she will work out her own salvation?"

"I know you care for Randolph . . ." Lesley said carefully. "Don't you think he will work out his own salvation? You cannot help thinking about the Baxter end of their welfare, just as I can't help thinking about Alice's end. I expect that is only human nature."

"It's my job to think about Coolaroo Downs. I'm the head of the company whose welfare is wrapped up in the station. Including Alice now."

"Company?"

"Yes. We don't really own a million acres of Australia, you know. We—a company of people—lease them. The homestead is ours, of course, and everything on the land, but so as not to have too much responsibility vested in one person the lease is taken out for the company. That's Randolph and Betsy and Brian and young Neil. Also Con. You see, we all have a vested interest in Coolaroo. Alice will have her share now, too."

Lesley felt as if she was standing outside a firmly closed gate. Alice was inside with all the Baxters. When Randolph had carried her over the threshold he had carried her into that company and it was the company's business to look after her. Not Lesley's—the person outside the gates. The outsider.

"I see."

What Lesley saw was a glimmering of understanding of Dan's manner towards herself. So long as she was the guest, the visitor, the person who, because of that privileged position, must not work or go out in the sun; who might be taken with great courtesy and impersonal attention to see the foundations of a new house in the moonlight; she was the recipient of his kindly and formal attention. But let her put her spoke in Coolaroo business! Ah, that was a different matter. There was an almost invisible line which she must not cross. That was what she had done this afternoon. She had crossed the line between visitor and relation or intimate of the "Company".

Alice was "Company" business now. She, Lesley, remained the visitor who may not look in the kitchen or lose her way below stairs.

"You are very hard, aren't you?" she said unexpectedly. It was almost as if she had spoken her thoughts aloud.

"It's a hard country," Neil said. "Dan says you've got to be tough to take it. Dan says we do things the hard way in the North-west and if you harden up it all turns out easy."

Lesley let her arm slip along Neil's shoulder.

"You'll make a fine Baxter, young Neil," she said lightly. "It won't be for want of a good master if you don't."

Dan had said nothing but stood looking down the long slope towards his house. "I planned it about four years ago," he said at length. "That was before Randolph went to England and met Alice."

Lesley could think of nothing to say to that. Was it Dan's way of telling her he didn't do everything in relation to Randolph's future and happiness?

They turned again towards the homestead.

"What does the night make you think of, Lesley?" Dan asked more easily. He was back again in the role of pleasant host.

"It's brilliant—and yet, soft . . ." She couldn't tell him about the pain in her chest and the memory of a person who wasn't worth remembering. Perhaps it was pity for her own love, her own wasted heartache that caused the pain. It couldn't be love itself. She almost squirmed away from the thought of Alec.

"It's like a moth," Dan said. "Silent, soft and beating around one like wings."

Casually he took her arm and, flashing on the torch, showed her the way home.

"Why, that's almost poetical," Lesley said, turning and looking up in his face. The moonlight touched the edge of his profile. He turned his face a little towards her. She could see the white flash of his teeth in the shadowy darkness. His face seemed very near.

"I guess it is the night makes me feel that way."

Lesley had the incredible feeling that he was going to kiss her. Then she realised, of course, that Dan did not kiss anybody. Dan was lovable, but unloving. It was her own silly thought. She was astonished at herself. It must have been his nearness—the lovely night—his descriptive words. It wasn't even herself. She didn't want to kiss him. She had never thought of such a thing. She thought he was hard—though very nice, of course. And there was Neil on her other side!

Lesley felt as if she were guilty of some impropriety. Her heart pounded under her ribs; she felt the warmth of her flush under her skin. Her eyes smarted with tears. If only he wouldn't be so nice—when he wasn't being so hard.

Betsy had not stirred from her seat on the veranda. The only diversion she had provided during their absence had been to burn her finger with the lighter as she lit her fiftieth cigarette for the day. On the little table beside her were the evidences of Mrs. Collins's first-aid administrations.

"Where's everyone?" Dan asked.

"Gone to bed in a huff," said Betsy. "They couldn't stand my moans or your absence. Neil, go to bed; you ought to have been there an hour ago."

Neil kicked the doorstep to register rebellion but when Dan said "Good night, son," he went without another word.

"He ought to be your son, Dan," Betsy said idly. "He has complete faith in every word you utter."

Dan went over to the tea tray and poured himself and Lesley a cup of tea. There was a cold little silence on the veranda. It had something to do with Betsy's words.

Betsy got up, gathered her chiffons around her, and as she passed Dan on the way to the door she kissed the tip of her first finger and planted it gently on Dan's nose.

"We'd have to put the clock back a few years to achieve that," she said. She gave Lesley a seraphic smile.

"Good night, sweet. Go to bed early if you want to keep

57

that dewy complexion. Riding about on a jeep in the sun won't help you."

Lesley's heart sank and she didn't know why. Was it because of Betsy that Dan didn't fall in love with anyone. And why should he fall in love anyway?

Oh blow!

"After that farewell from Betsy you won't want any sugar, will you?" Dan asked.

"Life isn't worth living without sugar in one's tea and cream in one's coffee," Lesley said. "I know, because I tried it once when I wanted to slim down after a too-hearty holiday."

"The Port Hedland station opens up in a few minutes and we might hear if the Flying Doctor service got on to that smoke signal. Would you like to listen in, Lesley?"

"Yes. I would indeed." She got up and, carrying her tea in one hand, followed Dan into his office. He put a cane chair for her against a wall and went over to the transceiver set and began to operate the dials.

The transceiver set made sudden noises. Lesley found it enthralling to hear the doctor prescribing over the air and then a few minutes later the voices coming back from all over the north of this vast continent telling of the problems, difficulties and anxieties of sickness. Then the doctor speaking again advising, comforting and promising a visit. Some were told the doctor would fly in to their station the next day. This told the listening world that the sickness was real and required immediate attention. One station after another was called and one after another the voices came back.

Then came the call for Coolaroo.

"Calling Baxter of Coolaroo. Baxter of Coolaroo. Come in, Baxter, if you're listening."

Dan turned the dial.

"Righto, Doc—what's cooking?"

He dialled again.

"I'm going out to the range about twenty-five miles north of Mars, Dan. We got that smoke signal through from Brennans at Witchery. They think the sergeant's out there with someone sick. Probably he's found that prospector. How's the landing dead south of White Gum Mountain? I'll repeat."

Dan's fingers were at the dials again.

"You can land south of White Gum, but we picked up that smoke signal east of White Gum. I'll get the boys to send out a signal in the morning to keep smoke rising for you, Doc. If you can't make a landing near enough, we'll send out a

Utility to take you across the foot of the mountain. You'd better come over Coolaroo and drop a message after you've seen the layout. The Macfarlanes are here and could fly the Anson over. I'll repeat. Come in, Doc."

"I'll fly over myself, Dan, and land if it's feasible. I'll fly over Coolaroo and drop a message. Okay, Dan, good night to Coolaroo."

In the still dark brilliant night it seemed as if voices all over the north were calling . . . "Good night to Coolaroo." As each station had gone off the air one had breathed "Good night."

Lesley remained silent. Dan switched off and reached for his cup of tea which must have been quite cold by now.

"What do you think of that?" he said.

"It seemed as if they were all in the room—all in the house—just round about——"

"Instead of five hundred miles away. Oh well, that's the north. We're very near—and yet very far. Think what it was in my grandfather's day when there were no aeroplanes and no transceiver sets. People lived and died without their nearest neighbours ever knowing they had existed. "

"I think you ought to keep Alice alongside the transceiver set," Lesley said. "She'll get used to the feeling of people about her then."

Dan was looking at her under level brows.

"There you go worrying about Alice again," he said. "Alice is my worry now, you know."

"I feel I take my courage in both hands when I oppose you, Dan. You're so used to being the head of the company, aren't you? But on the subject of Alice I refuse to believe that I—her cousin—am not allowed to feel that her happiness is my concern. You will have to think of me in an open state of rebellion on the subject."

Dan drank his cold tea and didn't even make a face.

"Don't fuss her, Lesley," he said. "Don't sympathise. Nobody who was sorry for herself ever got used to the North-west. She's got to look it square in the face, size up its difficulties and take a broomstick to them."

"I agree. Between us we don't seem to be giving Alice a chance before she has started. I would like to think—for Alice's sake—you were a little unfair to her just now."

"Supposing you leave her to me?" Dan said quietly.

"I'm blowed if I will," said Lesley. "You see, I am getting in the way of slang myself! If I stay over to the next ship I'll have about a fortnight with Alice. I intend to make the most of it . . . after all, I may never see her again."

Dan stood up and, taking Lesley's empty cup from her, put it beside his own on the desk.

"Open war between us from now on, hey?" he asked with an ironical flick to his eyebrows.

"Let's call a truce until Alice and Randolph come back," Lesley said lightly.

Mrs. Collins had come to the office door.

"Aren't you two going to bed? The rest of the homestead is in a state of somnolent exhaustion."

"Have you got some sunburn cream for Lesley, Con?" Dan asked. "The back of her neck and her arms will be sore in the morning."

"I've put some on her dressing-table already," Mrs. Collins replied. She turned to Lesley. "Do put it on, like a dear. The wind burns as badly as the sun, you know, and it can be very painful."

"Good night, Dan," Lesley said, looking at him squarely. "Thank you for the walk and for the radio fun." She didn't know it but Dan was admiring the proud tilt of her head and the dignity with which she said "Good night."

"I've really made her angry," he said ruefully to Mrs. Collins. "Go after her, Con, and smooth out the ruffles. She's too nice to be cross with me."

Mrs. Collins patted his arm and stood on her toes to kiss him good night.

"She *is* nice, Dan. Be nice to her."

He looked at his elderly cousin with surprise.

"I'm the soul of courtesy," he said. "What do you mean —'be nice to her'? Haven't I always been nice to everybody?"

"Yes, that's the trouble, dear. You're nice to everybody instead of being specially nice to one body. Good night and put out the lights."

She followed Lesley through the house, down the covered way to the bedroom in the annexe. She put her head in the door.

"There's a lantern in the shower-house, dear. Leave it for Dan. Put the sunburn cream on and to-morrow *I'll* take you to the stockyards. But only if you're well creamed and stop being cross with Dan."

"*I'm* not cross with Dan. I just want to help Alice get used to Coolaroo. As a matter of fact, when I come to think of it, I haven't really said anything about helping Alice. Dan sort of anticipated it and scolded me."

"Scolded you? That doesn't sound like Dan. He's kindness itself."

Lesley sat down on the edge of her bed, the sunburn cream unstoppered in one hand and a look of puzzlement on her face.

"No, I don't suppose he did scold me. It's just a 'feeling' as if I'm intruding—or something."

Mrs. Collins took out Lesley's pyjamas from under her pillow and lifted her towels from the rack and put them beside her on the bed.

"That's because he wasn't happy to see you drive out in the Landrover this afternoon, isn't it? My dear, Dan is quite right. The sun does burn—and he does rather admire that lovely soft skin of yours. These Australian girls have an extra layer of epidermis that is sun-proof, you know. That's why they can go galloping all over the paddocks and just get a little browner."

Lesley looked in the glass at her skin.

"I'll put layers and layers of cream on it," she promised. "And after that I don't even want it mentioned again."

"It shan't be. And to-morrow I'll find a pair of jeans that will fit you—and a good horse——"

Lesley smiled at Mrs. Collins's reflection in the mirror.

"I believe you see right through me," she said. "You knew I didn't like being left behind——"

"Why not? And all those nice young men around! You're only human—in spite of that little preoccupied air of yours. And my dear—if you are keeping yourself heart-whole for someone in England—there's no reason why you shouldn't enjoy yourself while you are here. The young fellows, like the Macfarlanes and Joe Brennan, are a bit wild but they're the soul of honour."

"And Dan too!" Lesley could not forbear the little sardonic note in her voice.

"And Dan too!" Mrs. Collins said as she went to the door.

CHAPTER EIGHT

Sun-up, and the station was astir.

It was astir at sun-up every morning but to-day the house party too was out of bed with the first crack of dawn. There wasn't time for laughter, muddled beds or an occasional pillow thrown. Everyone wanted to be down at the stock-yards from the moment the black boys brought in the horses. There were enough saddle horses to provide everyone with a seat for the muster but at least half of them were not good stock horses and as no one proposed to stay out of the muster it was necessary to find enough stock horses for everyone.

The girls, on this morning, sat along the lower rail of the adjacent tank-stand waiting for one another to finish in the washhouse.

" Hurry up, Mary! For goodness' sake, are you drown-ing?"

They shook their tousled heads and yawned while the sky went grey then pink and an orange sun sprang over the sky-line between them. The young men—all in khaki shorts and a towel wound round their torsos, danced impatiently on the edge of the veranda.

" Blow me down, look at the cockatoos on the tank rail!"

" Stiffen the crows—it's the girls!"

Lesley jumped off the veranda and ran down to join the queue. There was a wail from the men.

" There's another of 'em!"

" They don't have showers in Pommyland, Lesley. Wait till Dan builds a bathroom. We're in a *hurry*."

Hannah and Christine conceded the men's dire need of a shower and went in together. They were still rubbing their heads as they ran out with wet feet and Lesley hurried under the shower.

A shock of water—no time for a proper soaping—and half dried she pulled on her blouse and shorts and went outside.

" Charge! "

Lesley was whisked up on to burly shoulders and run triumphantly to the veranda, where she was deposited with more haste than decorum. Khaki figures raced back to the tank-stand and all disappeared inside together.

Mrs. Collins came along the covered way and looked at Lesley as she picked herself up from the edge of the veranda.

"It's just their fun——" Mrs. Collins said. "Sky-larking. They didn't hurt you?"

"No, of course not?" Lesley said laughing. "I'm glad they think I'm worth fun-making. I'm not quite as spry as Hannah and the others, you know."

"Oh, yes, you are. It's just that it is all so strange—a different way of living—of behaving—isn't it? But those boys would guard you with their lives, you know. And the same for Hannah and Mary—and all the girls."

"I know," Lesley said.

Dan, heavily booted, his long, heavy drill pants tucked in the tops of his boots, an open-necked shirt and his slouch hat on, all ready, came out of the passage doorway. He looked at Lesley in surprise.

"You're up early. Betsy won't be astir for another hour."

"I'm coming too," Lesley said. She wished she didn't feel like a small child pushing herself into somebody else's party.

Dan's eyebrows went up. His face had the closed, reserved look that sometimes made a puzzle of what he was thinking to those who were looking at him.

"Lesley and I are both going," Mrs. Collins said. "We have sun-creamed ourselves and I've got out my old habit. You don't think I'm going to stay home when everyone— everyone—even Winnie Brennan, is going out?"

Winnie was Mrs. Brennan's name and she had already stated that where her girls rode she would ride—and better.

Dan allowed himself a small conceding smile.

"How's that old habit of yours, Con? You're not going out in jeans, are you?"

"I'm going in my habit and Belle took it out yesterday and cleaned it for me."

Mrs. Collins actually tossed her head. Lesley was still standing silent, wondering how much, if at all, she would spoil anybody's pleasure by going out on the run.

"Okay, Lesley," Dan said. "I'll see there's a good hack for you. Don't forget the sunburn cream and a big hat."

He nodded his head and went on round the veranda.

Mrs. Collins looked at Lesley with a smile.

"That will teach him not to be so bossy," Mrs. Collins said warmly.

"I feel like a schoolgirl who has just had permission from the headmaster to play hockey."

"Or hookey?"

They laughed together.

"Run along, Lesley. The others will beat you to it. There's a pair of Hannah's jeans on your bed. They'll fit."

They did fit, and Lesley emerged from the annexe looking as much like an Australian girl as she could with her soft, fair skin. Someone found her a straw sombrero and planted it on the back of her head. Hannah Brennan walked round and round her, appraising her from head to foot.

"You'll do," she said.

"Do?" said Mary Brennan. "Why, she looks exactly like Elizabeth Taylor. What chance has anybody got with Lesley showing off that nice boyish figure. What have you been doing with it under all those tucks and pleats and things, Lesley?"

"Oh, nuts," Betsy said languidly. "You've all been looking at her figure with envy ever since she came."

"Envy!" said Hannah loudly. "I like that! What's wrong with my own figure?"

"Nothing. It's long and lean—that's the way it's supposed to be. Lesley's is different. That's all. She's petite—as you say—like Elizabeth Taylor." And Betsy was not being sarcastic!

"Well, thank you all kindly," said Lesley. "Shall I tell you about your figures now?"

"No fear," Mary laughed. "You might forget the compliments. After all, we did say you were like Elizabeth Taylor."

"That could be a compliment to Elizabeth Taylor," Betsy said as she helped herself to cornflakes and milk.

"It would be lovely if it was," Lesley said as she reached for the cornflakes herself. What had come over Betsy?

"She not only looks like an Australian," Hannah said to Christine, "but she's getting so she talks like one and, look —she reaches like one."

Leslie laughed.

"I wish I could ride like one," she said fervently. "It will be your turn to have a good laugh when we get on the horses." There was a staggered silence and everyone put down their spoons.

"But we all ride wrong. Didn't you know? We sit wrong, we hold the reins wrong, and—horror of horrors—we have long stirrups!"

"You ride magnificently," Leslie said. She took a mouthful of cornflakes. "But please, someone shorten my stirrup for me. Otherwise I'll come off."

Dan, who had been breakfasting with the men down at the cook-house, came across the gravel square and jumped on to the veranda where the girls were eating.

"What did you say about coming off, Lesley? Can you ride at all?"

"Yes, I can ride," Lesley said. "But not bareback; at breakneck; or back to front. Also I'd rather have a shorter stirrup."

She felt as if she had been giving cheek to the head.

Dan looked at her studiedly. She thought he was angry but in reality he was thinking how pretty she was and how starry her eyes had become in the last day or two. The girls—Hannah and Mary and Christine—were being good for her.

"Leave her to Con, Dan," Betsy drawled. "You're getting a fusspot. After all, they're not going to muster to-day. They're only going to see the colts broken in. Lesley won't get thrown sitting on the stock-rails. After all, that's what she's going to do for most of the day."

Dan turned to Mrs. Collins.

"I've told Abe to saddle Lalla Rookh for you, Con, and there's Maggie for Lesley. I guess Mrs. Brennan will pick her own mount when she gets down to the stables."

"Are we all going to pick our own, Dan?" asked Mary.

"What's left," he said. "The boys have got their horses."

There was a wail from the girls.

"That leaves the old hacks to us—oh, the mean things!"

"It might have been kinder of Andy—or even Bill Daley—to take a nice weathered lady's hack and leave you with the stockhorses, of course," Dan said with a smile.

The girls jumped up and pulled their straw hats down on their heads.

"Bye, Betsy . . . sleep well!"

"At least I won't do it through my nose the way some people speak," said Betsy. "Have you got post-nasal growths, Hannah?"

Lesley stopped by Betsy where she sat alone at the table, her lovely fair, plump arms resting in front of her.

"You won't be lonely, Betsy?"

"Good God! I'm always lonely. What do you think I wander about between Alexander and Coolaroo for? My health?"

Lesley hesitated.

"Well, go on, off you go," Betsy said petulantly. "Don't hang about, for goodness sake. You might miss Dan. That's what everyone comes to Coolaroo for, you know. Those Brennans and Macintoshes and Jenkins, anyway."

Poor Betsy!

Impulsively Lesley kissed the tip of her finger and planted

it on Betsy's nose as she had seen the other do each night to Dan.

"He's nice," she said. "I suppose one of them will get him one day. Shall we bet on it?"

"No, we won't," said Betsy. "I'd lose too much sleep worrying about my money. I wish to goodness Brian would hurry up and come for me. I'm getting tired of this merry-go-round here."

Lesley jumped down from the veranda and followed the others towards the stables. Was Betsy bored? Or jealous? Or just unhappy because she was left behind? Why hadn't she come too? Bill Daley had said she was a champion horse rider. It couldn't be all laziness and therefore must have something to do with the unseen Brian.

The stockyards were almost shadeless and for those who sat on the rails and watched the young horses being brought in, looked over and discussed, it was something of an endurance test.

Mrs. Collins and Mrs. Brennan had dispatched themselves to the shade of a clump of ghost gums in a little cutting between the sharply denuded ironstone rocks about three hundred yards from the yards. Here they unpacked the pack-horse—jingling chains and billycans and all—and made ready for an early picnic lunch.

Lesley sat on the stock-rails with the Brennans and Christine. There were two fine fillies being led around by a black stock-man: on the far side Dan sat on the top rail with Bill Daley, Andy Macfarlane, Abe—in a pink satin shirt to-day—and an older stockman whose face was entirely surrounded with long, grey, wiry whiskers.

Those who didn't smoke chewed straw. Intuitively Lesley knew this was the perfect picture of a day on the run. Even the girls were serious—the business of picking the right horses for breaking was important and ticklish.

The judges sat on their top rail in silence for the most part. Only after a lot of pursing of lips and puffing of cigarettes did someone utter a remark and then it was seldom more than a word or two.

By morning tea break they had picked a dozen young horses to break. Half an hour later they started to break the horses. This was exciting, but Lesley could not help her heart going out to those lovely young wild creatures that fought for their freedom so gamely. Though she admired the horsemanship of the two blacks taking it in turns to buck-ride the colts, her heart ached for their victims.

The men, Dan, the Macfarlanes, the stockmen and rouseabouts sat on the top rail and barracked them. After a while Dan jumped down and came round to the far side where the girls were watching .

"How's it going?" he asked Lesley. "Not tired yet?"

Lesley looked down at where he stood beside the rails, an impersonal smile on her lips, and even as he asked his eyes straying into the yard. He was being the good host again but his mind was on the business of the day.

"When I'm tired I'll cry," Lesley said quietly. "You'll hear me because I cry out loud."

Dan looked at her quickly. Again she was aware of the shaft-like appraising look in his eyes. For an instant they sprang fiercely to life and a minute later were lazy and tired and a faded blue like everyone else's.

"It's not much fun so far," Dan said. "You'll see something when they bring in that young colt from Mars—the one that broke away and Bill chased. Remember? He'll take some breaking."

"How can you tell that?" Lesley asked, wondering.

"Pedigree—and recent behaviour. A rebel, but will be first-class if they can beat him."

"You better pay attention to Dan," William Macfarlane said. "He's the best judge of horse-flesh in the North-west."

Interest now shifted to the black stockman tussling with a young brown horse in the entrance to the short race that led into the sandy yard.

"Here's it," said Dan. He went back to his former place on the rail beside Bill Daley. The latter jumped down and crossed the yard. He climbed the rails above the race and looked down on the colt. Between the wooden rails the girls could see the flashing white of the young colt's eyes. His hoofs were flaying the wooden uprights.

"What do you reckon, Bill?" Dan called.

"Tony wants a go at him."

"Okay, Tony—let him go."

Tony, the black stockman, clambered down on to the colt's back from the high rails of the race. Bill Daley leaned forward and opened the gate. The colt sprang through like a shot from a gun.

"Stick to him, Tony! Stick to him!"

"Give him whatzit, Tony! Let him have it!"

"Keep your boots out of his side," Andy Macfarlane yelled.

"What the hell you think you're doing, you black son of a dingo. You want to ruin that horse?"

"You must be goin' to buy it, Andy," William said. "You sure are mighty careful what Tony does to somebody else's horse."

Tony was on the ground and the horse was flying around, heels in the air. Abe jumped into the yard and caught the colt. Together with Tony they pushed him back into the race. While the horse was being taken to the through yard and turned round there was a general flying about of comment.

"Let's have a go on him, Dan?"

"Whose turn next?"

"If he threw Tony he'll throw the lot."

"Nuts. He was pig rooting. He wasn't bucking."

"Bill Daley could break him."

"Well—maybe."

"You want a go, William?" Dan called.

"Too raking right," said William Macfarlane.

William was round the corner of the stockyard and on top of the rails along the race.

Bill Daley leaned forward again and the gate swung in. William and colt came flying in a turmoil of dust and flying feet. One turn and William was off too. He addressed the colt with a flood of North-west language. There was a shout of laughter and everyone said what they thought of the colt and none of it was complimentary.

"I just don't agree with you," Lesley said indignantly. There was a silence at her unexpected words and at the real anger in her voice.

"All you men—with all your experience—on to one little horse. And he's game enough to fight you all."

A respectful but embarrassed silence continued. Everyone who carried the makings of cigarettes—and that was all the stockmen—took them out and began to roll cigarettes while the colt was taken back into the through yard.

"Nobody means what they say when they swear at a horse, Lesley," Mary Brennan said.

"Whatever they say they don't mean anyway," Hannah said. "Did you hear William and Andy? Yet they both want the horse so much they've almost got their wallets out."

There was a shout of laughter at this for the potential buyer of a horse was supposed to keep a poker face if he wanted to keep the price down.

Lesley bit her lip because she felt she had made herself look foolish. She realised the girls were right. The forthright and picturesque language the stockmen used did not have a dictionary meaning here. She glanced across the yard at Dan but he was looking down at the cigarette in his hand. He had made no comment.

"How about it, Andy?" someone said. "You want the hoss? You ride it!"

Andy took his turn and fared no better than the others.

"Okay, Bill!" Dan's voice came across the yard. Everyone knew what he meant and there was a general straightening of backs. Tony the black stockman, took the post over the gate from the race and Bill climbed along the top rails and eased himself down on to the back of the colt. Tony let the gate fly and Bill and the pony entered the yard at a sedate drawing-room trot.

"You going somewhere, Bill?" Andy said with a grin.

"What's your average at that speed, Bill?" William called.

"Let him be," old Wire Whiskers growled. "That there colt knows somethin'. Somethin' rakin' well told 'im what 'ud happen with Bill Daley aboard 'im. 'E's waitin', 'e is."

"You better put him on the defensive, Bill—or you'll catch it in a minute."

The pony was still ambling round the yard but every inch of him was electrified with concentrated rage. Cunning was in every step. One felt that in a minute Bill Daley would hit the heavens. But Bill was a master horseman. He knew that too. He was judging to the last second the colt's endurance in a patience match. Suddenly he let him have the spurs. A convulsion stirred the horse. He plunged forward, then propped back till man and horse were perpendicular. Bill stuck with him.

Down on front feet the pony came and then went into frenzied action. A sharp swing to the side and a buck forward as he kicked up. He then charged the fence and brought his hind legs in the air as he pulled up within six inches. Bill still stayed.

The gallery was hooting and whistling. The tussle between the man and beast was sheer joy to everyone but Lesley. Though she wished no harm to Bill she longed that the lovely little horse should remain free—unbeaten; his soul his own.

Once she caught Dan Baxter's gaze on her face. She hunched her shoulders down a little and licked her lips. There was dust in her eyes and layers of it on her face. Her mouth was dry. She didn't know her small, eager, heart-shaped face was so full of compassion that Andy Macfarlane—vested interest and all in the horse—would willingly have called the contest off. Dan said nothing of what he thought but every now and again his glance flicked in Lesley's direction.

Hannah became aware of it and turned her head to look at the other girl.

"He'll have a better life in the paddocks than on the ranges. What are you looking so sorrowful about?" she asked.

"I reckon you'll have to stop home next time, Lesley," William said as he snatched a glance in her direction. But the thrill of man and horse was too much for him to waste any more reflections on Lesley.

The colt flung himself high in the air, and then clean backwards. Bill Daley's spurs stood up in air and a minute later he was on the ground. There was a shout of derision all round. Lesley relaxed and let her shoulders droop. The horse was trotting amiably round and stopped to stare at his late victim.

"That's about it," said Dan. "You take him now, Tony."

The black man walked over to the colt and vaulted into the saddle. There was a last buck or two, one rash race against the railed sides of the yards, and the colt pulled up quietly by the gate of the race. He stood shivering and sweating while Tony slowly dismounted.

"How about that feller, Tony?" Dan asked. "You muster with him?"

"I take him out, Boss," the black man said with a wide smile. "This feller make good stock horse bime-by."

When the homestead turned out to the muster the next day six of the young horses broken in were taken out by the blacks to train.

It was a glorious morning; warm, brilliant and not too hot. The musterers left the homestead at the crack of dawn. The evening before one or two rouseabouts and the black stockmen had taken out camping gear and food supplies to Mars. Abe took out Maggie and Lalla Rookh on a string with one or two other saddle horses and Lesley, with Mrs. Collins, Mrs. Brennan and Christine Macintosh, were ordered into the Utility.

Christine had woken up with a fiery headache and Dan wouldn't allow her the long ride out to the stock camp by the ranges.

Lesley was declared insufficiently experienced and Mrs. Collins out of exercise. Mrs. Brennan said she would do all the riding she wanted to do when they got to Mars.

The Brennan girls were abreast with Bill Daley and Wire Whiskers as they galloped down the stretch towards the waterourses. Dan and William Macfarlane were last to leave the omestead.

Andy had taken the Anson out to the foot of White Gum Mountain to help the Flying Doctor. The latter had flown low ver the homestead late on the previous evening to say he had ocated the sergeant and his charge: the lost prospector, no ess. Sergeant Holland's tracker had stepped in a hole and roken his leg and the prospector was too ill to travel. The octor only had his Tiger Moth plane on hand and couldn't ake the whole party out. The plane at Coolaroo had been eeded for the rescue and Andy had perforce to miss the first ay of the muster. When the parachuted message descended n Coolaroo Andy said . . .

" I'll take the raking plane out, but why the so and so, so nd so, didn't he say how far off the mountain the blighters re."

The Flying Doctor's voice came through on the transceiver et that night and he detailed the plan of the rescue. Dan pared a young jackaroo who had recently arrived from the outh to go with Andy.

Mars—a stock camp or poddy station—out on the outskirts f the vast Coolaroo property, was a hive of activity. The utter's cottage had been scoured so that camping gear and ood supplies could be stored. The hutter had rounded up the tock that had already come in. In the shallow gullies and on he slopes of the first hills could be seen the green swathe of rass. All around the camp was the jingle of hobble chains as he horses—belonging to those who had camped the night efore—grazed on the new-grown grass. This was an oasis in he wilderness.

" I suggest you all make camp and have some tea," Dan said. " I'll find Abe and get Maggie for you, Lesley. I think you'd etter stay along with me or William for an hour or two until ou get the hang of things. The boys will go out on the range his morning so we won't be too far afield."

Still the good host, Dan was impersonal but careful of his guest's welfare.

" Do you want to camp in the cottage or would you like he open air," Mrs. Collins asked her.

" The open air sounds nice. What do the others do?"

" You won't catch Mary or Hannah inside the hut," Mrs. Collins replied. " They'll camp like the men. But there's an art in it, you know. Can you roll yourself in a swag? It's necessary because it gets cold in the middle of the night. And the ground is hard."

"So is the hut floor," put in Mrs. Brennan. "And if on is not likely to get a snake there one is certain to get flea Probably bugs—now I come to look at that crazy old hutt of yours, Con."

"I'll sleep in the open air," Lesley said hastily.

"Then hang your swag on the branch of a tree and befor night scoop out a hollow with the heel of your boot. I helps."

"What do I do for a swag?"

"Dan's got one thrown in the Utility for you, Lesley. On of the boys will bring it over."

Dan came back from horseback activities a few hundre yards away. He hitched his horse to a sapling gum.

"Tony!" His voice lost its soft drawling quality. Ther was a sharp command in the single word. The blac boy, heavily booted, his bridle over his arm, came towarc Dan.

"Okay, Boss. What do you want?"

"Throw that thing down a minute, Tony. I want you fell get roll'um swag out of Ute."

Together they walked over to the Utility and Dan bega throwing bundles of canvas out on the ground.

"That one," he said, pointing to a roll a little bigger tha the others. "Take that one fella over by small tree." H looked to where Lesley was hanging her canvas bag wit a change of shirt and washing things. "Here comes you bed, Lesley," Dan said. "Don't let anyone else get it."

The black boy deposited the roll at Lesley's feet.

"I *thought* Dan had that one commandeered for a purpose Mrs. Collins said with approval. She showed Lesley how t undo the tie strings. When the canvas was unrolled it cor sisted of a double layer with a thin padding betwee

"You'll be all right," Mrs. Brennan said. "That's mor comfortable than a ground-sheet and you don't have to ro yourself in it. You get in it—see—like a long envelope."

Dan came across to look the canvas swag over.

"Seems all right," he said. "I didn't have time to look over before we left."

"Thank you for thinking of it, Dan," Lesley said a litt self-consciously. "I'm sure it will be comfortable, and eve if it isn't, I find this all so interesting I'm thrilled to be her anyway."

Dan looked at her thoughtfully.

"Mind the sun, won't you?" he said. "And don't g right up in the ranges when I let you off the string. It doesn pay to take a risk in country you don't know. Maggie is

72

good horse and will give you plenty of speed without breaking either of your necks."

"I hope I'm not too much trouble—and that worrying about me is not going to take your mind off the cattle, Dan." She bit her lip as soon as she had spoken. The words sounded ungracious and she had not meant them that way. At the same time she didn't want to eat humble pie with Dan. She would rather be just one of the others and be as little trouble—if not as useful—as they would be. Though she appreciated the thoughtfulness that Dan showed she really longed for the same casual happy-go-lucky relationships that seemed to exist between Dan and the others in the mustering party.

Dan looked out across the ranges. He screwed up his eyes as they all did when looking into the distances.

"Hannah and Mary seem to be looking after the cattle," he said with a grin.

Away in the distance could be heard the occasional call and the whip crack of a stock-whip. Thin trickles of cattle were already coming out of the pockets of broken country and leading towards the grassy patches at the foot of the hills.

"You'll miss Randolph, Dan," Mrs. Brennan said as she busied herself taking the billy tea from the Chinese cook, who had come across from the fire with it.

"He can't do two things at once," said Dan. "You can't get married and muster cattle at the same time, you know."

"Oh tut! You sound as if cattle were more interesting than a pretty bride."

"Not necessarily more interesting. You just can't have them at the same time."

"Why not? Old Rafferty and me took our wedding journey on horseback. My pillow for my wedding night was my saddle and the roof was the heaven and the only light the stars."

"They all did things that way in those days," Mrs. Collins said. "Dan's own parents came down here to Mars for their honeymoon. And Mary had that padded swag Dan's just brought over for Lesley—and a saddle for her pillow."

Dan looked at Lesley quizzically.

"Rather different from an aeroplane ride round Australia," he said. "Which do you suppose Alice would prefer?"

"She may have the aeroplane—but she's also got company," Lesley said. She forgot for the moment that Mrs. Brennan was within hearing distance. The older lady flushed.

"Joe won't worry Alice," she said. "Joe's a good boy and he and Randolph grew up together."

"I didn't really mean it that way," Lesley apologised. "I just meant that when one travels by aeroplane one generally goes to cities—and crowded places. Perhaps Dan's parents—perhaps you and your husband—were happier with the stars for company."

"The stars were for light and they weren't the only company. There were ten of us in that journey. We were over-landing cattle to Derby."

Lesley said "Oh," for want of saying the right thing. She glanced unhappily at Mrs. Brennan and crossly at Dan.

"I've no doubt about it you would prefer horseback and the stars, Dan," she said. "I don't think Alice had any choice. Did she?"

Mrs. Collins looked uneasily at Lesley.

"You two seem to be sparring," she said. "Let's leave Alice and Randolph to fend for themselves. I think you and Lesley, Dan, are all set for a pleasant camp. You don't want an aeroplane, do you?"

Lesley fought down her inclination to be cross with Dan, for again bringing up the subject of Alice and Randolph. He had been extremely kind and thoughtful to her as his guest. It was worse than bad manners for her to bridle this way. She couldn't think what had come over her.

Standing there beside the clump of ghost gums, with the smell of burning eucalyptus leaves scenting the air, the three kindly Australians standing around her holding steaming mugs of tea, she suddenly felt engulfed in loneliness.

She didn't belong to them. They were so hospitable, so friendly, so charming in their easy-going way. Yet she didn't belong. There was a gulf between them. Was it her own fault? Did it have something to do with the care Dan gave to her comfort? He didn't have to do that for the others. They belonged, like a family.

Mrs. Collins carried a mug of tea to Lesley and there was something nearly tender about the way she put sugar into it and stirred it with the communal spoon. There was something understanding in her eyes too.

"Go away, Dan," she said. "Go and rustle up those rouse-abouts and get them going into the range. By the time they've fanned out we'll be ready to come with you through the lower hills."

Dan shook out the last dregs of his mug and threw it to the cook.

"Thrown out of the ladies' boudoir, am I?" he said with a laugh. "Okay. I'll get your nags hitched up by the stock-yards in about half an hour and we'll shoot through that gully

74

over there." With a half smile in Lesley's direction he was gone over to his horse.

He leapt up in the saddle easily and the horse cantered beautifully away around the stockyards. Lesley was looking after him and wishing they could agree on the subject of Alice. When she turned back to her tea she was conscious of the curious glances of Mrs. Collins and Mrs. Brennan. Without looking up she spoke.

"I'm crabby, aren't I?" she said. "I expect it's because I'm hoping for a letter from England. Perhaps I'm jealous of Alice that I'm not on my own honeymoon."

That, she thought, would put a period to what those two kindly-disposed ladies were thinking. She knew quite well they were thinking she, like everyone else, was falling in love with Dan. In fact, Betsy quite palpably thought there was something wrong with any female who did *not* fall in love with Dan. Was it for his acres? And his thousands of cattle and sheep? Or for his standing in the vast North-west? Or was it just because he was Dan—reserved but kindly; commanding yet using the gloved hand; affectionate to his elderly cousin and his younger but more heavyweight one?

Well, Lesley had dropped her hint of heart preoccupations in England and perhaps that would tell them she was not in the competition herself. Now they would let her get on with being natural with Dan instead of being on guard.

Dan, of course, would have to leave the subject of Alice and Randolph alone. Lesley didn't want to be constantly on the defensive where her own cousin was concerned.

And please God, Alice would look happy and contented when she came back. In the meantime she, Lesley, would agree to transferring her booking to the next Orient liner passing through Fremantle.

Neil woke Lesley from her reverie.

"Howya, mate? Maggie's ready and fretting to go. I'm coming with you and after lunch Dan says I can go out on the ranges."

"Good for you, Neil," Lesley said with a special smile for the boy. How he loved this open-air station life! What would happen to Neil if he were suddenly transferred to smoke-bound England and long winter evenings indoors. He would probably pine away and die.

With a short gallop Neil brought himself up alongside the stockyard fence and unhitched the horses. He trotted up to the clump of trees with them.

"Neil, do you ever do any school work?" Lesley asked as she mounted.

"Too right, I do. Correspondence classes. Dan'll make me spend nearly a week inside catching up after the wedding and the muster."

"A week? Aren't you ever going back to Alexander?"

"We'll go back in time for the races. Never fear. People come from all over the country."

As they rode out towards the mesas Dan joined them.

"You better take it easy, Con," he said.

"You go and teach your grandmother how to preserve pickles, Dan. I knew these hills before you were born." Dan gave Lesley a grin.

"That's just it, old girl. That was thirty-odd years ago." Mrs. Collins turned in her saddle.

"And how many mountains have you moved since then, my boy?"

"You win," said Dan. "Let's take a gallop through that gully to your right. You and Mrs. Brennan scout the left side. Neil, you take up the top end of the gully and keep anything you see driven into the centre. I'll keep Lesley along with me. Then I know nothing will happen to her. Everyone right? Good. Then let's go."

Dan galloped in moderation and Lesley was thankful for that. She knew she had a good horse and she had more or less to shut her eyes and leave the scrambling up the hillside to her mount's sure-footedness.

They reached a pocket in the side of the hill where the ground was level. They scouted out three bullocks and sent them racing towards the centre of the big gully. Dan pulled up.

"Like to get down and have a rest?" he said. "I don't suppose you've galloped up a rough hillside like that before."

"I haven't," Lesley said, thankfully getting down. He was looking at her with a smile.

"I wasn't scared, you know," she said. "I just left it to you and Maggie. Between you I thought you'd take care."

"You're all right with Maggie," he said. "Shut your eyes when you come to a bad spot, and hang on. Maggie will do the rest."

He swung his leg over the horse and dismounted.

"There's a bit of shade over here under the rock face. We can sit down and have a cigarette."

Lesley sat down thankfully. Dan began to make himself a cigarette. It seemed as if they were on some little shelf about halfway up the hill and from it they could see the stock camp below and men away over to the west raising a lot of dust.

Lesley had a faint feeling of exhilaration. She liked being in things and not just a spectator. She thought she had come off rather well considering she had never ridden anywhere before but along the green sward of a village green and on nothing but a nicely behaved lady's hack.

Dan looked at her curiously.

" You enjoyed that?" he asked.

" Was I smiling? I was thinking of telling them at home about racing up a rugged mountain and driving stock out on to the plains below. They'll think I'm exaggerating."

" Will they? Why?"

" It's so like a wild west film. One doesn't think of films as being real—so this won't sound real."

Dan wrinkled his eyes as he looked out over the plain. He drew on his cigarette.

" Where do they think the beef comes from for their Sunday dinners?"

Lesley laughed.

" It's a long time since they had much of it, you know," she said.

" They'll get plenty of it now if the rains come down. And it looks like the drought will break at last. If the outlook stays the same as it is now these hills will be running streams in three weeks' time."

" It's hard to believe it. They look as if they've never seen water."

" They haven't for three years."

Lesley liked this impersonal conversation. Dan was just a very nice stockman with courteous manners and a not over-boring interest in his own livelihood. When he was like this Lesley felt she had misjudged him when she thought of him as wishing to dominate everybody else at Coolaroo. There was a steady easy-going air about him at the moment. Lesley wished she hadn't been so hard in her judgment earlier.

" Like something to eat?" Dan asked.

" You haven't got anything, have you?"

He smiled quietly.

" I always carry a saddle-bag," he said. He got up and went over to his horse. He unstrapped the water bottle and saddle-bag and brought them to where they had been sitting. He threw them both on the ground and squatted down beside them.

" One doesn't travel far without these fellows," he said. He opened the saddle-bag.

" A beauty, isn't it?" he asked, looking up quickly. Lesley

thought there was something eager and boyish about the way he asked for her admiration.

The saddle-bag was indeed a beauty. It was of hard, polished leather and the inside was divided into three compartments. In one an aluminium tin exactly fitted the pocket. Dan took this out and opened it. It contained some buttered damper and biscuits. The other two compartments had little leather cases in them.

"What are those?" Lesley asked. Dan took one out and opened it. It contained a set of shining silver instruments.

"That's called a 'travelling surgeon'," Dan explained. " See the surgical scissors, the pincers, the little surgical knife —the hypodermic syringe. Elastoplast and Band-aids."

"Do you ever use it?"

Dan's laugh rang out.

"I should say so. Snake-bite—a bad thorn—a jagged cut. Something's always happening, you know. Quite often to the horses and dogs too."

"And what is in the other case?"

"Those are some first-aid drugs. Morphia, hyacine, antiseptics, aspirin, toothache drops and earache drops."

Dan turned over the flaps of the bag and there, neatly strapped to the under-side of the flap, was a small saw, a knife, a small hatchet and a small telescope.

"So you do have a spy-glass," Lesley said.

Dan looked at her in surprise. "Who's been telling you about my spy-glass? I use it to spot straying cattle—a horseman stranded on the other side of a swollen river—anything in the distance, you know."

"Bill teased me about it the day he drove me down to the stockyards. He assured me you would be looking at us—and do you know—I felt quite guilty that day—as if I oughtn't to be there with Bill."

"Bill doesn't worry you, does he?"

Dan asked this with a slightly embarrassed air. Perhaps he thought it was his duty to protect Lesley from overt advances from his jackaroos. Lesley laughed.

"No. He doesn't worry me. I rather like Bill."

Dan was unscrewing his telescope and adjusting the sight. "He's much more able than he gives anyone to believe," he went on. He was squinting with one eye and looking out over the plain. "He can do everything a pastoralist needs to do from field surgery to mustering, droving and flying an aeroplane."

"You can't fly an aeroplane, can you, Dan?"

He lowered the telescope and smiled at Lesley.

"No," he said with a grin. "But I can navigate a ship." He raised the glass again and suddenly burst out into laughter.

"Are you seeing something funny?"

He handed her the glass.

"You have a look around the hills first," he said. "You'll see the cattle coming down, and the men over on the other side. Then look at the camp. You'll see Hannah."

Lesley did as Dan told her. It took her quite a while to get things in focus and then she could see the great worth of this little instrument. Through it one could see what was being done by everyone within range. Lesley could see Lee, the Chinaman, moving about the camp. By the small stockyard there was a horse and on it sat Hannah. Hannah had a telescope to her eye and it was directed towards where Dan and Lesley were sitting on the hillside.

Lesley lowered the glass and looked at Dan. He was smiling to himself.

"What is she looking for?"

"I think Hannah is looking for us all," he said, not unkindly. "She likes to know what everyone's doing. I hope William knows she's got hold of that telescope."

"Why William? I didn't think Hannah really returned William's affection. He is so obviously attached to her, isn't he?"

"Hannah's been receiving William's attentions all her life," he said. "So she doesn't appreciate them. But let him show defection! Now, if it were William sitting up here in this eagle's nest with you, Lesley . . . why, Hannah and that horse would burn their way up the hillside."

His face was full of affectionate amusement and Lesley looked at him in astonishment. Didn't he know that Hannah was in love with himself? Impossible that he could be so blind!

"I don't think she'd worry overmuch about William," she said thoughtfully. "I'm going back so soon. It wouldn't matter anyway, would it?"

Dan said nothing. He was putting away his telescope. While they had been talking they had eaten a little damper. Dan now unscrewed the water bottle top and handed it to Lesley.

"You first," he said. Lesley lifted the bottle to her mouth, tilted back her head and drank a little of the unsweetened lemon water that was in it. Dan took the bottle from her and then drank some himself. He screwed up the bottle and returned it and the saddle-bag to his horse.

"Well, on your way," he said. He gave Lesley a hand up on

to her horse. He sat very still a moment, looking out over the plain.

"You look like the monarch of all he surveys," Lesley said with a smile. He glanced at her quite seriously. Then he turned back to the distant reaches of the great tableland.

"You know, that's what I feel," he said. He pointed to the south. "If we could run water through there . . . There's water underneath. . . . We pump it up. The question is how to measure the underground reservoir! How to conserve the rain that does come with the cyclones!" He raised his arm and pointed to the dried bed of the Coolaroo River. "An underground stream runs under the river bed through the sand. How to measure it? What is the volume and capacity that reaches the sea? What would happen if we dammed the underground stream before it got to the sea. Would the water surface and dry out?"

Lesley looked at his thoughtful face. How many Dan Baxter's were there? This man was a dreamer and a builder. He wasn't the easy-going stockman who had proudly displayed his saddle-bag on the hillside. Nor was he the reserved, pre-occupied homesteader who said *who* was going to stay *where* amongst the womenfolk of Coolaroo. He was a man on the ranges changing a desert into a fertile land of plenty. He had taken charge of her and had provided for her; but at this moment, although he was talking to her, she didn't exist.

And neither did poor Hannah Brennan.

Lesley had no sooner completed this train of thought than she did see Hannah and her big roan " burning " up the hill-side. The horse was coming on full pelt towards them.

Lesley glanced at Dan. Surely he would register something now! But no, he shook his head and came down out of the clouds to look at Hannah in surprise.

"Where you going, mate?" he said. "Thought you went over the range. Something wrong?"

Hannah pulled up. Her rather sultry good looks were a little blemished by the mask of dust and the sulky frown on her brow.

"I didn't know Lesley was with you. Cousin Con and Mama and Neil have come down the gully—and Lesley wasn't with them. I thought I'd better see . . ."

"That was mighty nice of you, Hannah." Dan gave her a brotherly smile. "I took charge of Lesley this morning—she's a new chum, you know. But I tell you what. She's fine and dandy on Maggie. I think I can trust her to you this afternoon."

"I might spoil their riding——" Lesley said hurriedly.

"You won't," said Dan. "I'm going to ask Hannah to take the east wing on that mob we've rounded out so far. That's flat riding on the plain—and it's quite a lot of fun."

Hannah turned her horse and let it follow Dan and Lesley down the hillside.

"She won't get into any mischief with me," said Hannah.

"I thought not," Dan said with a grin. "That's why I've handed her over."

When Dan's horse was close to Lesley and Hannah some distance away he leaned towards Lesley conspiratorially.

"Hannah's got a heart of gold," he said.

Lesley reflected she would hate any man to say she, Lesley, had a heart of gold in that manner. No man who approved of a woman the way Dan approved of Hannah would ever love her.

She still didn't know whether Dan was as blind to Hannah's regard for himself as he pretended to be.

In the afternoon Dan disappeared out on to the ranges with the men and Lesley spent the day with the girls riding round and round the gradually swelling mob. By night she was hot, dirty and exhausted. During the morning and afternoon, interest in all that was going on around her had taken her thoughts away from herself. There was something in the age-old saying that a change of scene often meant a change of heart. "Send 'em away to get over it!" That's what everyone said about people who loved hopelessly—or loved the wrong person. The very pessimism of these thoughts added to Lesley's feeling of exhaustion. It may be a saving grace that the heart was capable of forgetting, but somehow youth didn't take gladly to that knowledge. Youth liked to believe that love was invincible, was eternal. Perhaps if the person one had loved had been worthy of that love, one would never really quite forget. One would always remember with tenderness and be glad that one had loved—that person in that way. The bitterness of waning love lay in the knowledge that the things that would be remembered would not be happy things. If one remembered at all . . . it would be the embarrassments, the little shabby humiliations . . . the disappointments.

Lesley's thoughts shied away from the past. She must not think about it. She must force herself—even in moments of physical fatigue when mental effort was almost too great an effort—to think of the day's happenings and all they meant. Think of the great dry plain; the cattle; the shouting, riding stockmen; the surgeon's case that rendered first-aid to men injured out-back . . .; the quiet man on the hillside who actually had the temerity to think there might be a way to turn the desert into a fertile land.

Lesley, after having washed at the water-hole and put on a clean shirt, lay back, her hands under her head, and listened to the desultory talk around the camp. A concertina was being played dolefully over at the stockmen's camp, and its sad melodies, gave Lesley's heart that restless burgeoning feeling she had known so often before she left England. It was her physical being making her restless, and her heart, wanting something with all the force of her temperament and personality and yet knowing the want was foredoomed. It was unattainable.

In England she had focused that need on Alec. She had refused to hear the still small voice that warned her it was a waste—Alec was never good enough for such devotion.

But here . . . under the starry banner of an Australian night? What was wrong with her now? What *was* her need?

She had wanted to be one with the girls, to cease to be the visitor, the person set aside, the stranger within the gates. Here at the camp she had been as much one of them as was possible. If she hadn't, it had been her own fault.

The old pain was back in Lesley's chest but it seemed to have changed its nature a little. Perhaps it had just grown an extra barb or two that only functioned on those occasions when she had taken a day off from pain and had the temerity to forget it. She felt it doubly when she returned to it.

Lesley dozed a little. Suddenly she felt someone beside her.

"What is it, Lesley?" It was Mrs. Collins's voice. "Is something hurting you?"

"It's all right," Lesley said. "I was thinking—or dreaming—about something in England. It wasn't very pleasant. Did I make a noise or something?"

"You've been restless for quite a while, dear. I got up to see if I could get you something."

Lesley sat up.

"I shouldn't keep you up. You're so very kind——" She drew her knees up and rested her clasped hands on them. Suddenly she bent her head down and covered her eyes with her hands.

"If only I'd stop remembering——"

"Remembering what, my dear? Can't I help you?"

Lesley shook herself and regained her control."

" It's just something that hurt once—and I keep remembering."

"Were those girls—or perhaps Dan himself—tactless with you to-day? Sometimes it happens innocently with people from other countries. They tease one another so much—they tease visitors——"

Lesley shook her head vehemently

"No, it's not that. They were kindness itself. Even Dan—even Dan bothered with me, and probably spoilt his morning on the ranges looking after me. He was so nice—so very kind and considerate." She broke off.

"No," she said at length. "It's not them. It's myself. I had a dream——"

Something suddenly clicked in her own mind. Subconsciously, all day, she had thought of Dan's kindness in taking out a stranger and giving up the morning to her—just out of courtesy. Alec hadn't treated her with courtesy for years. That was what was disturbing her. It was the differences—and the almost wild regret that the one wasn't more like the other. And a fear that she could not put all her trust in the second's kindness because she had been let down so often by the former. She would never again be quite self-confident. She would always doubt.

If Mrs. Collins hadn't been there she would have groaned again. Instead she straightened her back and threw back her head.

"I feel ashamed to admit it, but I think I've got just a touch of indigestion. You know, a pain in the chest. That's enough to make anyone dream——"

"That's what hot buttered damper does to you just before bedtime," Mrs. Collins said. "I thought I should have warned you at the time. I'll get you some indigestion mixture."

From the first-aid chest she brought out a white powder and mixed some for Lesley. Lesley drank the mixture and shook her head. Her change of mood from earlier in the day was not really inexplicable. Deep down she was becoming dimly aware of its causes, but she was not yet ready to delve and start turning over her innermost feelings and examining them. They were too sensitive, just now.

She slid back into her sleeping-bag. Mrs. Collins brushed the hair back from her forehead.

"Good night, my dear. Sleep well."

CHAPTER NINE

In the morning Dan was gone. During the night, shortly after the camp had really settled down, a motor cycle had come down from the homestead with an urgent message from those marooned out on White Gum Mountain. The Flying Doctor could take out the sick prospector but the black tracker who had broken his leg was suspected of further injuries and a truck and litter were required to get him across the base of the mountain. So Dan had gone back to the homestead to take out the big Utility with gear.

"Won't he mind missing the muster?" Lesley asked.

"Very much. So will Andy Macfarlane and Neil—but they had to go. *Noblesse oblige* operates in the desert just as it does in the ancestral homes of England," Mrs. Collins said. "Where human life is involved it's not enough just to send a stockman or a rouseabout. The owners, traditionally, go to the rescue."

Lesley was sorry Dan had gone away. Bill Daley, who had taken over the management of affairs at the cattle camp, and William Macfarlane, could hardly fill the gap. Lesley thought they were all probably in the habit of looking to Dan for direction and as the head of affairs. They had a somewhat suspended feeling now.

As Christine went towards the cook's camp to get her breakfast Bill rode up, slipped a lasso over her shoulders and with an easy flick, imprisoned her against his saddle. Amidst cries of protestation he bent down and kissed her.

"That's enough of that, Bill," Mrs. Collins cautioned. "You've had your fun. Let her go."

"The only way I can kiss a girl is to lasso her first," grumbled Bill as he loosened the coils. "Hop it, young Christine, or I'll do it again!"

He tilted his hat rakishly and ambled his horse towards the breakfast camp himself.

Lesley had taken little notice of the matter, thinking it only one of Bill's rather gauche pranks, until when leaning forward with her plate to rescue a spitted sausage from the fire she caught sight of Christine's face. Christine's face was rebellious and her eyes full of unshed tears.

"Christine——" Lesley leaned towards her sympathetically.

"Oh, go away. Mind your own business!" The girl turned away and almost ran towards the water-hole.

Lesley turned perplexed to Mrs. Brennan, who was on the other side of the fire.

"I didn't mean to hurt Christine. Should I go after her?" Mrs. Brennan shook her head sagely.

"Leave her alone, Lesley. I don't think Christine minded the kiss. She only minds that the one person to kiss her is so plentiful with his offers to do the same to everyone else. She'll get over it."

Lesley was astonished.

"Is Bill her special friend? Have I trespassed——"

"No, my dear. Don't give it a thought. I think Christine, like everyone else, likes Dan best. But Dan is the kind of hopeless love that keeps everyone happily lovelorn while they look around for something more likely. Just between you and me, Lesley—Christine would not dislike Bill kissing her— even publicly. She just doesn't know how to pass it off."

"Neither would I," said Lesley severely.

"Ah, but then you wouldn't be liking the kiss. That's the difference."

Lesley looked at Mrs. Brennan.

"Don't look so shocked, my dear. I'm Irish and I've got two Irish girls of my own, you know. There's not much you can tell me about young people—and their propensity for falling in and out of love."

"But you *do* something about it, don't you?"

"Well, did your parents?"

Lesley dropped her eyes. She was caught on that. Her parents had done absolutely nothing about it because Lesley had herself been bent on her own way. She had not taken them into her confidence in matters of the heart. How much difference would it have made if she had felt a bond of sympathy between herself and her mother, and had been able to go to her in the first instance? And even when mother and daughter had that bond of sympathy was a young girl ever really frank about love?

The day was full of activity for Lesley. In the morning she rode around the growing mob with Mrs. Collins. Later in the day, from the top of the stock-rails she watched Bill Dalcy rounding up the strays and packing the mob along the outskirts. He was a flash horseman—but very agile and clever. Some of the blacks on the newly broken-in colts were having a fine time training them with the cattle.

In the evening they found that the old transportable pedal wireless that had been brought down from the homestead was successfully installed in the hutter's hut and there it would remain. They learned from it that the Flying Doctor had flown back over White Gum Mountain and that Dan had just arrived there with the truck and gear. The doctor anticipated they would get the tracker out from the rough side of the mountain early in the morning and Andy Macfarlane would fly him out in the Anson.

"That leaves Dan having to bring in the truck," Mary Brennan said.

"If the sergeant comes with him it'll take days. They'll have to lead the police party's horses," Hannah said crossly. "I do think Dan should let that jolly policeman get himself out. After all, there'll be seven hundred steers in that mob, and that's a mighty lot of money to leave lying around the North-west."

Bill Daley threw a tree nut at Hannah.

"Who said they're going to be left around? I'm going to move that mob down to the coast."

There were exclamations of doubt and surprise.

"You heard the forecast," he said. "The raking cyclones are stirring up again. I'm gonna get that mob out before one of 'em hits Ninety Mile End."

Bill's statement was followed by a thoughtful silence. At last Mrs. Collins spoke.

"I think you're right, Bill. If Dan was here he'd shift what we've got out of the ranges already. I thought that when I heard the weather forecast."

"And I'm the boss," said Bill Daley, putting his thumbs under his armpits and leaning back grandiosely. He beamed on everyone as if challenging them to deny it.

The next day passed in a similar fashion. This time Lesley made short excursions up the hills into the cuts and gullies to drive out occasional strays. The older women hurried these bullocks along to join up with the mob.

The pains and aches attendant on one's first few days' strenuous riding had left Lesley and that night, as she lay back on her swag beside the coals of the camp-fire, she felt relaxed more than tired. She felt as if she had a place—oh, so minute a one—in the scheme of things that revolved around Coolaroo and its unseen master. She suddenly wished Alec could see her in this situation. How he would marvel—if he even believed it! If he were there, if he came walking across the plain now she would rise and toss her head and say, "See? Now you know where your Sunday dinner comes from. I hunted it out of the ranges on the edge of the West Australian desert my-own-very-self."

The concertina player down at the stock camp was playing

sentimentally again. Presently, Bill Daley came around the camp-fire while they waited for tea and sat down beside Lesley. He began to tell her snake yarns.

"I don't believe any of them," Lesley said. "You know, you people are famous for snake yarns. They're like fishermen's tales."

"Some of them are true," warned Mary Brennan. "Don't be too sceptical, Lesley. You might meet a snake next time you take a swim in the water-hole."

"If you see a ripple of water moving out in a fan shape it will be a crocodile—or a snake," said Bill. He moved a little nearer to Lesley.

"Now I'll tell you some dingo yarns," he confided. "Do you want me to hold your hand? A dingo yowling in the night can fairly make your blood run cold."

"Not enough to have my hand held," Lesley said quickly.

"Not even in matrimony?"

Lesley could see why Bill, good-natured and all though he was, was not the social success with the girls he longed to be. He made jokes that were pointless; that didn't come off.

"Go and pay your attentions to someone else, Bill," she said with a laugh.

"You'll be sorry," warned Bill. "To-morrow I won't be here."

"You won't be far enough away," put in Hannah sharply. "We'll still hear you singing to the cattle, from this distance."

"Singing to the cattle?" said Lesley, perplexed.

"Would you like to come and hear? We won't be so far out by to-morrow night and we've got the best singing drovers in the North-west."

"If it's anything like that concertina player——" Lesley began, but everyone cried her down.

"It's not!"

"It's important. It settles the cattle."

"Like children, you mean?"

"You come out to-morrow night and you'll see," Bill said. "There's a couple of men round them to-night but the cattle can hear the noises of the camp mostly and that keeps 'em quiet. To-morrow when they're out under the stars they got to keep hearing noise—soft noise, mostly, to stop them getting the jumps. If they get the jumps they can stampede. And theres no fences out on the plain!"

"So someone sings to them?"

"All night long a drover rides round 'em snapping sticks, speaking smartly to one or t'other, but mostly he sings. You see, singing, he can keep up the soft noise all the time. And he can get some fun out of it, too."

All the time Bill had been flirting thus mildly with Lesley, Christine had sat in silence nearby. Lesley grew more and more uncomfortable. She wished she knew whether Christine was afraid that she, Lesley, was being taken in by the jackaroo's brash ways or even encouraging them.

Lesley found the girl somewhat inexplicable. Christine was a daughter of a pastoralist family herself, but except for her very fine horsemanship did not seem to be as tough as the others. She was full of bright ideas and fun and yet subject to sudden fits of moodiness. She seemed over-eager in her advances to Dan and the two Macfarlane brothers. Only Bill Daley she left severely alone.

Lesley thought that Christine was a girl who had had many advantages in life—and yet was neither as enterprising nor as happy as a girl with her background would be expected to be.

Faint and far away could be heard the drone of a bee.

"What do you hear, Con?" Mrs. Brennan asked.

"I think it's a plane."

"It's the Anson," said Hannah from a distance.

"It's the Anson, all right," said Mary. "They must have got that tracker out safely. I guess Andy will take him up to the homestead. They'll land before dark."

"Will they fly overhead and drop a message, do you think?" Lesley asked.

"No fear," Mary and Mrs. Brennan said almost together.

"The plane would stir up the mob. Andy will see the cloud of dust and know they're on the move. He'll keep away."

"Then we won't be able to know how they got on," Lesley said with disappointment.

"We'll wait till they open the air station," Mrs. Collins said. "We can pick up what he says on the pedal wireless. They might have news of Joe and the young couple up at the homestead."

Lesley wondered how Betsy was getting on up there all by herself. Would she sleep the whole clock round? It would be fun for her to have Andy back for a night anyway.

"Poor old Dan," Mrs. Collins bewailed. "He'll be bursting to know how the barometer is and if Bill's moving the cattle. And he might be stuck out there at White Gum Mountain— or on the way in—for days."

"Pity he's so stubborn about flying, you know," Mrs. Brennan said with a faint air of pride in the aeronautical triumphs of her own family. "What's the good of being a sailor when you live in the middle of a desert."

"Dan loves those pearling luggers up and down the coast," Mrs. Collins said. "The war brought a dream true for him when he joined up. When Dan takes a holiday—as you know—he doesn't go south to the bright lights; he goes to the sea."

"He could still fly."

"He hasn't got time to learn. I guess Randolph won't be long, though. All the boys in the North-west had an advantage learning to be pilots in the war. Randolph likes the sea too—but not so much as Dan does."

Hannah and Christine came from the cook's fire with a billy of boiling tea between them. The Chinese cook pattered behind them with two plates of scones.

Hannah put the billycan down and turned to watch the Anson against the eastern sky.

"He's landing," she said. "Old Harry is sleeping in his hut, so goodness only knows when we can get the wireless going. Andy might just have come in for supplies—or something."

"Well, if that's all we'll see him fly out again. Then we'll know."

Mary poured the tea into the mugs and Christine handed round the scones.

"I vote we all go to sleep," Christine said. "It's too hot to talk."

"You girls sleep your lives away."

"Why not? Look what fun Betsy has."

The talk did in truth drift away in spurts as the last of the sun struck down on the camp, still with the wrath of God in it.

Lesley, from under the shade of her hat, tried to count the dancing diamonds of light shooting in between the plaits of straw.

How easy and natural these girls were. It was all because of the simplicity of the life here on a station in Australia. Everyone was nearer to the earth. They were more volatile because less inhibited; more emotional. And more naïve. This thing called "reserve" which she was supposed to have was in reality no more than a protection against people. One had to protect oneself against people in a land where one mixed with millions all the time. Here they only had to protect themselves against the land and the sun.

But Dan! He was reserved—or wasn't he? Was he just on guard—always protecting his acres?

Lesley decided Dan was what she called "funny" and not meaning "funny" at all. He was so easy and unaffected half the time. The other half he was like a closed oyster.

Perhaps he was only closed to herself. And Alice!

Poor Alice! Lesley sighed for Alice. She would have a real battle getting her own way with Dan riding round and round Randolph and keeping things going his way. Alice did like her own way too! Lesley had the most curious mixture of feelings on this subject. In the hidden recesses of her mind she knew that Dan was right and that Alice had made her choice when she engaged herself to Randolph and had therefore to face and fit in with the life that Randolph could give her. On the other hand, a contrary streak in Lesley herself wanted to see Dan as an overbearing overlord—master of Coolaroo— who was going to see that Alice toed the line just as Bill Daley and Cousin Con and the stockmen did. Even though Dan ruled with a gloved hand, he ruled. That easy-going manner of his changed like lightning when he gave an order. How his voice crackled out!

For all the terrible isolation of people in the North-west they managed to have a lot of fun. They had it the hard way— but they had it. Lesley's mouth curved in a smile as she recollected Hannah trying to rescue chops from the barbecue when the fat on them had caught fire. Hannah had lost her temper and let the lot drop in the coals. Two stockmen rushed to the rescue of the chops and they told Hannah what they thought of her and she told them the same thing back, in no uncertain terms. Hannah had stood by the fire, the light from the flames licking over her and giving her temper a fiery aspect. Nobody would have dared to laugh.

Lesley laughed now in retrospect. Then suddenly she remembered she had not laughed to herself in years. Laughter she had reserved as a studied thing to assume as part of the façade that hid her inner self. Her inner hurt self.

And here she was laughing with nobody around to see. Lesley lifted her hand up and let it rest on her chest.

She even felt irritated she had to remember she had had a pain.

She didn't know what had happened to her. She felt that in the girls' company, in the point and recover of their by-play, she herself had been through some experience and out of it she had come whole.

For the dinner barbecue next night Bill Daley, five miles away with the cattle, sent back a stockman called Reynolds.

He rode into camp at sundown, a fossil of a man, dust-coated and grimed from head to foot.

"Sent back to see if youse all right?" he said. "Wire Whiskers should be down in the mornin'. Bill says I gotta stay to-night with youse all. Reckon that's all right. Bill says Andy Macfarlane will probably be down here sometime soon. Reckon youse all saw the Anson land."

"That's all right, Reynolds," Mrs. Collins said. "We're grateful for your company. How's the mob going?"

"Five miles, Miz Collins. Reckon that's fair goin' fer the first day. Bill's happy, anyway. Mob's quiet enough."

The dark had barely begun to close in on them when a light in the distance heralded the approach of a motor cycle.

"Thought I heard that a few minutes ago," Mrs. Brennan said. "I guess that's Andy coming down from the homestead. The plane didn't fly out again so all must be well out at White Gum Mountain."

The chug-chug of the motor cycle could be heard and the jumping light spread a path of gold across the spinifex plain.

"He'd better go slow," Mrs. Collins said anxiously. "Those things aren't safe at night time. It isn't as if there was a track. A horse, now——"

"He'd be all night coming on a horse," Mary said. "I bet he's bursting to know how the muster went and if the mob's really moving."

"Come on, let's go and meet him. He'll stop the other side of the broken country in case there's any cattle loose around here."

Mary and Hannah jumped up.

"He's all yours," said Christine complacently. "Lesley and I don't believe in running after Macfarlanes. We're stopping here."

Lesley thought she would take Christine's hint. Next to Dan the Brennan girls loved the Macfarlanes.

She threw a stick into the fire and quietly got up.

"You can stay here, Christine," she said lightly. "I'm going to have a look at the stockyards in the moonlight. We waste too much moonlight sitting round that fire."

"You ought to have been a drover yourself, Lesley," Mrs. Collins said kindly. "They live by moonlight. They only endure by daylight."

Lesley dug her hands deep in the pockets of her jeans and strolled away from the camp. Down at the yards she turned round, spread her arms along the top rail and leaned back looking towards the camp.

She was conscious of the immeasurable vastness and loneliness of the country. It did not intimidate her as it did Alice. Somehow she admired the country for its enormity, its silent, inscrutable strength and the incredible endurance of the ghost gums and spinifex that they survived and prevailed.

She saw and heard Hannah and Mary coming over a silver rise with Andy. She could hear them, laughing and excited. All must have gone well out at White Gum Mountain for there was nothing subdued about the exuberance of the girls. They had Andy back—that was one man recaptured from the desert!

Lesley stayed alone in the moonlight for a few minutes and then she started to stroll back towards the camp. She could see the figures of Mrs. Brennan and Mrs. Collins reaching up and kissing Andy welcome. How affectionate everyone was! Those young men—Dan and Randolph and Andy and William and Joe Brennan really belonged to everyone. Everyone had the right to kiss and be kissed.

Lesley suddenly thought it would be rather nice to be in on the kissing business too. One wouldn't feel so lonely. Perhaps that's why they all did it. The country was so lonely, the life would be so intolerably lonely if it weren't for one another.

Andy's black shadowed figure came away from the firelight across the camping ground to meet her. He seemed bigger—is that what mountains did to men?

"Hallo, Andy!" she called gaily.

"Hallo, Lesley," he said. "But I'm not Andy. I'm Dan."

Lesley's heart quite literally and unexpectedly turned over.

"Oh!" she said awkwardly.

Dan was right up to her now and he held out his hand. Lesley put her hand in his. Her voice wouldn't come.

"They haven't killed you off yet?" Dan said.

"No. No—I've managed all right—I think."

"I'm sorry I'm not Andy. I seem to be a general disappointment all round."

Lesley had recovered her poise now.

"You're not that, Dan. Everyone was expecting Andy, that's all."

They had turned and walked back towards the fire. Dan stooped down and lifted a leather mail bag.

"A truck passing through from Ninety Mile End brought out the mail and there are four letters for you, Lesley."

Lesley took the letters from him and as she did so marvelled at how her hand trembled. Even in the firelight she could recognise the handwriting. An Australian stamp! News from Alice at last! One from mother, one from aunt—one from Alec.

"Go away and read them in a corner, Lesley," Mrs. Collins said. "I know what mail from home is like—you're bursting to hear the news."

"I'd like to read Alice's letter anyway."

"Yes, rather. We all want to hear the news."

The letter was shorter than Alice's usually were. Randolph was a pet. He really was a pet of a husband. Joe, of course, was frightfully amusing but he wouldn't go home. She didn't really mind now—she'd got used to him. She was really having fun, but the heat! And the dreadful country without a blade of grass . . . and the flies! Lesley had no idea, but the country went on like that for hundreds and hundreds of miles. What did Lesley think of the idea of persuading Randolph to sell out his share in the station to Dan and buying a nice farm in the south of England? Randolph had been *crazy* about England when he was there. He'd never seen such lush grass, such fat cattle, such hefty sheep. She hadn't mentioned the idea to Randolph yet, but she wanted to ask Lesley to get in some groundwork with the other Baxters at Coolaroo. She knew that Lesley was staying on a week or two because Betsy's voice had come over the Flying Doctor circuit about the black tracker with a broken leg. She had also told the whole world about Lesley. Did Lesley know that *everything—everything* that was uttered over the wireless was listened in to by *everybody* in the North-west. It was like having a morning and evening gossip service!

And so on.

Lesley realised she couldn't pass the letter around as she would have liked to do. She folded it and put it in her pocket. As she opened the envelope of her mother's letter she was conscious of a little silence as everyone watched her. It mattered very much to them—about Alice. They wanted to know, all of them, if everything was all right. Randolph was theirs and they wanted to know if all was going well with his marriage. Lesley swallowed hard.

"Alice says Randolph is a darling and a pet of a husband. Also she loves him. Also she thinks Joe is amusing and she likes him being with them."

She could almost hear the unison of expelled breaths.

"Go on and read your home letters, dear," Mrs. Collins said.

"Are you going to be homesick, Lesley?" Hannah asked.

"Do you want a loan of a handkerchief—or just a hunk of privacy?"

"I've got two handkerchiefs, and my mother never makes me feel homesick."

She read the letter quickly. Dad was well, the garden was shining; Branks, the dog, was in good health though he had got off his lead in the village the other day and had his usual altercation with Mrs. Smithson's terrier. Of course, the Smithsons' chauffeur had had to separate the dogs and quite a crowd collected. Too embarrassing! And how could she argue with a Rolls Royce and a chauffeur! She just had to appear to be in the wrong. Aunt was well, but just too worried for words about Alice. How was Alice getting on in that strange country—though really, from the newsreels about the Queen's tour it seemed to be very much more settled than one dreamed. Quite big cities and they all hoped that Alice had one of those lovely houses overlooking the harbour—like the one the Queen visited in private. Everyone assured her that pastoralists in Australia were really frightfully rich. They all had mansions round Sydney Harbour. Alec hadn't been to see them since Lesley's departure, which is exactly what Lesley's mother had said would happen!

Aunt's letter also explained her deep anxiety about Alice's happiness "so far from home". She, too, expected that Alice would live in one of those lovely houses on Sydney harbour. Was Coolaroo Downs within motoring distance of Sydney? And what enormous cars the Australians seemed to have! How very comfortable and wealthy Randolph must be with all those cars and trucks and things. Even neighbours with aeroplanes. Alec hadn't been to see anybody—and what did anybody expect anyway!

Lesley folded that letter and put it away in her pocket too. Something hard and burgeoning swelled in her breast again. If she let the tears shine in her eyes everyone would think she was soft—was homesick. So she put on a hard little smile and looked up at everyone brightly.

"All's well," she said. "Everyone is thrilled with Alice's wedding, and the dog's had a fight with our aristocratic neighbour's dog."

She couldn't bring herself to tell them the joke about the house on Sydney Harbour. They wouldn't understand how anyone from Europe would misunderstand distances.

Everyone noticed that the fourth letter went unopened into her shirt pocket.

"Right over her heart," Christine whispered audibly to Hannah.

Mrs. Brennan nudged Mrs. Collins.

"That's it," she said, nodding her head and pursing her lips. "There's someone in England!"

Dan finished rolling himself a cigarette and lit it. He stood, his back to the fire, his slouch hat still on the back of his head, the fire flames casting his legs in long shadows across the ground until it seemed as if his shoulders and head were climbing the gum tree.

"All's well with Alice and Randolph?" he asked. "They're getting on all right? No word about when they're coming home?"

"Break it down, Dan," said Mrs. Brennan. "They've only just got married."

"Besides, Joe's got to have his holiday," Hannah said.

"She didn't say anything about coming home," Lesley said. "She devoted most of the space to telling me what a nice husband she had married."

There was something challenging about the way Lesley said this. As if she were on the defensive. Dan lifted his head in sudden surprise.

"That's what we all thought," he said gently. "But then we're prejudiced, of course."

"As long as you're prejudiced in favour of people—not against them——" Lesley said.

Dan looked at her steadily across the fire.

"Are you tired, Lesley?" he asked.

She bit her lip and said nothing.

"She can't afford to be tired," Christine said. "She's got a date with Bill Daley. She's going out to hear him singing to the cattle."

"Nonsense," said Mrs. Collins. "That was just a joke. Christine, you go and get the billy of tea like a good girl. Dan wants some tea."

"Would you like to go out to the cattle, Lesley?" Dan asked gently. "I'm going out myself in the Ford 'Ute'. I'll take you if you would like to go."

Lesley was still struggling with her voice. She felt that Dan's studied kindness was real kindness, yet underneath she suspected his determination to have his own way with Alice and Randolph. As Master of Coolaroo he would be a wonderful master, provided everyone did what he wanted them to do. Or was she doing him an injustice? Was it her own anxiety—or own insecurity—that made her suspicious of him.

"Yes, thank you, I would like to go," she said at length. "By the way, what did you do with Neil?"

95

"He's coming in with the sergeant. They're bringing in the truck together. I came in with Andy but he stayed at the homestead to overhaul the Anson engine to-morrow."

"I suppose he wanted to make the trip with the sergeant?"

"He did. And we believe in teaching the tough way when they're young. They'll be days coming in because they've got the horses behind."

That, thought Lesley, disposed of Neil. Yet Dan was so fond of him!

Christine came up with the tea and once again all mugs were out as the boiling brew was passed around. Dan was first finished.

"Go on with you," said Mrs. Collins. "We all know you're itching to get out to the mob, Dan. Lesley, there's a jacket in the 'Ute'. You'll need it coming back."

"Aren't we invited?" said Christine with an injured air.

"No," said Dan firmly. "You know what the cattle're like at night, Christine. One unexpected sound and they stampede. I can manage one fractious young lady but not a bevy. When they've settled down—say to-morrow night—you might come out. I'll see."

"How far will they be to-morrow night?" Lesley asked as she went with Dan towards the Utility.

"With luck another six miles."

He opened the door of the car and switched on the dash-board lights. Lesley got in and Dan bent to pull some sacking away from her feet. His hand rested for a moment on her boot and he looked up into her face with a smile.

Lesley looked down into his face. There was nothing there but quiet kindness. He wasn't really being hard on Alice. It was only herself, Lesley, who was wrong. For a moment her mouth trembled.

Dan straightened himself. With one hand he lifted off the hat that clung perpetually to a man's head when he was out in the open air.

"You're very pretty, Lesley," he said softly.

"Thank you, Dan."

He walked round the car and got in beside her.

He sat, leaning back, his hands on the steering-wheel. He stared straight in front of him for a minute. Then he looked at Lesley and grinned.

"That was quite a struggle," he said.

He started up the car.

"A struggle?" she asked.

He began to move forward slowly and carefully, craning his

neck so he could see every hump and spinifex, every rut of ironstone.

"I never really wanted to kiss anyone before," he said, smiling but not looking at her. "That kind of a kiss anyway."

"Oh, Dan!"

His left hand dropped off the steering-wheel and took hers. She didn't know whether he squeezed her hand tight or whether her hand clung to his, but for a moment she felt safe and happy.

CHAPTER TEN

Dan drove through the moonlight and Lesley had the eerie feeling of being alone in a forsaken world. The silver plains stretched away, as clear as in daylight, until only the night sky looming black on the horizon put a period to them.

They were silent and yet it was not an uncomfortable silence. Lesley felt quietly happy. It was almost a homey feeling to be sitting there away from the noisy, happy-go-lucky girls and the motherly watchfulness of Mrs. Collins and Mrs. Brennan.

Glancing sideways, Lesley could see Dan's face. It was pale because of the moonlight, yet there was something strong and firm about it. Yet so easy. They had gone a little over five miles when Dan pulled up.

"We'll leave the 'Ute' here," he said. "How are you at walking in the moonlight, Lesley?"

"I've always been waiting to try it," she said with a laugh. Dan opened the door for her and put his hand under her elbow as she alighted.

"Don't they have any moonlight in England?"

"You should ask Randolph that. He and Alice did their courting by some kind of light—and it wasn't electricity."

They began to walk across the plain towards the west. "See the Southern Cross? That group of stars there, and the two pointers?"

Dan had stopped and was pointing to the brilliant stars hanging low in the sky.

"The upper and the lower stars serve as pointers to the south pole of the heavens. So you keep your eye on an imaginary line drawn along that meridian, Lesley, and keep that line on our left. Then we're going due west—that's where the cattle are."

"Like the pointers on the Plough as we see it in the northern hemisphere."

"Exactly. If you get lost don't travel by daylight. You only walk round in circles, and the heat—and shortage of water—are exhausting. Travel by night, and get your direction from the Southern Cross."

"There's not much chance of my being lost—is there? I'm too well looked after."

"You never can tell. Con was the only whole person in a car crash about ninety miles this side of Witchery. She set out for Witchery, lighting small fires at mile intervals, and she was picked up."

"Well, I'll only be here another two or three weeks. With luck I won't be in any car crashes in that time."

There was a little silence. Dan helped Lesley over a broken cut in the ground.

"Dan, you did fix up that booking on the *Arcadia*—didn't you?"

"The Bank is looking after it. They'll let me know when they've got the thing tied up."

"But there shouldn't be any difficulty. I've got an option on a berth."

"I guess it will be all right," Dan said without much enthusiasm.

"Alice will be home in at least a week or ten days," Lesley said.

"You sound defensive," Dan said. "Don't you feel you *ought* to go? Or why go at all? There's lots of time in the North-west, you know. You could stay for years!"

"Don't be silly. I have my own life. A home and a job. My job won't wait for ever, you know."

"Why not make Coolaroo your job?"

"What you really want is a wet-nurse for Alice and Randolph, isn't it, Dan?"

She stopped quite still and looked at him. She was surprised that she had to look up so much. Dan was taller than she thought—or was he standing on a mound?

"There are quite a lot of reasons why we would like you to stay, Lesley. The most important one is that we like to have people staying. It makes the womenfolk feel less lonely and isolated. And they are very isolated, you know. I would be sorry for Alice to feel the impact of that isolation too soon. I am thinking of Alice and Randolph but only in the second place. We—Cousin Con and I—would like you to stay. Just because we like you staying——"

He broke off. Neither of them seemed able to see situations like this without the shadow of Alice across them.

"I do think you could help Alice a lot," Dan finished lamely.

"I might give her the wrong kind of advice," Lesley said. Some demon had got hold of her and was saying the wrong things for her. Even while she was speaking Lesley knew she was being tactless, and yet she couldn't stop herself. She had some indefinable desire to rouse Dan from his courteous quietness—to strike fire. Dan said:

"I think you're rather fond of your cousin. You wouldn't have come so far to be her bridesmaid. The kind of advice you would give her would be calculated to help her settle down and make a home of Coolaroo."

"I don't know. It's difficult at this stage. You see—Alice wouldn't really have a home, would she? It's yours and Betsy's and Cousin Con's. She wouldn't even be able to work out the day's menus—or rearrange the furniture. . . ."

They were walking on slowly now.

"That's it," Dan said warily. "Living on a station is rather like living in a compound in China—and the Far East. It's a community affair."

"I think they'd both be happier on a farm they could call their own—in the south of England. That's what Alice would like. Randolph would like it too. He was crazy over our pasture lands and the livestock. He'd never seen anything like it——"

Lesley stopped. She wished she could un-utter the words. When she had read the proposition in Alice's letter she knew it was ridiculous and had anticipated quite a battle getting Alice rid of the idea. And here she was propounding it as if it were her own. As if she, herself, supported the idea. She knew very well she herself would think less of Randolph if he were so easily weaned away from his own country; from his life's occupation and from the family heritage which he shared in Coolaroo Downs.

Something inside Lesley was goading her on. If she had wanted to hurt Dan—really to strike fire—this was the way to do it. Yet she *didn't* want to do this. What was the matter with her?

Dan's silence did nothing but goad her on.

"Alice would no longer be a problem to you—thirteen thousand miles away, Dan."

She could have cried. She was hitting him with words as a child would drum her heels on the floor or her hands on the table. Personal pride would not let Lesley see into her own heart and understand that frustration was making her strike the person she liked best in all this million miles of North-west. She was not yet ready to look inward and understand that frustration or the sources from which it stemmed.

Dan's silence made her bite her lips to keep silence herself. To continue thus would cause her to lose her own dignity. And she regretted each word as she uttered it.

Lesley stumbled and Dan put out his hand to help her. She could not even bring herself to thank him.

What had come over her? It was as if suddenly a great black cloud had enveloped her spirit.

Dan had nearly kissed her, and she had been flattered. They had driven together in a kind of cosy silence that she had enjoyed. The "Ute" had come as near the cattle as Dan dared drive it without scaring them, and he and Lesley had got out and were walking through the moonlight in the direction of the drovers' camp.

What in all that had caused this avalanche of regret?

Lesley ceased to notice the silence between them as she sought to recover her poise and recover her spirits. They had come up a little rise and Dan again touched Lesley's arm. This time to ensure silence. They stood listening. Down below them they could hear the crackle and thud of a horse as it passed noisily over a strip of spinifex. The drover riding the horse was singing throatily:

"Wrap me up with my stock-whip and blanket,
    And bury me deep down below,
    Where the dingoes and crows can't molest me,
    In the shade where the coolibahs grow.

"Hark! there's the wail of a dingo,
    Watchful and weird—I must go,
    For it tolls the death-knell of the stockman
    From the gloom of the scrub down below."

The voice stopped and there came the sound of the clink of hobbled hoofs. The drover's voice came loud, throaty and peppered with blasphemy.

"What the rakin' hell you doing there, Jonah? Git yourself to rakin' hell some place else."

There was a subdued sound of a flat-handed smack on the

rump of a horse, a snort and blow from the animal and the jingle of hobble chains.

Dan began to speak very softly and his voice rose steadily and slowly until he was speaking quite loudly.

"The drover makes a noise to get the mob used to sounds in the night. Everything is so dead still otherwise, the crackle of a stick would frighten the cattle. The sound of the "Ute" would be too foreign to them to risk it. By now—" Dan's voice was raised enough now so that the drover could probably hear him—"they will have heard my voice. It's not frightening them."

"Am I allowed to speak?" Lesley whispered.

"Yes. Quietly at first and then bring it up to ordinary conversation level."

The drover had either seen their figures silhouetted against the pale sky or had heard their voices. His own came, carefully modulated in the same tone as he had previously used for swearing purposes.

"That you, Boss? Kinda thought you'd come. Reckon'd it wouldn't be Andy at this hour of night. All right, Boss, come in. They're keeping pretty quiet."

"Walk softly at first," Dan said to Lesley. "Then get a bit more noisy."

Lesley did as she was told. There were seven hundred head of cattle somewhere in front of them, and the wrong sound would send them stampeding.

By the time they reached the drover, sitting high and hunched on a big horse, they were making any amount of noise with their boots.

"How's the camp, Dig?" Dan asked.

"They're snug and tight, Boss. They're dead to the world. Everything's okay. Bill's done a good job."

"Thanks," said Dan. "By the way, Dig, we got the prospector and the black out. The sergeant's coming into Coolaroo in the next few days. He's bringing in the truck. I came in with Andy. I'll take over from Bill, and Andy can take over later in the week."

"Okay, Boss, suits me. Reckon Wire Whiskers'll do the night watch when 'e gits in from the ranges."

Dan and Lesley moved off in the direction of the camp. They could see the coals of the fire about five hundred yards away.

"We should keep talking," Dan said. "Just to let the cattle know we're around. Do you know anything about the price of wheat, Lesley? The Chicago free market is falling, which looks like a stock-pile is coming on the market. In June,

Australian wheat was 18/6½d. a bushel. In the depression my father got 1/6d. a bushel, so why should I complain?"

"I didn't know you grew wheat on Coolaroo."

"We don't. I'm merely talking about wheat so as to keep talking. My father did get 1/6d., however, because he came off Coolaroo in the depression. He left Betsy's father as manager. We went share farming in the wheatbelt to grow the food to feed ourselves. You can't grow food in the North-west. We've only got the engines for pumping water since the war. Before then it was windmills—and no money to keep them in repair. Without water you can't grow anything."

They were on the fringe of the camp now.

"So ends the first lesson in talking to the cattle. I'm sorry to bore you, Lesley. If I'd been Bill now—I'd have sung you a serenade."

Around the dying embers of the fire were rolled the swags. Dan went from one to another—evidently knowing by its length or outline which would be Bill Daley.

"Up, you son of a gun!"

A well-aimed boot—striking in the right spot—brought a swag to the sitting position. In some incredible way it unwound itself too.

"What the hell——"

"It's okay, Bill. And there's a lady here, so don't swear."

"Crikey, Dan! I'm glad to see you. I'm fair done in."

"I hear everything's all right."

"Too right, it is. What did you think?"

"Just that. You want a spell to-morrow, Bill? I'll take over if you like."

"Too right I want a spell."

He was peering through the flickering light of the fire and suddenly realised the lady present was Lesley.

"I wish I'd taken that turkish bath before dinner," Bill said ruefully. "Truth is, I told the servants to turn the tap off and I forgot to turn it on again."

Lesley knew there wasn't water for miles around and she rather appreciated Bill's wry humour.

"You've got to get up and sing for the lady, Bill," Dan said. "That's what she's come for?"

"What? In these whiskers? In this dirt?"

"You haven't got whiskers on your larynx, have you?"

Bill had unwound himself completely by this time and he stood up. Except for his boots he was dressed as for the day. He reached for his boots and began to pull them on.

"You want to go round the mob, Dan?"

"Got anything saddled up?"

"Jinx is tied up and Jonah ought to be around somewhere. He's in hobbles."

"We met Jonah—he's east of the mob. I'll take Jinx, Bill. You take care of Lesley, will you? And you might stir up the fire and get the billy going."

Bill lurched away in the darkness and came back a few minutes later with a horse on the lead. It was saddled up. Dan sprang up.

"They all bunched, Bill?" he asked.

"Yeah. Follow round where you come from. Dig's out that way and you can spot the mob from that side easier."

"Give me about an hour," Dan said. "I'll come in for some tea. You'd better stir up Sam and get him on the mouth organ. Between you, you'll entertain Lesley. And don't forget the tea."

With the stumbling of hoofs against ironstone Dan rode away into the shadows. Except for his discourse on wheat he had not addressed Lesley. And that discourse had been for the cattle, not for her. Was she angry? Hurt?

Lesley thought sadly that she merited his disapproval and his absolute silence was a sharper punishment than he would have realised. From it Lesley could not tell whether he was angry or whether he was just going to take some kind of action that would make things harder for Alice.

Dan would have to be kind to Alice—in order to help her settle down. If she sensed displeasure or disapproval the spoilt child in her would react badly. She would be more "spoiled" than ever.

Bill Daley had kicked another swag into life and there was an altercation going on as to whether the inhabitant of the swag should get up and fetch his mouth-organ, *and* the billy of tea, *and* a dozen chops, *and* a tin of tomatoes.

"Oh, please don't wake him up," Lesley said. "It seems so unfair."

"He'll like it—when he's up. I do."

Bill threw some wood on the fire and by the sudden up-leaping of flame Lesley could see he was indeed unshaven and very dishevelled.

"I'm no sight for ladies," Bill said regretfully. "Well, that's the life on the land for you. No room for a change of clothes when you're droving."

The man called Sam was alive at last. He brought a wire frame and threw it on the coals. Some carcass meat was hanging in a bag from a small tree and he took this out and cut off some chops. These went on to the wire frame and began to sizzle over the coals.

"Feed the brutes," he said. "First thing a feller wants when he wakes up is a feed."

He handed Lesley a grilled chop on the end of a small spiked stick.

"Use yer fingers, miss. That's what we all do."

Bill had found some damper in the store tins and, cutting a piece length-wise, he advised Lesley to put her chop between the two layers.

It was a lovely meal. Lesley felt unexpectedly hungry and the chops were sweet and succulent.

"How you getting on without me?" Bill asked Lesley. "Breaking your heart, eh?"

"We seem to be getting along fine, Bill," Lesley said. "Of course, the girls never stop talking about you. They must miss you . . . *terribly*."

"You don't say!" said Bill. He sounded surprised but pleased. Lesley realised rather ruefully that Bill had taken her teasing as fact.

"What do they say about me? A bit brash, eh?"

"I think everyone thinks you're one of the finest horsemen in the North-west, Bill," Lesley said with greater truth. "When I hear people talk about you—they never fail to admire your ability on a horse."

"Do you hear that, Sam? What do you reckon about that?"

"I reckon the young lady's pullin' yer leg, Bill. But she does it so smart she deserves a song. Now where's me mouth-organ?"

After much rummaging in saddle-bags Sam emerged with his mouth-organ. First he had to settle himself comfortably and then, prefacing his tune with much mouth wiping and furtive blowing into the instrument, he began a tune.

Doleful ditties followed and at last he broke into the Australian classic. Impulsively and quite unselfconsciously Bill Daley's light tenor took up the tale.

"Once a jolly swagman camped by a billabong
Under the shade of a coolibah tree;
And he sang as he watched and waited till his billy boiled:
You'll come a-waltzing, Matilda, with me!

"Up rode the squatter, mounted on his thoroughbred,
Up rode the troopers—one-two-three:
'Where's that jolly jumbuck you've got in your tucker-bag?
You'll come a-waltzing, Matilda, with me!'

' Waltzing, Matilda, waltzing, Matilda,
    You'll come a-waltzing, Matilda, with me.
    And he sang as he watched and waited till his billy boiled:
    You'll come a-waltzing, Matilda, with me!"

Having started, Bill and Sam kept on. Song followed song and Lesley leaned back, gazed into the fire and listened. Presently the sound of a horse picking his way over the uneven ground told them that Dan had come back.

" That sounded fine from the other side, Bill. You're in good voice."

" That's because he was singing to something more suitable than cattle," Sam put in.

" The cattle just keeps me in practice," Bill said.

" I think you've got a fine voice, Bill," Lesley said generously. " I like it because it's so soft."

Dan swung himself down off the horse and while Sam threw several chops on the fire for him he went into a technical discussion with Bill Daley about the mob. He had not spoken to Lesley.

Later when he was drinking his tea and munching his damper and chop he looked up across the fire at her. There was something curiously direct, almost challenging in his face.

" Bill will drive you back, Lesley," he said. " I'm staying with the camp." He turned to the jackaroo.

" Bring Hannah and Mary and Christine out to-morrow night, Bill. Hannah can drive the 'Ute' back and leave you here. I want you to spell off to-morrow."

So! Lesley was disposed of. And unless Bill decided to include her she was not going to call on the cattle to-morrow night! Hannah would drive the 'Ute' back, which meant Dan was going to keep on staying on with the cattle drovers. Lesley wouldn't have any opportunity of making up for her ill grace and bad manners on the way out. Was this Dan's way of punishing her or had he simply dismissed her from his presence—for ever?

Dan had minded Bill Daley driving her out to the stockyards the day they brought the horses in, but he didn't mind him taking her back in the dark of night!

Lesley felt as petulant as a small girl who has been told she cannot go to a party. Like a small girl she longed to please but found herself almost wilfully doing the opposite. She carefully said nothing now. She had begun to think that her tongue would disobey her and say the opposite to what she

intended if she unleashed it. Perhaps that was why Dan kep
silence. If one is silent one *can't* say the wrong thing.

"All right, Lesley. Up and at it," Bill said, getting up and
stretching. "I'll have a day's sleep to-morrow."

Lesley jumped up and brushed the leaves and twigs from
her jeans.

"Thank you for bringing me out, Dan," Lesley said. "I
was fun."

"Now you know what night life is like on a station. I'm
glad you enjoyed yourself. Bill will take care of you."

He might have been on top of Everest.

As they walked the half-mile to the "Ute" he talked to
Bill about the mob. Lesley stumbled once, but it was Bill
Daley's quick hand that went out to her. They did not talk
across her but rather into space. They seemed to assume
that Lesley either knew all about or likewise was intensely
interested in bulls, bullocks, steers, weaners, nuggets, clean-
skins, and about the newly broken-in horses being able to
"hold a cut" or "tighten up the wings".

When they came up to the Utility Dan opened the passenger door for Lesley.

"Good night," he said to Lesley. "Bill will get you back
within half an hour. Sleep well." His words were formal,
polite, and Lesley felt that Dan couldn't have been more remote
than if he were in truth on Everest.

Bill started up the engine and swung the car round. In a
minute they were bumping over the plain, with the Southern
Cross, this time, on their right.

"I guess Dan knew you were safe with me in these whiskers," Bill said ruefully. "Just my luck."

"Wouldn't I be safe with you without them?" Lesley
asked lightly.

"Why should you be? You're a girl, aren't you—and a
darn pretty one?"

"You shouldn't make so many passes at girls, Bill. You
should let the girls make a few at you."

"Blow me down. Who'd have thought you were so worldly
wise?"

"I'm not so much wise as observant. You make overtures
—amorous ones, I mean—to all those girls who came to
Coolaroo for the wedding. Nobody attaches much importance
to them because they can't be very sincere, can they? I mean,
you'd kiss *any* girl who'd let you, even if you were only
doing it for fun?"

"I wouldn't be doing it for fun if I kissed you," Bill
said, and all the raillery had gone out of his voice. "I'd

like you for my girl, Lesley, only, what would be the good. I couldn't marry you and give you a station, or even a cottage in a city. So why not make a joke of the whole thing."

"If you married someone—not me, incidentally, I'm not open for offers—you'd be given the management of a station, wouldn't you? You'd turn serious, Bill, and in no time you'd be a 'Boss' too. There's nothing serious about you ——"

"What's the lecture for, anyway?" Bill asked. "What have I done?"

"Nothing. That's the trouble," said Lesley. "You're such a wonderful horseman you're a legend. You know men and you know cattle so well that you can take over the responsibilities of the owners of Coolaroo without a worry. All you want is *one* girl and *one* girl only to settle you down. Stop making sheep's eyes at them all."

"Who's the one girl to be?"

"Why not Christine?"

"Christine! Phew! You don't know what you're saying. She's a Macintosh of Bengarra in New South Wales! They're big guns in the pastoralists' world."

"Christine doesn't seem like a 'gun' at all to me. She seems like a nice girl. And what's wrong with you? The Macintoshes, whoever they might be, would hardly turn away from someone as able and as well known as you must be in the cattle world."

Bill was silent for a few minutes.

"You know what?" he said after a while. "I never even thought of it. Christine Macintosh, and settling down, managing a station! Say, you got big ideas, Lesley."

"So have you when you think you can kiss any girl anywhere anytime. That's what I call real cheek!"

"Were you ever a schoolma'am?"

"No. Do I lecture as much as all that?"

"More so. Christine! Well, well, well!"

"You like the idea?" asked Lesley.

"Listen, beautiful one. Christine's like all the rest of 'em. She's got eyes for only one man in the North-west. That's Dan Baxter. What do you think her people send her over to the West for? Not for the love of her cousins—the Macfarlanes. They aren't the same religion. They just want to net Coolaroo Downs into their big fat ring of stations. The Macintoshes want to corner the beef business, in the next generation, if they can't in this."

"Christine strikes me as being a very simple, nice girl. I don't believe she has any such ideas."

"She hasn't. She's nice, like you said. But she's dead nuts on Dan. They all are. There won't be any peace in the dove-cotes anywhere till Dan gets himself married off. Tell you what . . ." Bill glanced at Lesley and the light from the dashboard showed a devil's grin flickering over his face.

"You rope in Dan," he said. "That'll leave the field clear for the Macfarlanes and me."

"A few minutes ago you were asking me to be your girl-friend. It seemed only a little matter like a station or a cottage standing between us."

"And you've handed me on a platter to Christine. Christine! Phew!"

"You try it, Bill. Only take my advice and stick exclusively to Christine. Don't let her think that Hannah or Mary, or even Lesley have any interest for you at all."

They slowed down as they neared the camp and beside the stockyards they pulled up. Bill unwound himself from the driver's seat and opened the door for Lesley.

"Okay," he said with a grin. "I'll give it a go. Put myself under your direction, as it were. Mind if I come to you for advice?"

"Don't do it too obviously. Christine would think you were dividing your attention—as usual."

"Well, I certainly have had an interesting time," Bill said, rubbing his chin. "Don't call me in the morning, young Lesley. I'm going to dream on your advice."

They stealthily approached the sleeping camp. They stood looking down as the moon shone full on the swags lying around the embers of the fire.

"Do you suppose they're only sleeping?" Lesley asked. "They're so still!"

"Bet you Cousin Con's awake. She'd keep a chaperoning eye even on dear Dan."

Bill stepped over the debris of the camp and stooped down beside Mrs. Collins's sleeping-bag.

"Don't you be playing fox, Cousin Con," he said. "I know you're awake."

"I'm very anxious to be otherwise," Mrs. Collins replied tartly. "You just get yourself to bed and let the rest of us sleep, Bill Daley."

"It's an awful pity," said Bill.

"What is a pity?"

"That I'm covered in whiskers and dust——"

Lesley did what she had seen Betsy and the girls do to

Dan. She kissed the tip of her finger and placed it gently on the side of Bill's nose.

"You just want any girl who'll be nice to you, Bill. And Christine would—if you'd stick to her exclusively. Try it. I'll be batting for you in the wings."

As she crawled to bed she was quite aware that everybody —though utterly silent—was wide awake. They had been waiting for Dan to come home.

CHAPTER ELEVEN

A week later they were back at the homestead. The muster was over and Dan and his men were away fifty miles towards the coast. Andy flew his sisters back to Hannans Downs and was then to return overland to meet Dan and the cattle outside Ninety Mile End. The Brennans, with many sighs, left for Witchery on the Coolaroo heavy truck.

Betsy declared she was only waiting for Neil to return to Alexander. Coolaroo, she said, really was the most primitive homestead in the North-west and thank goodness Dan was building a new house. She was bored and acid and was only barely polite to Lesley.

"Good heavens!" she said. "You have got yourself *burnt*. Funny how a person loses her good looks when she loses her complexion."

"Something that will never happen to you," Mrs. Collins said with equal acidity. "You and the sun are strangers, Betsy." She began banging curtains and shaking mats and stirring cushions. "Let us have some sunshine here anyway."

Later she confided to Lesley that the aftermath of a celebration was always a lowering of spirits.

"The fun is over, so Betsy wants to go home," she said. "Well, it will only be a week or two to the Fitzroy Races, so she won't be in the doldrums for long."

Two days later Brian Baxter, Betsy's husband, arrived in his own Dove plane. Lesley was really interested to see what sort of a person Betsy was married to. Like all the North-west men he was tall, burned, slight, with very blue eyes that were barely discernible between the slits of his eyelids when he looked into the light. He came through the garden, stood on the step surveying the veranda party, and said . . .

"Well, how goes it?"

He was very like Dan.

Mrs. Collins was delighted to see him and said so vociferously. Betsy was delighted too, but except for a heightened colour she declined to show it. She remained lolling back in her bucket chair, one hand behind her head, one foot jogging slightly in the air.

"Well," she said. "Look what an aeroplane's flown in."

"Who'd 'a' thought it," said Brian. He walked over to her and bent down to kiss her cheek. He meant it casually but as soon as his face was near hers their eyes met and something passed between them.

"How are you, old girl?" he said.

"Tired!" said Betsy. "This climate is more filthy at Coolaroo than Alexander."

Something had happened like magic to Betsy and though her manner remained bored and languid she seemed as if she had softened like the opening of a lovely rose. That was exactly what Betsy was, Lesley thought. She was big and a little blowy, but she was lovely in a soft, feminine way. Only her light blue eyes did not soften.

That afternoon the sergeant came in with the other heavy truck—three horses in tow. Neil tumbled out—burnt to a cinder, waveringly tired but with a smile of seraphic joy on his face.

"Golly, that's terrible country out there," he said. "Fit only for blackfellows and madmen."

He sounded so grown up and was so obviously quoting Dan that they all laughed.

Sergeant Holland came on to the veranda and shook hands with everyone. He was a stocky, powerful-looking Irishman. His brown sombrero went on to the floor under his chair and he favoured Mrs. Collins with a piteous glance.

"I haven't tasted Irish whisky since last I passed this way."

"It's on the way, Sergeant," Mrs. Collins consoled him.

"It's been out of the store-house these two days awaiting you."

At that moment one of the lubras came on to the veranda with a tray on which stood the whisky and a soda water syphon.

The sergeant sat down, took a loving sip of his drink and favoured Lesley with an appraising look.

"Your face is pretty enough for you to be coming from the Green Isle itself," he said. "But they're after telling me you're an English lady."

Lesley smiled, showing her lovely white, polished teeth, her blue eyes looking more blue because of the tan of her skin.

"I'm English," she said. "But it's very near to being Irish, isn't it?"

"About three hundred miles—but a powerful lot can happen in three hundred miles. They tell me you're the young lady's going to marry one of these here Baxter boys."

"That was my cousin, Alice. And she married Randolph. The wedding's a thing of the past now, you know."

The sergeant raised his eyebrows in astonishment.

"You don't tell me! Did I miss a wedding and all? And Randolph himself—the creature."

"You mean to tell me Andy Macfarlane and Dan and Neil have been out on White Gum Mountain with you and not mentioned a wedding?" Brian Baxter asked with a grin.

"Not a word. Well, not a word that conveyed the right kind of meaning, if you understand. It was this beautiful, charming young lady here now that I was after thinking about."

"Don't think too hard, Sergeant Holland," Mrs. Collins said. "You might crack your head."

"And that's the sole prerogative of the rye whisky. Ma'am —your good health." He sipped his whisky and looked over the glass at Lesley. His bright Irish blue eyes beamed on her.

Neil came out on the veranda.

"Come on, Dad. Come on, Mum. If I've got to go home, let's get it over and be done with."

"Okay, son," Brian Baxter said, getting to his feet. "The bags down at the plane?"

"I guess so," Neil said without interest. He looked tired and a little forlorn now. He walked over to Lesley.

"Tell Dan from me that I really did want to see some of those walls going up on the foundations, and can I come back with him after the races up north."

Mrs. Collins had got up and she put her arm around the boy's shoulder.

"We'll be seeing you soon, Neil," she said. "And Lesley and I'll tell Dan everything—just as you've said it."

"Okay, Cousin Con. Good-bye, Sergeant Holland. Thanks for a beaut time."

"Thanks for your help, boy. I couldn't have managed without you." The policeman stood up and solemnly shook hands with Neil. There was a general hand-shaking all round. Betsy, in a blue linen suit and her hair dressed and face made up, looked the true beauty she was.

"Good-bye, Cousin Con," she drawled, as she kissed Mrs. Collins on the cheek. "Too bad Dan's going to be away so long!"

By this time she had reached Lesley and her blue eyes were faintly ironical. " Not even Bill Daley around to amuse you. What a pity."

" There's the sergeant," said Lesley with spirit. " I think we'll get on famously together."

Sergeant Holland bowed low.

" At your service," he said. " Tread gently when you tread on me—you tread on my heart."

Betsy favoured him with a superior smile.

" You've no heart, Sergeant," she said. " Only a stomach. Well, good-bye, Lesley—I guess they'll keep you long enough to bring you to Alexander for the races."

They all walked through the tropical garden to the gate and stood and watched as Brian took his wife and son down the long, dry, shadeless paddock to the plane.

" I'm always glad to see Betsy go—and always glad to see her come," Mrs. Collins said with a sigh. They turned back to the house.

" Now there's no one but you and me, Lesley. I hope you won't feel the solitude—and the silence."

" Silence?" They stood at the foot of the steps and looked at the sergeant. His glass was on the table by the soda water syphon, his hand hung down by his side and reached the floor. His chin rested on his chest and a loud, penetrating snore told them he had fallen asleep.

" So quickly?" said Lesley in surprise.

" That's his life," Mrs. Collins said gently. " He must fall asleep when he can—when he's out on a patrol. He trains himself to do it."

They tip-toed past him. The sergeant lifted his head, opened one eye then closed it and let his head sink back and was asleep again.

Mrs. Collins and Lesley walked through the homestead to the veranda on the west side.

" We'll have tea—and then think about what we'll do for the next few days."

" I'll make the tea, Mrs. Collins," Lesley said. " Please let me. I'm not a visitor any more—and I've made tea in the pantry before."

Mrs. Collins looked at the girl for a moment.

" It would be nice," she said. " I've got a headache. I'll sit out here by the breakfast table and have a rest."

If Mrs. Collins had a headache it wasn't a bad one, but she was both wise and kindly. She knew that Lesley would feel more at home—and less like the last visitor—if she had the freedom of the house like one of the family.

Lesley brought the tea from the pantry and poured it out.

"Lovely. You make a good cup of tea, Lesley, and I can't say that for everyone."

"I've noticed that you like it rather strong."

They sat, their elbows resting on the table, their backs sagging a little, and drank their tea in silence.

"What do you usually do when the homestead empties itself like this?" Lesley asked.

"You'll be surprised at what will turn up. The lubras will cut themselves and the piccaninnies will get bung eyes from fly bites; a delicate horse will decide to foal; and the cake tins will suddenly empty themselves."

"Haven't all those things been happening while the wedding and the muster were in progress?"

"I suppose so. But they don't seem to matter then—and nobody takes any notice. Now they'll be urgent. Anyhow, the first thing you and I are going to do is have a good long rest. Both of us. Just sit and lounge about for a day or two—then when we're rested and bored we'll set about getting the annexe ready for Alice and Randolph."

"I think that's a splendid idea. But what about the sergeant?"

"He'll sleep for a day and then go back to Ninety Mile End. If time's not urgent with him he'll probably travel a day with the mob. If Wire Whiskers will take his horses for him he can go out in the Utility."

"They're not so very far away, are they?"

"No. Dan'll probably send someone into the homestead every other day—for mail or news—or even with mail."

"How would he get mail?"

"Everyone in this part of the North-west would know he's got a mob travelling for the coast and anyone passing his way from Ninety Mile End would take his mail for him."

"Does Dan like being out with the drovers?"

"Yes, if he can be spared from the station. He'd make time now because they're travelling against the weather. The barometer's dropped a point again to-day and the weather's too muggy to be good. He's got to get that mob over the Coolaroo before it floods and into Ninety Mile End before the cyclones come down."

"Then his troubles will be over?"

"No, indeed they won't. He's got to find feed and water and yarding while waiting for a ship. If the ships farther up the coast strike the cyclone season they'll either be delayed or they won't put into Ninety Mile End at all. They keep out to sea. There are more wrecks on this strip of coast than anywhere else in the world."

"Why does Dan like the sea? Why did he go in the Navy instead of the Air Force as most of the pastoralists seem to have done?"

"That coast—from Shark Bay in the south to Wyndham in the north—is the most unpredictable coast in Australian and Island waters. It has a fascination for Dan. He's even been out in the pearling luggers in the cyclone season. And, of course, it's his idea of heaven to sail into the north when the weather's hot and the sea is fine."

"Does he go often?"

"Every year he takes a trip—up into Timor or even as far as the Sundra Sea. He's due for his trip now. The wedding has robbed him of his holiday so far, and the cyclones—if they come—will probably settle them for this year."

Lesley was thoughtful for a little while. She found it intriguing that Dan should be interested in unpredictable things. She would have thought him to prefer the straight-cut, open and measured things of life.

The next day Mrs. Collins and she did just as the former had suggested. They lay about—idly looking through magazines; listening to the radio and hearing the gossip of the North-west as well as programmed entertainment. In the afternoon, Lesley went into the pantry and began going through the shelves until she had found a sufficient number of ingredients to make biscuits. She got a curious pleasure in making them. She felt warm and happy inside her and wondered if she were really cut out to be a housewife after all. As she put the tray in the little oven she remembered the letter from Alec. It was in the shirt pocket of the clothes she had worn out at the cattle camp. Lesley sat down on a chair suddenly. She put her hand up to her head and ran her fingers through her hair.

"I must be going mad," she thought. "I had forgotten it. I haven't even thought of it. I haven't even thought of Alec —for days—and days—and days."

She began to wonder what she had been thinking about. She had been preoccupied with the everyday affairs of Coolaroo: with striking camp, ready to return to the homestead: with the feeling of relief that Bill had included her in the party that had gone out on the second night to visit the new drovers' camp—five miles farther across the plains. With the feeling of relief that Dan—although he had not said very much to her—had at least let her come out of Coventry;

with the alarums and excursions of the Macfarlanes' and Brennans' departure. In other words, her thoughts had caught up with her physical presence on Coolaroo Downs. She was part of the station life—for the time being anyway—and she hadn't even noticed it.

Lesley sat and steadily watched the biscuits rise behind the glass door of the oven. She was happy and was going to stay that way. She wouldn't open Alec's letter at all. Well, not yet, anyway.

Lesley carried her new-made biscuits, with a pot of tea, on to the front veranda, where Mrs. Collins was having her siesta.

"I wondered what you were up to," Mrs. Collins said. "Are you bored yet, Lesley?"

"No. I suddenly feel that I would like to know all about station life. Not just about sheep and cattle and weddings and musters. But how it ticks."

"Ticks is the right word. It runs like a clock—that is, if it is well run. There has to be someone who winds it up regularly, though. On Coolaroo Downs that someone is Dan. Everything is going on here at the homestead without him. But it wouldn't for long. The rouseabouts would get lazy, the blacks would go walkabout and Lee would find someone to bring his own particular form of grog out from Ninety Mile End. You'll see that after a day or two Dan will come in and shake everyone up. Or maybe he'll send Bill Daley. Bill may not be very successful with the ladies, but he's very effective with the station hands."

"I suppose they respect him."

"They respect his horsemanship and they respect the toe of his boot. He can be very active, can Bill, when his ire is aroused."

"How does Dan deal with them?"

"They've got a lot of respect for Dan. There's never any trouble when he's around."

"It's just respect, then? And not the toe of his boot?"

"He'd use his boot if he had to."

"Yes, I think he would," Lesley said thoughtfully. "In his own way he gets people into line with what he wants, doesn't he?"

"You mean Alice? And Randolph?"

"Yes. I suppose I do mean them."

They were both silent as they drank their tea. Each was thinking of the same thing. How *would* Alice settle down.

After lunch the next day Bill Daley came thundering up the

plain, a cloud of dust, and himself whiskered and begrimed. He came through the garden to the steps of the veranda.

"Catch, Cousin Con," he said. A bundle of letters tied with string soared through the air and landed with a perfect three-point landing on the cane table beside Mrs. Collins's cane chair.

"Coming your way, Lesley." Several rolls of newspapers and magazines were withdrawn from inside his bulging shirt and came spiralling in Lesley's direction. "See you when I'm clean," he said as he made off towards the tank-stands.

"That's in your honour," Mrs. Collins said, untying the mail. "Otherwise he would have come stamping on to the veranda hollering for tea."

There were two letters for Lesley, both from England.

"Mother and aunt," she said as she glanced at them. "I wonder if the dog has had another fight with aristocracy."

Mrs. Collins was already deep in her first letter so Lesley opened hers without apology.

Mother was well, Dad was well, the dog was well. And nobody had seen anything of Alec! There were rumours that he was taking someone out, but, after all, they were only rumours. Aunt said the same thing except she implored Lesley for news of Alice.

So Alec was taking someone else out!

Lesley thought of his letter, still in the shirt pocket hanging up in her wardrobe. Perhaps she should read it after all! She would do so when she went inside to change for late tea. She marvelled at her own reluctance to open that letter. Was she afraid of its contents? Or didn't she really care any more, and was she ashamed she had no mourning to hang out for a love that was dead.

Lesley got up from her chair and walked to the edge of the veranda. She stood with her hands gripping the rail, looking into the heat haze of early afternoon.

All that pain and anxiety! Those sleepless nights and those tearless eyes! The family rows, the loss of her friends one by one, through neglect. Surely they couldn't so suddenly go for nought. What had happened to her? Here she was on the edge of the Australian desert with nothing real or tangible to take her mind off her sorrows, and yet she felt as if she had never known Alec and had never known what it was to have a heartache.

"Is your news all right?" Mrs. Collins asked solicitously.

"Yes. All's well at home, thank you," Lesley replied, turning round. "I was wondering if Bill would come back here for tea. Shall I go and make some?"

"Make it if you like, my dear. My guess is that he'll come here. The cook-house will be locked up and Lee fast asleep."

Lesley went into the pantry to make the tea. She was also trying to make herself walk through the house to her bedroom and get that letter out of her shirt pocket.

"Oh, it can wait till washing day——" she said impatiently. "What's a letter anyway?"

What indeed!

Bill Daley, thundering through the house in his riding boots, came into the pantry as she was pouring the boiling water into the teapot. He put his arm along her shoulder and looked over it down at the tea.

"Got plenty there, mate? I've sure got a hell of a thirst."

"There's plenty," Lesley said. "I was reckoning on that."

"Reckoning on that? My, oh my! That ain't no way for the English to talk. You go back to England talking about 'reckoning' this and 'reckoning' that and they'll think you've taken leave of your senses."

"No they won't. They'll think I've taken a jaunt in a wild west film. You shaved very quickly, Bill."

"You know what? I'm record shaver in the North-west. Whiskers off in three minutes."

"Is there any record in the North-west you don't hold?"

"Would you call yourself a record? Because I don't look like I'm holding you—yet."

"No, and you're not going to, either," Lesley said, ducking neatly under his arm and emerging behind him, a teapot in one hand and a strainer in the other. "Which will you have, Bill? Boiling tea spilled on your hands or a hit on the head with a silver tea strainer."

Bill turned round and looked at her glumly.

"Only obeying Dan's orders."

"Dan's orders?"

Bill shrugged.

"Sure thing. He was gonna send Abe in with the mail and all of a sudden he takes a special one-eyed look at me and says. 'Second thoughts, Bill, you'd better go. Lesley might be feeling the loneliness after the crowd's gone. You'll be more company for her than Abe'."

"The perfect host," Lesley said, picking up the tray and offering it to Bill to carry out for her. "It's a wonder he didn't think to come himself."

"Not Dan——" said Bill, eyeing her wickedly. "You don't count compared with the steers, lady. Dan's got beautiful manners when the cattle's not around——"

Lesley picked up the biscuits.

"And you don't care a fig for cattle—only ladies? Congratulations on your first overtures to Christine, Bill. They were effective. Don't spoil it by making eyes at everyone else."

"There you go, giving advice again."

"There you go, keeping up your reputation as a flirt. You won't keep any girl that way. Now just carry that tray carefully, please."

Bill followed Lesley on to the veranda like a chastened schoolboy.

"Goodness," said Mrs. Collins. "Your hair does look nice plastered down, Bill. It can't be in my honour so it must all be for Lesley."

"Bill's practising," Lesley said quickly as she began to pour tea. "In the not-far-distant future he's going courting. His effects are just a try-out."

Mrs. Collins didn't look convinced. She looked doubtfully from one to the other. There was fun and raillery between the two young people. She wondered what they were up to.

Bill Daley, Sergeant Holland and Wire Whiskers all left the homestead the next morning. They were heading west with a string of ponies with them. The sergeant had his pack-horse and his black tracker's horse and Wire Whiskers had three horses that were being sent up the coast for the Alexander races. One of them was Wildfire, the handsome stallion that Lesley had seen both Tony, the black stockman, and Bill Daley ride on the first day she had gone down to the stockyards.

"Well, things are on the move," Mrs. Collins said as she went back into the house. "Lesley, I think we'd better get the annexe fixed right away, or the races will be on us and Alice and Randolph back before we've done a thing."

"I suppose the first thing I'd better do, is move out," Lesley said. "Where shall I go?"

"The east room is the guest room, but it's got one disadvantage. The sun hits it first thing in the morning and there's no sleep after daybreak. Most people who come to Coolaroo just use it as a dressing-room and sleep under the nets on the veranda."

"Where Betsy was sleeping?"

"Yes. It's the best place for a good night's sleep."

"What's wrong with my having my bed there?"

"Nothing at all, except that English people are a little bit shy about sleeping out. Specially when the men's beds are just round the corner."

Lesley laughed cheerfully.

"Dan doesn't walk in his sleep, does he?"

"No. Do you?"

"No, and if I did where could I go anyway?"

"Come on then. We'll get a couple of the boys from the camps to help move the heavy stuff and we'll go down to the store-house and get out a fresh mosquito net."

They spent a busy day in spite of the heat. Lesley thought she did not feel it so much when she was working.

They moved her things out of the room in the annexe and then set up one room as the bedroom for Alice and her husband and the other as a private sitting-room for them.

When Lesley looked across the plain through her window that night it seemed as if every parched blade of grass, every tuft of spinifex, was etched in silver. The moon made a path across it like a path across the sea.

In her new iron bed under the mosquito net on the veranda she felt and enjoyed the freshness of the night and the cool, turfy smell of the earth all around her. In the distance she heard a dingo howl. A light went up in the stockmen's quarters and someone went out into the night.

That dingo had to be shot.

CHAPTER TWELVE

The following day Cousin Con and Lesley had news of Alice and Randolph over the transceiver set. The Brennans came through with some amusing anecdotes about Joe, who, like the prodigal son, had returned to the fold much chastened because he had missed the Coolaroo muster but was already planning a sortie on the Alexander races. Alice and Randolph were in Adelaide—the queen city of the south. They were seeing theatres and hearing music. They were to leave by air at the end of the week for Darwin where they would pick up an M.M.A. plane for Fitzroy. They would stay with Betsy and Brian until and for the races.

"So you see," said Mrs. Collins, "you can't go now, Lesley. You've promised to be here for a little while when Alice comes back."

"It seems to me the shipping company will get tired of me changing my mind. How do I find out about bookings, Cousin Con? Dan told me he had arranged with the Bank to fix me up."

"Then you leave it to Dan, my dear."

"But how can I? He's not here. Besides, I don't even

know what the Bank has arranged to date. I suppose any mail for Dan was taken out before Bill brought the letters in."

"It certainly was. If there had been anything for you to worry about, Dan would have let you know."

"I'm not worrying—but I'd just like to know what I'm doing. How does Dan know, for instance, whether I'm able to stay on or not?"

"He knows what's going on—don't you fret. If someone doesn't ride in here, then someone certainly rides into Ninety Mile End—and they'd pick up the radio news there. He'd know almost as soon as we do that Joe Brennan is at Witchery and that you'll be coming to the Alexander races. Dan will fix it all, don't you worry."

Lesley looked at Mrs. Collins with a faint exasperated frown on her pretty, fair forehead. Mrs. Collins burst out laughing.

"You're not used to having your comings and goings decided for you, are you? Dan's mighty masterful when he wants to be. I guess Dan's figured it all out that you'll stay on. He knows you wouldn't disappoint Alice."

"I wish I could get hold of him—just for one minute."

"What would you do?"

"He doesn't wear a tie, so I can't pull that out—I suppose I would be reduced to stamping on his toes and even putting my tongue out."

"Don't you want to stay, Lesley?"

"Yes, I think I do. But I would like to be asked—not just commanded—or arranged for."

"What Dan does is always right; and it's such a comfort not to have to worry. He does it all. You'll learn that in time, and just let your troubles slip off your shoulders on to his. We all do that."

"In time!" Lesley reiterated. "You sound as if you think I'm going to stay for ever, Cousin Con."

"I wish you were. I think Dan would like you to stay."

"As a wet-nurse to Alice and Randolph!"

"No, for yourself," Mrs. Collins sighed. "I know it is not likely. Coolaroo is not like a nice county home in England. A 'place' I think you call it there. We're so cut off here— hundreds of miles from anywhere and only ourselves to squabble with."

Lesley remained silent. She wondered what Coolaroo was really like in between weddings and such-like. How *did* the inhabitants spend their ordinary days and nights.

She did not have to wait long to find out. Dan himself came in that night in the Utility. He had injured his arm badly

nough to want some further antiseptics and some motherly
bandaging from Cousin Con.

From the veranda Lesley and Mrs. Collins had seen the
Utility bowling over the plain in its cloud of dust.

"I do hope it's Dan," Mrs. Collins said—her kind face
flushing in anticipation, her blue eyes growing moist with
anxiety.

When they saw the dust-covered figure with tight-fitting
working trousers and the slouch hat on the back of his
head get out of the truck they both knew at once it was
Dan.

Lesley had a curious feeling of having been in a vacuum
and of now emerging into life again. Nothing had stopped at
Coolaroo while Dan was away—and yet, nothing had seemed
to go on. Now everything was galvanised into life.

Dan lifted his left arm in a wave and disappeared around the
corner of the house. Mrs. Collins was peering after him.

"Was he holding his right arm against his chest, Lesley?"

"Perhaps he was carrying mail in his shirt the way Bill
Daley did. Why didn't he come through the garden?"

"Too dirty, I guess. You'll have had that much effect on
Dan, Lesley. He would want to scrape off his whiskers and
clean himself up."

Around the side of the house was a hullaballoo of noise.
The blacks had swarmed up from their humpies when they
saw Dan and Lee had come jabbering out of the cook-house.
Lesley wanted to offer to make the tea as she had done for
Bill Daley, but somehow she couldn't make herself say the
words.

"Lee will want to make the tea for Dan," Mrs. Collins said,
as if reading her thoughts. "It's rather late, after all."

Lee, however, came round the side veranda in a great
state.

"Boss got a pretty bad arm, Miz. You come lookee see.
You get some stuff ready. Black Sykes and me get Dan's
clothes off him quickee down shower-house."

Mrs. Collins was already on her feet and following the
Chinaman.

"Let me know if I can help," Lesley said.

"He won't be too bad," Mrs. Collins said as if consoling
herself. "After all, he drove himself home—and the men
wouldn't have let him come alone. . . ."

She was still reassuring herself—and Lee—as she disappeared from view and from sound.

Lesley sat in her easy-chair, the magazine she was looking
at open in her lap but her eyes looking out over the garden

to the Utility which stood, covered in dust, its door still open, just as Dan had got out of it.

The open door seemed to say such a lot. It was not haste to shower and shave that had taken Dan so quickly round the side of the house but rather the necessity to do something for his arm. And quickly.

Lesley sat still for quite ten minutes. When Bill Daley had come pounding up the paddock and stamping across the cement paths of the garden she had just felt a vague pleasure in one more human being coming to join the conversation piece at Coolaroo. Dan made her feel different. She felt disturbed. She didn't know why except that she expected it was something to do with his bossiness. He would want to tell her what to do about Alice—that is, if he was on speaking terms with her at all. He would loftily refrain from telling her what he was doing about arranging her bookings for England.

Funny if they kept her a prisoner here. How could she get out of Coolaroo if they didn't want to let her go? There was the transceiver set by which she could broadcast an S O S to the North-west. But she didn't know how to use it, and besides, no one in the North-west would believe anything against a Baxter of Coolaroo. *Any* Baxter for that matter.

Lesley shook herself because she knew she was letting fantasy run away with her thoughts. Still, she would have to come to grips with Dan on the subject of her ship bookings.

" It won't hurt me to make him some tea," she said, to herself as if conceding some point in a mental struggle that she imagined was going on between herself and the master of Coolaroo. " Lee will be acting as valet—by the sound of things."

She got up and went into the pantry. More or less without thinking, she prepared an attractive-looking tray. Dan would be hungry. On to the tray went her own baked biscuits and some honey bread thickly spread with butter she took from the small refrigerator in the breakfast room.

She heard Dan—and his army of attendants—come up the yard and step on to the veranda. She heard his voice. He was swearing, mildly by North-west standards, but effectively. Lee and at least half a dozen black boys and lubras were expressing themselves volubly, too.

" Now, get to hell out of it, the lot of you," roared Dan. " You breathe disease on me, you young blackguards. For God's sake go and clean yourselves up. Lee, bring me that raking chair and when you get the hot water from the cook-house, for hell's sake put a clean cloth over it. Now get cracking!"

Lesley smiled to herself. The Law had arrived. It's voice was clear and authoritative. It was comforting in its firmness. Perhaps there was something in the tendency of everyone on Coolaroo to leave their affairs in Dan's hands after all. There was a sense of comfort in being taken care of—in having that crackling, drawling voice settle one's affairs—without one having to have too many headaches.

Lesley felt herself slipping. It would be easy to let Dan run one. She had to be on her guard about that self-easiness. Not that it mattered to herself, Lesley. But it would matter for Alice. Lesley had to watch out for Alice.

Mrs. Collins, who had been opening and shutting cupboards and boxes in Dan's study, now went out on to the veranda where her beloved cousin was sitting alternately cursing at the blacks, mildly groaning, and reproaching Cousin Con for being " such a hell of a raking time ".

Through the pantry window Lesley could see the row of young aborigines standing mutely on the gravel below the veranda. They watched operations in reverent silence, only hopping anxiously on one foot when Dan swore. At last the first-aid attentions seemed to be over.

" There you are, Dan, old dear." It was Mrs. Collins's voice, tender and maternal again. There was no sound from Dan. Mrs. Collins raised her voice. " You there, Lesley? Get the brandy, some water and a glass out of the sideboard, will you?"

There was no urgency in her voice but Lesley knew that Dan needed that brandy. She ran into the dining-room and took a small decanter with the water and glass to the veranda.

Dan was sitting, his hair wet and tousled, cleanly bathed and in a clean shirt slit down the side of the bad arm. His face was white and his eyes had a tired, almost exhausted look. He raised them rather wearily to Lesley and a half grin was all he could squeeze out. His left hand must have felt to him like a weight of lead for he lifted it with effort on to the table and took the glass Mrs. Collins proffered him. He drank the brandy in one gulp. He sat silent a minute, then he looked up and caught the row of shining black eyes watching him in awed respect.

" And a good time was had by all," he said with a grin. " Now you can all go back to your slumbers. Get out!" The last two words came out like a pistol shot and sheepishly the blacks ambled back across the yard.

Mrs. Collins ran her fingers through Dan's hair.

"You want a cup of tea, boy?"

"More than anything else on earth."

"Can you walk round to the front veranda, do you think?"

"I certainly can."

Dan stood up and wavered a minute. Instinctively, Lesley put out her hand and steadied him. Dan looked down, unsmiling, at her. They stood a minute, Lesley feeling her face going almost as white as Dan's had been a minute before. Then very slowly Dan let his left hand slide along her shoulder and rest there. Lesley turned as if to help him along the veranda but Dan did not move. Mrs. Collins was taking away the bowls and debris of bandages.

Dan's hand opened and closed on the corner of Lesley's shoulder and he still stood looking down at her gravely. Suddenly Lesley no longer felt oppressed by him. Something in her rose and gave her a momentary ascendancy. She kissed the tip of her finger and placed it on the side of his nose.

"Poor Dan!" she said.

He walked around the veranda corner with her, his arm holding her tightly. When they got to his favourite easy-chair he looked at her quizzically.

"Thank you," he said. "You know, if Cousin Con wasn't shadowing us I think I'd kiss you after all."

Lesley pushed him gently into a chair.

"I've got the tea already made."

"A lot?"

"Gallons!"

"Then bring it out." He watched her go along the veranda and turn into the front doorway. He brushed his good hand through his hair and let his gaze wander out over the garden. The colour was steadily returning to his face, but his eyes were tired. He moved uneasily in his chair and his face was caught up in a spasm of pain as the movement disturbed his right arm.

Mrs. Collins came round the corner and eyed Dan tenderly.

"I should have given you an injection before I dressed the arm, Dan. I didn't realise it was so bad. How did you do it?"

"Glanced off a steer. His horn got me. Don't ask me how—I just wasn't looking. If any of the men had been so careless I'd have roared hell out of them."

"Have you got your mind on something, Dan?"

He gave her a quiet grin.

"I had just at that moment. My head was well and truly in the clouds."

Lesley came out on to the veranda with the tea tray. She put it on the table and began to pour the tea.

"I brought the big cups out, Dan," she said.

"Good scout."

She glanced up at him as she put his tea on the table beside him.

"Plenty more where that came from," she said with a smile. She was a little taken aback by the exhausted look in Dan's eyes. There was something startling about a man so strong and virile and active looking pale and exhausted. How are the mighty brought low! Dan wouldn't be bossy about Alice and Randolph now—like Achilles, he had a heel.

They drank their tea in silence, Dan having a second and then a third cup. This last he didn't finish. It sat on the table beside him half drunk—when his head began to droop sideways. For a long while he remained, his eyes half closed, looking wearily out over the garden. Then presently his eyes closed and he had gone to sleep.

Lesley no longer felt resentment—only compassion towards him.

"Poor Dan," she said gently.

"Let's straighten him," Mrs. Collins said, getting up. "You hold his head and shoulders, Lesley, and I'll lift his feet out. Mind his arm. . . ."

Lesley felt that her tenderness towards Dan was quite ironical at this moment. She supposed it was the proper feminine way to feel when the menfolk of the house had misfortune visited on them.

Dan half-opened his eyes, shrugged his shoulders, winced and then settled down to a more comfortable position.

"Let him sleep," said Mrs. Collins. They tip-toed quietly away.

Dan's defection from the position of the all-powerful, the all-strong, convinced the inhabitants of Coolaroo that he would be at least several days in the homestead. News of shipping came over the radio that evening and Dan was reassured that a small coastal ship would put into Ninety Mile End on its way north and pick up his mob. The horses for the Alexander races would go along too.

There was some disconcertment in the early morning when Dan came stamping round the veranda, buckling his leather belt and shouting orders to the blacks. Lesley had just risen and was emerging from her room in shirt and shorts, towel swinging, on her way to the tank-stand.

"Dan!" she said in surprise. "Do my eyes deceive me?"

"Not on your life," he said. "The arm's fit as a fiddle and I've seven hundred head of cattle to get to Ninety Mile End."

"It can't be right as quickly as that."

"It has to be," he said with a grin. "I'm no good as an invalid anyway, in spite of your ministrations."

"Cousin Con's ministrations."

"Do you mind an aeroplane ride, Lesley?" he asked, changing the subject. She shook her head. "Andy Macfarlane will take the Coolaroo load to Alexander for the races. Hannans Downs family are going overland for a change."

Lesley hesitated.

"Have you arranged my bookings back to England, Dan."

"No."

Lesley was so nonplussed by his staccato negative that she couldn't think what to say.

"But you said——" she got out at length.

"I'll talk to you about it when I get the cattle loaded."

"Dan. I'm not a good influence on Alice—you know, if that is what you're delaying for. I think it's a good idea for Alice and Randolph to take up a property in England. You could become a sort of international farming firm that way, you know. It's good business."

Lesley didn't even know herself what she was saying—or why. She just wanted to resist him, and this was the surest way of doing it. Anyhow, it *was* good business. Look at the English, and even American companies who ran big pastoral companies in Australia. Why couldn't the opposite operate— to the mutual benefit of both ends of the business?

The logic of what she had just said to Dan began to impress her itself, in spite of the fact that she hadn't even thought what she was going to say when the words tumbled out.

Dan looked at her for a moment and then stood gazing out over the plain. Was it indecision in his face? Or just thoughtfulness?

"We'll see Alice and Randolph at Alexander," he said at length. He looked at Lesley now. "Meantime I'll get in touch with the Bank again, Lesley. A hurry-up from me will get you a booking as soon as possible."

He reached for his hat, which was where he had flung it the previous day when he came up from the shower-house.

and he lifted his hand in a half salute to Lesley, but did not seem to look at her. She wanted to run after him as he leapt off the veranda and say she was sorry to have started fighting with him again. But she couldn't have moved. If she had opened her mouth it would have been to make matters worse. So she turned and went off in the direction of the tank-stand instead.

For the rest of the day Lesley felt ill at ease and restlessly inclined to try and force Dan's hand about that booking. Much as she sympathised with Alice's possible problems at Coolaroo, she could see that she, herself, would become involved with no particular benefit to anyone. One of the things that disturbed her most was the choppiness of her own thoughts and feelings. She was being as inconsistent as possible about Alice, about the station life of the North-west, and about personalities such as Dan and Bill Daley. Mrs. Collins seemed to her the only rock which was unchangeable in a sea of unexpected shoals.

Taking her afternoon siesta on Betsy's veranda lounge Lesley tried to explain herself to herself. When Dan was sick and injured she had felt only tenderness and compassion for him. Indeed, for one moment—when she had planted a kiss on his nose—she had felt elated that he was in her hands. Even for only a moment. When he was dealing with her own comings and goings, with Alice's potential for settling down, or otherwise, she thought he was authoritative and managing and she unconsciously resisted him. When he was just running his great pastoral organisation she thought him just a nice Australian with a brown face and a lovely set of teeth.

Clearly the trouble lay with herself. She resisted being organised—and on Alice's behalf resisted Alice being organised. It all stemmed from the years in which Alec had organised her; from the time during which she had been without a will—and little more than a cat's-paw for his selfish whims.

That experience had left her self-conscious, a little ashamed —and suspicious of man's selfishness towards woman.

Her reflections left her much happier. Lesley knew now that she had the past in true perspective and that she must not let it have too salutary an effect on her attitudes to people henceforth. Dan was all right. It was herself who was wrong.

With a light step Lesley went into the house, fossicked round for the shirt she had not been able to bring herself to send to the wash because it would have meant facing the letter still unopened in the pocket.

She took the letter from the pocket and as she slit open the envelope she sat on the chair by the window. She unfolded the single sheet of paper. It was a shock to see how short the letter was.

DEAR LESLEY,

By this time you'll be "Down Under" after (I hope) a bright and even enterprising trip aboard ship. They tell me that the chief occupation of passengers under the age of thirty is flirtation. Anyhow, I hope plenty came your way. You deserved it.

All's well here with the firm, though business is falling off due to import restrictions in U.S.A., and now Australia. However, Europe is opening up and we've got a man over there looking at markets. The girl in your place is satisfactory, but is going to be married about May. Don't let that hasten you home, however, if you've struck something worthwhile where you are. I have to confess I'm not exactly the "bachelor type" myself and I've been seeing rather a lot of Joan Wells (the blonde in the machinery department). She's got one good point in her favour—besides being darn pretty. She lets me do the running after. Well, it's fun while it lasts.

What I'm trying to get at, Lesley, and I'm finding it difficult to say, is that I don't want you hurrying home. The job can wait, or even go to someone else. And I think you and I had better change our old habits a bit. The thing was beginning to drag—wasn't it?

Yours affectionately,
Alec.

Lesley sat looking at the letter for quite a long time. She felt exactly as if she had had a slap in the face. She felt cold all over her. She didn't mind Alec's defection. She was suffering from defection herself, wasn't she? It was the manner in which it was conveyed. She had been cast off like an old and no longer interesting garment. She screwed up the letter and threw it into the corner. Then she covered her face with her hands.

To have let herself—her pride—come to such a pass! Never again would she put herself at the mercy of a man's love!

CHAPTER THIRTEEN

Ten days had passed. The cattle were safely shipped and Dan and his men home from the drive. The barometer had risen and now all were doleful as several times a day someone went to the glass and tapped it. They had wanted the rains to hold off for the muster—but now they were welcome to come. There had been no rain on Coolaroo for three years and if the drought didn't break this season the remaining cattle in the ranges would die and the sheep flock would have to be whittled down.

"Well—we don't want it flooding for the races," Mrs. Collins said consolingly. "Perhaps the rain is just waiting for that event to be done with."

Betsy came over the air twice to tie up final arrangements for the Coolaroo party, and the Brennans were full of their anxiety to join up with the Baxters again and " see more of Lesley!"

"How's your sunburn, Lesley?" was the inquiry that reverberated around the North-west on the open session. There wasn't anyone now, the length or breadth of the country, who didn't know Lesley was at Coolaroo and that Lesley had an English complexion that had to be guarded against the rigours of the climate.

Lesley herself didn't know whether to feel vexed with this publicity, but Mrs. Collins laughed her out of it.

"My dear, you're an object of interest to everybody. Even the jackaroos and lonely hutters right out on the fringes. Without change—and the news of change—we'd all die of loneliness and boredom."

Dan had made no further comment about his injured arm. When he came in from Ninety Mile End it was still bandaged but he insisted it was all but healed. Bill Daley had done the dressing. He still wore it bandaged, Lesley noticed, but it did not seem to inconvenience him. He had been quiet ever since he returned. The life at the homestead seemed very quiet and everything worked in a pattern of routine.

For two or three nights after the drive of cattle to the coast, the men—Dan and Bill Daley—sat silent, leafing over papers before they went very early to bed. On the fourth night Dan asked Lesley if she liked recorded music and invited her into his study. In silence they sat and listened to the "Ninth Symphony". After that Dan made the tea.

Lesley was puzzled. She wondered if he had really wanted to listen to music himself or whether he was feeling his duties as a host superimposing themselves over his fatigue and had made an effort to "do the right thing" by his guest. Moreover, she didn't know whether it was his fatigue or whether she had really and irrevocably angered him when he had come in with his injured arm and she had resisted his plans to delay her departure, that made him so very quiet.

Mrs. Collins did not appear to notice anything amiss.

"Dan giving you some music, Lesley? He must be feeling lively."

"I wouldn't have thought sitting in a chair, smoking home-made cigarettes and listening to music being lively. He was much more so when Hannah and Mary and Christine were here."

"We all were. But we couldn't keep that up in this climate. It saps one's energies so."

Lesley reflected that this period must be a fair sample of everyday life. So far, she could not find it in herself to dislike it. The heat was objectionable, but apart from that there was time to do the things for which she had never found time living an urban life. Things like catching up with her reading, and putting lace in the right spots on her petticoats, and doing fine embroidery on fine linen handkerchiefs, an art she had been taught at school and at which she excelled but in which she had not been able to indulge herself in years. Nevertheless, Dan was remote from her, which he had not been before. His conversation at the evening meal was formal and impersonal. When he spoke to her he fixed his blue eyes on her face as if absorbing what she was saying without being absorbed. He could almost be thinking of something else.

Bill Daley, on the other hand, was in his element. He had one fair lady to himself. He made no more amorous overtures to Lesley but he rarely left her side once he was in from the run.

"What you making there? Good heavens!" he said, picking up one of Lesley's fine handkerchiefs. "Fit for mosquitoes to blow their noses on."

Dan looked up from his papers and watched Lesley diving to retrieve her sewing. Bill was holding it aloft beyond her reach.

"Would you like to give one to Christine when we go up

north to Alexander?" Lesley asked. "I promise you she would like it—only don't say where it came from. It is the kind of present you could make, Bill, because it is un-ostentatious yet has both art and value."

Bill gave a laugh as if the idea was absurd. But there came a flicker of doubt in his eyes. Lesley saw it. She felt jubilant. Her planted seed had not fallen on barren ground then. It was even showing signs of budding.

"I'll work a 'C' on it?" she said.

"Well—I suppose something like that—at Christmas—or some such time. Old Macintosh over there in Victoria could hardly object to a handkerchief."

"Or to a crack stockman, a champion rider—or a record scraper of whiskers."

They laughed together like two conspirators.

"What are you two talking about?" Mrs. Collins asked. "You seem to be having such a good time, can't we share it?"

"Bill holds all the records in the North-west. I was just cataloguing them for him."

Dan put down his paper and looked at them. Bill was sitting on the veranda floor beside Lesley's chair. She was looking up at Mrs. Collins, her pretty face full of laughter. Dan did not say what he thought, but after a minute or two he went back to his paper. Every now and again his eyes would stray to the two who laughed and talked together like old friends.

Mrs. Collins thought she had never seen anyone bring out the best in Bill Daley before. He stopped showing off, and although he remained a tease he didn't go too far with his familiarities.

The day before they left for Alexander Station the homestead was galvanised into life again. Two of the stockmen, with Abe and Tony, the crack aboriginal riders, left for Ninety Mile End in the Utility. They were to catch the M.M.A. mail plane north for the races. Lee and his cohorts in the cook-house were doing their best with roasting in the big ovens.

The men polished their bridles and even their stock-whips. Saddles were looked over and spurs were brought out and tested.

"We take our nice frocks, Lesley," Mrs. Collins said. "After the races there'll be a party and dance but even for the races pretty dresses and big hats will be the order of the day. They're only bush races on a home-made bush track—but it's the best-dressed show in the year. People come from down south and even across Australia from Queensland—and they can't be allowed to out-smart the North-west."

Lesley began to catch the spirit of excitement as she packed. It would be fun seeing lots of people after these weeks of isolation. She was very anxious to see Alice. Moreover, Dan had said at dinner that the north was greener than Coolaroo —they had a better rainfall—and the countryside would be different. Lesley was quite anxious to see it.

Late in the afternoon the Anson flew in and landed on the plain a quarter of a mile from the house. Bill Daley went down in the truck to pick up Andy Macfarlane and bring him to the homestead. Lesley went down to the gate of the garden to meet them.

"You look like you're at home, young Lesley," Andy said with a grin as he came up. "Standing at the gate like that! Know your way around by now, hey?"

"Yes, I do," Lesley said with a laugh.

The three of them walked up the garden path and on to the veranda. Dan stood in the doorway of the homestead watching them. He looked at Lesley curiously for a moment and she wondered if by Australian usage she had perhaps presumed in going first to the gate.

"Hiya, Dan!"

"Hiya, Andy. How's the old bus?"

"She'll carry us. Lesley, of course, will have to slim down between now and the morning—but otherwise——"

Dan's blue eyes flickered thoughtfully over Lesley. Then he looked quickly away as if he, too, had been caught out in some presumption.

"Well—come in," he said. "Have a drink, or something."

"I'll have 'something', 'specially if it's got soda water with it," said Andy.

Their hats all went on to the floor under their chairs and they sat down lazily. Dan disappeared inside and came out a few minutes later with a tray and some cool drinks. Lesley thought that this was perhaps the hour for men's talk and started to go inside.

"Won't you have a drink, Lesley?" Dan asked, almost with studied politeness.

Lesley felt shy to sit down with the men in Mrs. Collins's absence.

"I'll be back presently, Dan," she said. "I've one or two last-minute things I want to do."

It was a funny thing, Lesley thought, but even after a week or two she was getting into the Australian habit of thinking men should be left alone when they wanted to talk business or get on with their everlasting yarns. When women were present there was only badinage or reading.

The next morning, shortly after breakfast, they packed into the Anson—plus roast carcasses of sheep and many tins of biscuits and savouries.

From the air Lesley looked down on Coolaroo.

Heavens, how isolated it was! It sat, a little village of homestead and outhouses, by a dried-out watercourse, the only evidence of which was the line of trees marking its bed.

The ranges humped up beyond the watercourse and beyond that was desert. Mile upon mile of endless desert.

"If I'd seen a picture of *that*," Lesley said to Mrs. Collins, "I think I'd have been too frightened to come."

As they went farther north there was more green visible below them but there were still vast arid stretches of what looked like pocket deserts in between mountain ranges and dried-out watercourses.

The Anson came down at another town—an enlarged version of Ninety Mile End. The houses straggled over a sandy plain, their iron roofs anchored to the ground by cables; the only secure, permanent-looking dwellings being the concrete ones.

There were Utility trucks to take the party to the hotel, where Lesley was amazed to find gathered what seemed to be the entire population of the town.

There was back-slapping and hat-throwing—this last a favourite way, seemingly, of saying "hallo" to someone at the other side of the room.

There they all were—the travelling Australians on their way to Alexander Station at Fitzroy for the races! They were slouch-hatted, brown-faced, blue-eyed. Their voices crackled and their faces wrinkled up with their impish laughter. They looked shyly at Lesley. First once to see who she was, then twice to take note of her pretty face, or petite figure and her "Elizabeth Taylor" eyes. This second glance was always from under eyelashes and was both wondering and bashful.

Dan noticed it and for a moment he felt proud of his guest. He took Lesley's arm and introduced her round. The women frankly looked her over, but their friendliness quite outweighed their frank curiosity.

"Come and sit down here—of course we've all heard about you. I'm Sarah Gibson from Railton Downs Station."

"Of course," Lesley said. "Your voice was familiar—I've heard you once or twice over the radio."

"I bet you have. They say I get into the air more than any other woman in the North."

She was tall, slim, and her face, though handsome, was a little too weatherbeaten.

"How'd the wedding go? And how'd you get on with Betsy?"

"The wedding was lovely. Randolph married my cousin, you know. That's how I happen to be here."

"You don't have to tell me, my dear. There's nothing the whole North doesn't know about you—down to the brand of cosmetics you use and the colour of your toothpaste. What the radio didn't tell us, the travelling bushmen, the bush wireless and Betsy herself told us. I saw your cousin, too. We were up at Darwin when Joe Brennan flew them in. My, she's pretty!"

"Thank you," said Lesley. "I think she's pretty, too!"

"You pass pretty well yourself."

Lesley said, "Thank you," again. She didn't know how to pass a similar compliment herself without embarrassment. Dan came over with a long, cool drink for her.

"Hallo, Sarah! Want a drink?"

"I always want a drink—you don't have to ask. Say, Dan —you going overland to Fitzroy?"

"Yes. I leave the party here. I'm going to take the horses out myself."

"We're overlanding too. Ask Jim about joining up, will you? There's a couple of trucks going out from the town too."

This was the first Lesley had heard about Dan leaving the party. She reflected rather sadly that his manner—very reserved during the last few days—must indeed reflect his coldness towards herself. He would surely have mentioned his plans otherwise.

She found herself following him with her eyes as he threaded his way through the crowded lounge to the outside bar. When he disappeared through the door she was conscious that the eyes of the women around her were on her. There was speculation in their eyes. A faint colour crept up Lesley's cheek. She sipped her drink. At any rate, Dan had remembered she liked the lemon drink flavoured with passion-fruit and mint!

"You going back to England soon, Miss Wilson?"

"A week or two, I think. I'm waiting to see Alice settled at Coolaroo."

"I guess you'll find Alice out at Baxter's now. They were due in there last night. The 'milk round' plane was taking them out from Darwin."

"Milk round plane?" Lesley looked puzzled. Everyone laughed.

"The mail plane that makes the round of the stations— in the morning."

Dan came back with a tray of drinks for the ladies who were standing around. They all smiled on him when he arrived and though he did not seem to make any attempt to charm them it was quite clear they all felt he did. There was something so natural and easy about him, and yet behind it all that rather intriguing hint of reserves of strength—it was certain that everywhere he went people took notice of him.

Lesley could not help but be interested in this effect he had on people. She found herself again looking at him, almost as if to detect the mechanism that made him tick so successfully. Then, catching a curious pair of eyes on her again she quickly looked away.

Dan emptied his tray as Mrs. Collins came up.

"I'll see you in two days, Con," Dan said. "If you don't hear from me by then, send out a break-down van, will you? The crocodiles will have had a hunk of me."

"I heard a steer had a hunk of you, Dan?" a rather shrill feminine voice asked him.

"What were you doing with a steer to get caught that way, Dan?"

"I wasn't even thinking of the raking beast," Dan said with a laugh. "That's the trouble with accidents, you know, take your mind off your job and you'll catch it."

He glanced at Lesley as if expecting her to say something. She was standing a little apart, her long glass in her hand. She returned his look coolly. Well, if she was really out of favour, she would have to accept that philosophically. Certainly after her experience with Alec she was not going to put herself in the position of being hurt by any man. *Any* man.

"Well, I'm off," said Dan. Lesley gave him a half smile which, she thought, was enough for good manners and not enough for Dan to think she was making overtures to overcome his coolness. It was on the tip of her tongue to ask him had he checked about her bookings before he left the town, but she caught herself in time.

It was some demon that took possession of her and made her say things to cut off her nose to spite her face. There wasn't any real need for her to hurry home now. She knew she would never go back to her old job. She would never expose herself to further humiliations from Alec. Besides, she felt herself to be slowly but surely awakening as if from some kind of Rip Van Winkle sleep and beginning to live again in the world of people. For two years she had lived only in the world of her frustrated love and her embarrassed pride.

Certainly the North-west was a strange world into which to awaken. But it was interesting. At least, the people in it were. She wanted to see out the various projects she had seen begin. She wanted to know what would happen to Bill Daley and Christine Macintosh. What would happen to Cousin Con if and when Alice really did establish herself in the homestead at Coolaroo? Would Randolph prevail on Dan to buy a plane, and would it be to take Alice on a roundabout of the great country as Joe had done? And would the rains come and relieve the drought farther south? And would Dan's house be finished? What would it be like and who would live in it? And here she was on the point of goading Dan into getting rid of her as quickly as possible.

Well, Dan didn't mind; that was quite clear. With something less than a half smile he had gone out of the hotel. Lesley could see his brown slouch hat disappearing down the wide, shapeless, hot road.

"Well, Dan's gone, we're in Andy's hands now," said Mrs. Collins. "We'll go upstairs and have a wash and brush-up, Lesley, then on our way. We'll be at Alexander in an hour."

Lesley put down her glass, smiled at her new acquaintances and followed Cousin Con upstairs.

"We'll have Bill," said Lesley consolingly. "Where is he? I haven't seen him since the plane landed."

"He went to look after the horses. Even Dan would be worried about them. You never know how they will take a sea voyage. Bill's set his heart on going out with Dan. They've got to swim the horses over the river about twenty miles out, and it's full of crocodiles."

Lesley wondered why she hadn't known that both Bill and Dan were leaving them here. Was it a conspiracy of silence, or did everyone take it for granted she knew. She would ask Cousin Con later.

A little later the trucks took them out to the plane again. At the last minute, on a borrowed motor bicycle with a black for pillion rider, Bill Daley came hurtling towards the plane.

"Changed your mind, Bill?" asked Andy.

"No. Dan's changed his, and he's the Boss. Thinks you ought to have some competition, Andy. Thinks I'd make a better success with Lesley than you . . . you raking well got to keep your eyes on the controls."

Lesley listened to this, unsmiling. Afterwards she would scold Bill. Christine Macintosh was already out at the station and Bill was not to be allowed even one regression to his old flirtatious way of talking.

"Tell you what," said Andy. "You take the controls and I'll take Lesley."

"Those are not my orders. Dan says. . . ."

"When'd you take real orders from Dan, Bill? Most times you please yourself. And Dan's not captain of my plane, whatever he is in Coolaroo."

There was an unmistakable edge in Andy's voice and Lesley looked at him in surprise.

"Now then, you two," said Mrs. Collins firmly. "I'll knock both your heads together if I hear another word. Andy, you fly the plane out, I've no faith in Bill at all. He hasn't touched the Anson for months. As for Lesley, *I'll* take care of her."

She hustled everyone aboard and Bill swung himself up and into a seat behind the women.

"Okay . . . okay . . . okay, Lesley!" he said when she turned to speak to him. "Don't scold, I won't do it again." He leaned over her shoulder conspiratorially.

"I'm just making some competition for Andy. He's gonna be so busy winning you in the teeth of opposition he won't notice Christine losing her heart to me. See? You don't suppose Andy or William Macfarlane are going to stand by and see Christine go to a mere jackaroo, do you?"

"What are you two up to?" Mrs. Collins asked severely.

"Christine!" Lesley said complacently. "She and Bill are in love with one another, and I'm just helping them along. What's wrong with being a jackaroo, Cousin Con? They all start that way, don't they?"

"Never mind about the jackaroo just now. What's this nonsense about Christine. As for Bill, he never stays in love five minutes. He's made wolf's eyes at every girl in the north."

"But he doesn't make wolf's eyes at Christine," said Lesley.

"That's the point. He's *different* about Christine."

"You know what?" said Bill, gazing at Lesley. "You've really got something. You've even got me believing that myself."

"Just wait till I start on Christine," said Lesley.

"You'll do nothing of the sort," said Mrs. Collins. "Lesley you astonish me. Whatever's got into you?"

When Bill had relapsed back into his seat, Lesley told her.

"Well, he wouldn't leave me alone, Cousin Con. And he's rather a dear really. He deserves to be successful with someone. So I picked out Christine—she wants someone too—and her cousins and the Brennans won't let her poach on their preserves, so you see?"

Mrs. Collins looked at Lesley in amazement.

"Whoever would have thought that was going on in *your* head." She chewed her lips thoughtfully a moment. "I guess you're having a little bit of fun, Lesley, but I don't approve. It's all right for Bill, but Christine is something different. As you say, she really does want someone, and one can't afford to play at love with people like Christine."

"She hasn't been touched yet," Lesley said sanguinely. "I've only been giving Bill the idea."

"I believe you mean it all."

"What is socially wrong with a jackaroo, Cousin Con?"

"Nothing. That's the trouble. He's socially in the top drawer, but generally he hasn't any property. If they've got ambition, jackaroos become managers for the stations owned by companies—stud managers—agents for the marketing firms."

"Bill's good enough to become any one of these things, isn't he?"

"Yes. He only wants the incentive."

"And the Macintoshes have got enough properties, haven't they?"

"Lesley, I'm ashamed of you, match-making like this." Lesley turned smiling eyes on Mrs. Collins.

"Of course, you and Mrs. Brennan, and Mrs. Jenkins, wouldn't think of doing anything like that," she said gently.

Mrs. Collins looked quite taken aback.

"I'm a lot older to begin with, but as if I would."

Lesley patted her hand.

"Of course you would. We all would. Everyone likes to see the right people meet and live happy ever after."

Mrs. Collins caught Lesley's hand a moment. Then with a little unusual fuss she opened her handbag and fossicked for a handkerchief. She mopped her brow, then fanned herself with the fine piece of linen that Lesley had embroidered elegantly for her.

"I don't want you to go back to England, Lesley. It was I who delayed sending Dan's letter off to the Bank. You see, I handle the mail after Dan has sealed it up. Joe was supposed to take that letter when he flew Alice and Randolph out. I just didn't put it in. Dan only guessed when he didn't hear anything in return. Then I persuaded him to leave it another few days, when he came in from getting the cattle off. He'd do anything for me, Dan would. I've been a bit lonely, and, well, how do we know what Alice will want to do with the homestead? She won't want an old, elderly cousin around. You see, I thought I'd have you, just to help over the difficult period. The same as Alice would have you. Then you're good for Dan—he likes you——"

Mrs. Collins broke off. Her face was quite moist with the effort of confession. Lesley listened to her in amazement.

So Dan hadn't been quite so arbitrary as she had thought! On the other hand, Mrs. Collins had had to persuade him to the delay when he had found out, so it wasn't his idea—it wasn't necessarily his wish at all!

But he hadn't given Cousin Con away when she, Lesley, had reproached him.

Lesley had the most extraordinarily mixed feelings as she listened to Mrs. Collins. Mrs. Collins she had thought of as the one secure person, the one about whom she did not have to conjecture at all, and here she was, a rather moist, hot little woman, afraid for her home and for her boys. All that cosy self-assurance, that rather endearing bossiness, was a fraud.

But why had she pinned her salvation on Lesley? Lesley, who had so little confidence in her own ability to steer a safe course through the difficulties of life, was astonished that Mrs. Collins attached so much importance to her own presence—other than the influence she might have on Alice.

She touched Mrs. Collins's hand gently.

"Why—why me?" she asked rather falteringly. "I mean, apart from being Alice's relative. That would make me more likely to take Alice's part if there were any difficulties, wouldn't it?"

"You're so gentle, Lesley. As soon as I saw you, I thought you were Alice. That you were the one Randolph was bringing home, and my heart almost swelled with relief. Then when it was Alice who was to be the bride, I made up my mind to like her just as well. I do, too—you mustn't mistake me, Lesley. She is so pretty and fair, and Randolph adores her. But she is a little delicate—surely—a little petulant——"

"Spoiled," said Lesley succinctly. "But not *too* spoiled. She doesn't always get her own way, you know."

"So I thought—you and Dan——" her voice trailed off with embarrassment. "Then I realised you probably had someone you cared for in England, and I thought if you stayed here long enough you might forget——"

"But why *me*?" Lesley persisted. "There's lots of girls here."

"You're so gentle, you're different. You see, Hannah and Mary are so self-assured and firm—they would push me right out of Coolaroo in time. I know that. Not that they're not nice girls—good girls—they are. But they're bossy too. Dan only ever liked one girl, and she was different. He's never liked anyone else—it needed someone very, very different to rouse him. Someone so different from all the girls and women in the north that he'd stop and look twice."

"Why didn't he marry the girl he liked? I can't imagine anyone turning Dan down."

"It wasn't wise. Everyone joined in frustrating it. She was twice his cousin. Her parents were cousin to one another and were Dan's cousins. In the end he might have married her, only she went off suddenly and married another cousin. Somehow one thought it was just to show Dan it could be done."

Betsy!

So that was it. All along Lesley had wondered. Betsy, with her faintly supercilious surveillance over Dan; her real and undisguised affection for him. All along Betsy had been an enigma to Lesley. Lesley had rightly thought her kindly and generous by nature and had been puzzled by the faintly feline qualities that raised their heads every now and again. In her heart Betsy still possessed Dan. No other woman might do anything more than be an off-hand acquaintance.

Lesley sat silent for a minute. She hardly observed the changing landscape below them.

Mrs. Collins looked at her anxiously.

"You're not angry, are you, Lesley? Does it affect you very much, not having made an early booking?"

"How could it make me angry? I'm so *gentle*," she said a little bitterly. Then she was instantly sorry. After all, Cousin Con had paid her the highest compliment imaginable. She had wanted her to stay for her own sake and she had wanted her to stay for Dan. Her beloved Dan.

"Has the letter gone to your Bank yet?" she asked.

"Dan had it with him this morning. He was going to post it by air mail to Perth to-day. That was why I was rather unnerved. I didn't want you to go, Lesley, and I knew if the

Bank did settle a booking for you that you really would go."

" So the die is cast! Oh, well, perhaps I won't get one for some weeks. I would like to stay on a while, Cousin Con, if I may, but not because of Dan. Because of you, and Alice."

Mrs. Collins looked moist and happy. Then she pulled herself together. She put away her handkerchief and closed her bag.

" Not a word to Dan," she said.

Lesley shook her head.

Mrs. Collins was her old self again; maternal and kindly.

" Bill," she said severely over her shoulder, " can't you keep those great clopping boots of yours still?"

" What's eating you, Cousin Con? My boots aren't any different than they always are."

" The boots are the same. It's the feet that are inside them. You're trying to draw attention to yourself, and it won't do."

" I'm trying to draw Lesley's attention to the river crossing. You're so busy talking you haven't got time to look."

Lesley looked out of the plane. Far below her she could see the same village-like formation of black and white buildings as at Coolaroo. The chief difference was in the countryside, which had both water and trees.

The plane began to lose height and presently they could see the paddock where they would come down. There were two small planes like silver moths at the side of the paddock. They weren't the first of Alexander Station's guests to come by air.

When the Anson landed and taxied nearer the home paddock a swarm of children, both black and white, of horses, dogs and a Utility truck came pouring over the brown grass. Foremost was Neil.

" Howya! Howya! Howya! Hallo, Lesley, Hallo, Cousin Con. Howya doin', Bill! Good day, Andy!"

Neil was noisily excited and yet obviously the young master of Alexander. Even excited he didn't lose his little air of dignity.

Bill Daley cuffed his head playfully and Andy threw the small packet of mail at him. Mrs. Collins kissed him and Lesley shook hands with him. He presented several of the children, but none of them had known names to Lesley though quite clearly Bill and Andy knew who was addressing them.

"Cripes, Jeannie, you've grown. Thought it was your mother—begorra and I did," said Andy.

"Good day, Cyril, how's your pa? How's the bull doin'?"

They knew all the children. They were playful and teasing and very popular. Everyone was thrown a bar of confectionery which Andy now discovered in a box alongside the pilot's seat. How it got there he did not profess to know, but supposed it was all right by the kids if he threw the stuff away. He threw the stuff, piece by piece, to one child after another.

The plane was unloaded and the children given cases and parcels to transport to the homestead. Lesley and Mrs. Collins got into the Utility with a shy young blackfellow who was driving.

At the homestead Alice and Betsy were waiting for them. Lesley tumbled out of the Utility first and went eagerly towards Alice. They kissed and then stood off and looked at one another. Alice looked happy and well, a little excited at the prospect of being with Lesley.

"Thank God for a familiar face," she said. "I've been with no one but strangers."

"You and Randolph, not to mention Joe. I thought most brides got all the company they wanted from their husband on a honeymoon."

"Yes, well, but it's all so different. Adelaide is nice but the people, they're all so different. But Lesley, how are you? You're thinner. What have you been doing with yourself?"

"Riding—I went to the muster—it was great fun——"

Lesley broke off. In her eagerness to see Alice and test how her cousin was reacting to the new life, she hadn't spoken to Betsy.

"I'm awfully sorry," she said, turning to Betsy.

Betsy was leaning against the little wicket gate watching the two English girls greet one another. There was nothing but mild curiosity in her face.

"Go right ahead," she said. "Don't mind me——"

Lesley held out her hand and Betsy took it idly. "I suppose you want some tea?"

Lesley's interest had suddenly moved from Alice to Betsy. This was the girl whom Dan had liked. Betsy was Dan's fair angel. How lovely and soft and even warm her face was! Only her eyes lacked that warmth. Their blue was of too light a variety—it was cold.

Betsy looked neater to-day than she generally did. She had on a pink linen dress that was beautifully tailored. Her hair waved wispily round her forehead but was more or less tidy.

"Come on inside," Betsy said and led the way to the veranda. The homestead, except for the greater area of garden and tree shrub about it, was much like Coolaroo. It was a squat, square building, partly of wood and galvanised iron, partly of stone. All around it was the wide veranda—the widest veranda Lesley had ever seen. It was quite clear from the tables and chairs and lounges on it that most of the family living was done here. There was even a radio set against the wall and farther down a pick-up wireless. They stepped up on to the veranda and Betsy bade them sit down.

"They've all gone down to see the horses," she said. "I sent them off so that you two could have five minutes to yourselves."

She stood on the edge of the veranda and called Andy and Bill.

"Down at the stables!" she said. "I'm sending big tea down there for them all!"

Andy waved his hat and he and Bill went around the garden and disappeared from sight. Betsy caught a young piccaninny by the neck of his shirt and dispatched him to the gate.

"You tell'm Neil, and young fella, Missy said take parcels belonga plane round house." She turned to the cousins. "That'll get rid of the kids too." She went inside.

Lesley looked at Alice. For a moment they were both at a loss where to begin. At the gate words had tumbled out and they had nearly forgotten their manners to their hostess. But now they were alone they felt shy of one another. Alice had ascended to another plane—she didn't belong to the sisterly ranks of spinsterhood any more!"

"How is Randolph?" Lesley asked at length.

"He's well. Full of himself, of course. Getting back here he feels he's back to earth again and truth to tell, Lesley, he no sooner got with Brian Baxter than I simply ceased to exist."

Was there a faintly peevish note in her voice?

"I think that's the way with men. You're just not a novelty any more, Alice. You're his wife and part of his life as a pastoralist. You wouldn't want to be any different, would you?"

Alice looked at Lesley in surprise. Clearly she had expected sympathy from her cousin. She did not realise that Lesley saw nothing in Alice's circumstances that needed sympathy.

"Lesley, you don't really think it's a woman's place to

stay in the background—keep the home fires burning—his slippers and his pipe ready?"

"I can't see Randolph with either slippers or a pipe," Lesley said dryly. "I don't think a woman should remain in the background. I think she should be at her husband's side. You know, Alice, I've learned quite a lot at Coolaroo. I know we were both rather taken aback by the men's habit of segregating themselves when they want to talk about cattle and wool. I think it's as much the women's fault as the men's now. They just don't find cattle and wool good conversational topics. Yet out on the run they can do, and do do, as much as the men. They're with them all the way. Those Brennan girls can ride like demons. They didn't expect, and they didn't get, any cotton-wool treatment because of their sex. I was the only one who was cotton-woolled, and it was because I was English, not because I was useless. They just took it for granted I would have to be taken care of— fussed over—given sunburn cream——"

Lesley stopped, aghast at herself. When had she been thinking all these things that now they came tumbling out unbidden. She looked at Alice sheepishly.

"In England I like a man to take care of me," she said lamely. "But in Australia—I'm afraid—I rather envied the relations between those girls, between Mrs. Collins and Mrs. Brennan, and the men. They're equals!"

Alice looked petulant.

"Of course I don't know what you've been doing with your time at Coolaroo, so I can hardly judge what's come over you. You're different from me, Lesley. Perhaps you want to be a horsewoman. I don't. I agree with Betsy in so far as I don't believe in getting my skin burned up to a frazzle. I don't want to be like Mrs. Collins. Or Mrs. Brennan. I know they're good, honest, likeable people. *I just don't want to be like them.*"

"Maybe you just don't want to grow up and take responsibility."

"Nonsense," Alice said. "I want to be young as long as I can, that's all. I don't want to frizzle up in that desert they're pleased to call a 'station' at Coolaroo. I don't want to sit in a wood and iron building all day waiting for my husband to come home, too tired, and too dirty, to be of any interest. And they do get dirty. Lesley, why do they have to go out looking like working men and getting themselves into as bad a state as the stockmen? Why can't they leave it to the stockmen and the blacks?"

"I don't know," Lesley said. "I expect it is because there is so much money wrapped up in a mob of cattle or a flock of sheep. Twenty thousand sheep must be worth a great deal of money. Then there are so many people depending on them. A station seems like an industry to me——"

They sat silent a minute. Lesley was not exactly disappointed in their conversation. It was so like Alice to have a grievance about something.

"You know, Alice——" Lesley said slowly at length. "I think it's rather fun to go out and get mixed up with the sun and the earth and the grass. One is freer. I enjoyed every moment of the muster, and I slept in the vest and shirt I'd had on in the daytime. I was grass seeds and ironstone and spinifex from head to foot. The stuff was in my hair. And I felt as free as the air. It was rather wonderful."

"You should have been the one that married Randolph." Lesley looked at Alice, startled.

"Alice, don't say that. You do love him—don't you?"

Lesley knew it was terribly important that Alice loved Randolph. Otherwise her life on the station, hating the heat and the climate the way she did, would be intolerable.

Alice had the grace to look shame-faced.

"I can't help being in love with him," she said. "There's something very lovable about him——"

"Of course there is. Well, hang on to that quality. Never let it go. You'll settle down in time."

"Oh, no, I won't," said Alice, tossing her head. "I'm going back to England. And I'm going to take Randolph with me."

Again they were silent, while Lesley earnestly sought for the right thing to say. She did not want to give way to her cousin but she did not want to antagonise her by opposition. Her only chance of helping Alice was to keep her confidence.

"Promise me not to bring that subject up for a few days, Alice. You might get your own way about that, if you are patient and play your cards the right way. I think it could be good business, but Dan will fight it tooth and nail if it is suggested to him by you and me."

"Dan! Both he and Randolph have got to get one thing straight. My life is not going to be ordered by Dan. And if I get my own way Randolph's won't be ordered by him either."

"Dan's all right——"

"Don't tell me you're another Dan fan, Lesley. Betsy

145

tells me he has the devil's own time shaking off the girls already staking a claim on him—without one coming from over the sea."

" Never mind what Betsy said, and never mind what I feel. You've already had a lot to think about and a lot to say in connection with Alec. But when it comes to a girl from over the sea, don't forget you're one. You've taken Randolph and it might have been better for the North-west if an Australian girl had won him, and been prepared to settle down here."

Alice looked nettled.

" I don't understand you——" she said.

" I just want you to be happy. That couldn't be more simple. And I know you love Randolph, so your only chance of happiness is with him."

" I can be with him in England——"

Lesley could hear the sound of a traymobile coming up the passage.

" Promise me you won't mention that till we've had another talk. I might be able to help you, but promise!"

Alice nodded.

Betsy came out on to the veranda with the tea.

" Well? Told one another everything you've been doing?"

" I did get around to reporting that I'd been at a muster," said Lesley.

" Stale news," Betsy said laconically. " I told Alice that myself. Also about the state of your face when you came in."

" Do you know," Lesley said easily as she took her tea. " I wasn't even thinking about my face when I came in. What was it like?"

" Burnt up like brown paper."

Lesley looked at Betsy.

" Well, I must admit that I think your skin is very lovely, Betsy. It's rather a hard choice to make, isn't it? Stay inside and keep beautiful, or go outside and have fun."

" If you call rolling in the hay having fun——" said Alice.

Lesley decided she had had enough. If she listened much longer she would lose both her patience and good manners. After all, neither she nor Alice had had even time to exchange news of home or of one another's health. Their conversation had been complaint and criticism.

" Does Alexander Station run sheep as well as cattle?" she asked Betsy, to change the conversation.

" Don't mention sheep round here," said Betsy. " Cattle men hate sheep."

146

"Do they? Why?"

"Sheep eat out the place. No, we run cattle only up here. Dan likes the cattle on Coolaroo, too, but gradually the sheep are taking over. They pay so well when the price of wool is high. Randolph is one jump ahead of Dan in those things. He brought the sheep on to Coolaroo. He went to Sydney to get the stud stock—and he'll get an aeroplane on to the place before the year is out. He looks after the cars and trucks too."

"I see," said Lesley. "Dan likes the horses and the cattle—and boats. What a good partnership it is. That way they can have both."

"They wouldn't without Cousin Con," said Betsy. "She is the silent power behind the throne. She's modern, like Randolph, and she can influence Dan. That's how things move forward on Coolaroo."

Alice looked at Lesley triumphantly.

"Who says Dan is boss now?"

Lesley felt a little grieved for Dan. Somehow she had rather liked him as "boss". Was he master of Coolaroo in name only?

Betsy was looking at Alice speculatively.

"Don't you underestimate Dan, Alice," she said. "If you come up against him you come up against a brick wall."

Alice shrugged. "I'm married to Randolph," she said. "Not both of them."

CHAPTER FOURTEEN

For the next two days there were comings and goings on Alexander Station at Fitzroy. Once a year all the people of the North congregated at Fitzroy for a try-out of skill and horse-flesh. This gathering at the Brian Baxter's station was a kind of preliminary test that was something of a dress rehearsal for the big show. It was smaller, more intimate and was not attended by the big racing punters and book-makers as was the bigger meeting later in the year.

This was the origin of all horse racing. Men brought themselves and their horses to try them out against one another and not to make—or even lose—money thereby. If there was a bet it was a private one and made as a joke rather than in anxiety to "make a few bob".

The culminating event of the week's business was the polo match—Coolaroo *versus* Alexander—with Dan Baxter captaining one side and Brian Baxter captaining the other.

People camped all over the run, especially on the rise above the river. All day horses were pounding between one camp and another with supplies, news and interchange of persons. The Baxter fraternity, Brian and Randolph, made it their business to call on everyone, inquire after the health of the stock, the blacks, the children, the adults—in that order.

On the third morning after her arrival at Alexander Lesley rode down with Christine to the yards. Dan and Wire Whiskers had come in shortly after breakfast with the horses.

"I want to see Wildfire," said Christine. "There's nothing up here that will beat Wildfire."

"I want to see Bill Daley on him," said Lesley. "Will he race him, do you think?"

"Dan will have a job deciding that one. Joe—the black stockman—rides Wildfire most of the time."

"But it's Bill who draws the fire out of him—don't you think?"

Christine was thoughtful and a little grudging.

"I suppose that's the right way of putting it."

At the yards Bill Daley was already exercising a fine stallion that Randolph claimed as his mount for the heavy class race.

"Coolaroo's already bought that raking horse," he said. "He's mine. What you think you're doing, Bill?"

"I'll toss you for him as a mount—if I can't have Wildfire." Wildfire was being lovingly groomed by Joe. There was no sign of either Dan or Wire Whiskers. The only evidence of their presence was the horse.

Lesley could not help looking surreptitiously amongst the groups of men lounging about, yarning, smoking or giving a horse "the once over". She half hoped, half feared to see Dan's familiar brown slouch hat, familiarly parked on the back of his head, somewhere amongst the men around the yards.

She could hardly explain to herself the embarrassment of her feelings. She had been unkind and a little rude in her insistence that Dan get on with the business of booking her return to England, and she had wrongfully thought him to be deliberately delaying it out of "bossiness". She had been unjust to him, as Mrs. Collins had explained, but strangely enough she was disappointed that Dan had *not* wanted to delay her departure out of concern for Alice, for Coolaroo, or any other reason he liked to think up. He hadn't really cared about delaying her at all—seemingly.

Dan was nowhere about the yards. Perhaps he had gone

up to the homestead for a shave and a bath. Lesley remembered what the men looked like when they came in from the muster. Two days on the road had probably left their marks on Dan and Wire Whiskers.

Bill Daley came rolling across the yard to the girls. He climbed up on the top rail and sat looking down on them.

"As fine a pair of fillies as ever I did see."

Lesley frowned a little, but she could not help laughing at Bill's lugubrious expression when she remembered that he was to compliment no other girl but Christine. He scratched his head—obviously trying to think of something to say that would exclude Lesley from his compliments without appearing to be rude to her.

"Christine wants to see you on Wildfire, Bill. Can you take him out yet?"

"Why not? He spent the night only a few miles out. He's as fresh as a daisy." Bill looked at Christine, head a little on one side. "You interested in how *I* ride Wildfire, Christine? You better put in a word for me with Dan."

Christine rather softened at being thus appealed to.

Bill clambered down off the top rail and took Christine's rein for her.

"Come on over and chasten Joe for me," he begged. "He won't be game to say no to you."

Lesley turned her horse's head.

"There's Dan," she said. "I'll go across and say hallo. I'll be back with you in a minute."

In her anxiety to leave Christine and Bill alone together she unthinkingly clutched at the first good reason for escape. Dan was coming at an easy canter down the track from the homestead.

Immediately she had said it she felt confused. She didn't want so obviously to ride to meet the one man whose coming had attracted all eyes. Along the rails of the fence was a row of women and half-grown children watching the little scenes in and around the stockyards. They had all looked up—all straightened their backs—all let their faces wreath in cheerful grins.

"Here he comes!"

"Here's Dan. My, ain't he clean, all of a sudden!"

Lesley let her horse walk slowly in the direction of the track, but at the corner of the near yard she reined him in alongside the fence as if finding something of sudden interest there. She was still in Dan's direct line of approach and she blushed to her forehead as she feared that not only would everyone there think she had purposely drawn attention to herself—but, worse, Dan might. She did not realise that from the back view she looked like any of the half-dozen girls on the station. Her blue denim jeans, her gay tartan shirt and the wide-brimmed straw sombrero were identical with Hannah Brennan's and Christine Macintosh's. Dan rode on past the corner of the stockyard to the group of men appraising the young newly broken-in colts.

Lesley's feelings were again mixed. She was relieved that he had not seen her and had not, therefore, thought her to be pushing herself forward. Yet there was a vague disappointment. Could she really—in spite of everyone present—have wanted Dan to stop and speak to her?

She brushed the thought aside because she knew very well that when she did speak to Dan she would want it to be in private so that she could tell him she was sorry to have been so abrupt with him the last time they met.

She turned her horse and rode quietly back to the homestead. Perhaps she could do more good for herself by furthering her advice to Alice and generally allaying Betsy's suspicions that she had a predatory eye on the beloved Dan. She felt forlorn, and didn't know why.

That afternoon a dingo-shooter from out-back rode into the station on a beautiful little blood mare that had spirit and ambition written all over her lovely lines. The dingo-shooter hitched up to the stockyards and mooched over in the direction of Randolph and Brian Baxter.

"Good day!" he said, spitting a stream of tobacco juice at the fence post and hitting it dead centre. He allowed himself time to appreciate his own marksmanship before he went on:

"Thought I'd ride in," he said. "Thought I'd ride Pat alonga your races."

"Okay," said Brian. "Rub her down and get yourself a doss somewhere. What you call that mare? Pat? She's a nice little horse."

"You're telling me. Beat anything in the North-west."

Randolph shoved his hat forward on his head and looked at the newcomer. "They all say that," he said. "But she's nice."

"Thought I'd ride her—but I can't," said the dingo-shooter. He hit the fence post a bull's-eye with another stream of tobacco juice.

"Why the hell can't you?" said Brian—also shoving his hat forward on his head.

A few of the rouseabouts and bystanders drew near. This moving of the hats from the back of the Baxters' heads to the front meant there was business afoot. No one could talk business without shifting his hat first. It was like your learned professor holding forth at the fireside. First, he had to shift his feet. Only then would his opinions flow freely.

" Hurt me ruddy hand. Broke the danged thing."

" How'd you do that?"

" Horse trod on it."

" What, Pat?"

" Yeah. You wouldn't think it, would you? Quiet as a kitten, that's what she looks like. But she's got spite. She's got a nice spittle of spite."

" Too bad!" Brian Baxter eyed the mare from under the brim of his hat. He was suspicious of the horse. . . .

" Well, just looks like you can't ride," Randolph said finally. There was silence all around as everyone deliberated these weighty words. Brian and Randolph looked at the horse; the dingo-shooter looked at the Baxters.

" All the same—she's the best horse in the North-west," said the dingo-shooter, slowly. " She oughta take a ride. She oughta get a chance."

Everybody thought about this.

" And you can't ride her," said Brian Baxter again.

" Nope. Danged if I can."

" Know anybody who can ride her?"

" Well—now—there's Tony Coolaroo—he's mighty fine with a horse that's got a dash of spite."

" Tony Coolaroo's going to ride Wildfire," said Randolph.

Lesley, who had ridden down to the stockyards with Mary Brennan, was fascinated by this conversation. Its tardiness, its weightiness—all portended momentous things to the happiness of several people standing about. Only gradually did this unfold itself. Bill Daley, astride the young colt, sat in silence while the Baxters dealt with the young mare. Christine, since the morning Bill's constant companion, sat her horse beside him. There was a complete circle. Then Dan came across and one or two edged sideways a little and granted him room. Nothing was said to Dan of what had taken place, but it was quite clear to everyone that he knew. The silent group around the dingo-shooter, the mare; the swollen hand—told their tale.

" You see," said Brian Baxter thoughtfully, " it's all set for Tony to ride Wildfire."

Then both he and Randolph turned towards Dan and by

this gesture included him in the conclave. Dan's eyes flicked over the horse. Then he looked steadily at the dingo-shooter. He glanced at Bill Daley and then at Tony, the black stockman from Coolaroo.

"Tony!" It was that quiet voice with the edge of command in it. He nodded his head in the direction of the mare. Tony detached himself from the top rail by jumping to the ground. He walked over to the dingo-shooter's horse and ran his hands over her. He looked in the mare's eyes, and his mouth broke into a broad grin.

"She runs pretty fast, this one," he said. "This'm horse win plenty race up Territory way. I hear'm 'bout this fella long time."

The dingo-shooter spat on the ground. Tony hitched his pants and eyed the man. He stood thinking. Everyone was silent. Tony was weighing up his love for Wildfire against the adventure of racing the mare. Then he looked at Dan, shrugged his shoulders and spread out his hands. The decision was now Dan's and everyone looked at him. Lesley noticed the far-away look in his eyes. He looked into the light and his eyes became mere slits. Then they came back to the dingo-shooter.

"You want this horse to run?"

"That's what I brought her in for, Boss."

"Okay, she can run. Tony—you ride Pat. Bill—you ride Wildfire."

The circle eased. Bill Daley grinned and a smile spread all over Christine Macintosh's face. Tony took the mare's bridle.

"I make you plenty fella win—you——" and a stream of white man's language addressed the horse.

Lesley looked at Mary.

"Is that a good decision Dan has just made?" she asked.

"Yes. And it wasn't easy. A man won't often deprive a black stockman of his favourite horse for a white man. Only Dan could do it and everyone—including Tony—feels he's right. Anyone else would have taken the easy way and given Wildfire to Tony."

"And Pat wouldn't have been any good for Bill Daley?"

"Bill's too big for her. It was a lucky break that mare being brought in—otherwise Bill would never have got Wildfire."

When they all trooped up to the homestead Lesley felt as happy as the rest. She could see why Dan was so highly regarded. The afternoon's incident had brought a lifting of the tension all around. It was quite clear that everyone wanted to see Bill Daley on Wildfire—for the sake of his horsemanship; but everyone had thought the decision would have to be made in favour of Tony.

The dingo-shooter was the most popular man in camp that night. The fires burned brightly, the concertinas played in competition with one another. Round the fires the night voices of the drovers soared out in their cattle songs, some bawdy, some tuneful, and nearly all of them nostalgic and sad.

Lesley, lying on her stretcher on the " visitors'" veranda, her hands under her head, her eyes on the brilliant purple canopy of the night sky, smelt the bush, heard the songs and the concertinas, and loved every minute of it.

If only Alice could feel this way.

Lesley herself was filled with nostalgia too. Soon she would have to depart. If she hadn't been so hasty—so irritable with Dan—that letter wouldn't have gone off. She hadn't had the opportunity to speak to Dan alone since he had arrived in the morning. Only once had they been near enough to each other on the veranda after tea for one to speak to the other, but while Lesley had been summoning courage to mention her earlier conversation and tell Dan she was sorry to have seemed so importunate, Betsy had put her hand on his arm and asked him to go with her to look at one of the dogs that had come in lame. Dan had gone away without speaking to Lesley at all. She began to wonder if he was avoiding her. It seemed odd that Dan—the perfect host—should not come up to speak to her at all.

Lesley tried to think back to Dan's usual behaviour at Coolaroo. How much did he keep at the elbow of his guests when in his own home. She had not *wanted* his attention formerly and so she had not noticed how much of it he did, or did not, give. Lesley hastily told herself she did not *want* his attention now. It would be very embarrassing with every woman in the North-west watching " developments ". But she did want to speak to him *just once* without there being an atmosphere of quarrelling—either over Alice or her own projected departure.

Lesley turned on her side and gazed out over the paddocks. Inside the homestead a light was turned off and several men went out on to the front veranda. Lesley could hear their voices as they talked together, every now and again the crackle of a laugh. That was Randolph! Then a loud shot-gun of a laugh. That was Brian! Lesley listened. Who was telling the yarn this time? Could it be Dan? She had not heard his laugh. Perhaps he wasn't even with them.

For quite a long time their voices murmured on and then there was the sound of heavy boots going around the far veranda. Randolph and Brian? Somewhere in the dark vastnesses of the other side of the homestead they had their wives waiting for them.

Very quietly a pair of boots had come round the gravel below the veranda where Lesley and the entire female population of the Brennan family were sleeping. The boots stopped while the owner of them lit a cigarette. The glow from the match lit up Dan's face. He held the match up as if counting the beds on the veranda and then he dropped it. Lesley could hear him putting his boot on it.

Something like a warm hand seemed to touch and close round her heart. As he walked away she wondered how many other listening ears knew he had passed by.

Dear Dan!

CHAPTER FIFTEEN

When Lesley woke up in the morning she knew something had happened to her. She felt as she had felt after she had had her first Turkish bath in London—years ago. She was different. She was walking somewhere a little above the earth.

She was in love with Dan! She had known it for days but would not face it. For the moment it didn't matter that he was not in love with her or that she was only feeling what all the other girls felt. She was really and truly one of them now. She could do all the things they could do. She could ride out on the run without having to put a plaster mask of sunburn cream on. She could go backwards and forwards to the stockyards without anyone feeling she had to be escorted. She could sleep on the ground, on verandas; take cold showers; eat her dinner round a barbecue: keep Bill Daley in hand; and feel that heaven opened up and the sun shone through when Dan went riding by.

And it didn't matter a fig that she was only one more girl in Dan's gallery. She would live for the day—and let tomorrow take care of itself.

She didn't want to speak to Dan any more. Indeed, she wanted very badly that he should not even come near her. All that she felt would shine out of her face and embarrass her and confound him. So she just wanted him to *be* there, where she could see him in the distance and where Betsy's watchful eye would not torture and destroy something which at this minute, anyway, was sweet and precious; wholly altruistic because she asked for nothing in return.

The greatest effort Lesley ever put forward in her life was the effort—the dressing and at breakfast—to appear natural and unconcerned.

The homestead was a bustle of excitement—of movement, noise and anticipation. This was the first day of the races. Already the horses were being groomed down under the trees and the mounts for the spectators were hitched to the garden fence. They could do their saddling themselves.

Betsy, galvanised into real activity, was supervising the loading of food on to the truck. Along with the food went a barrel of beer, a barrel of ginger-beer and the vacuum urns with ice-cream and iced fruits and salads.

From Geraldton a plane had brought crabs and lobsters straight out of the sea. Last night they had been cooked in kerosene tins on an open fire in the back yard.

" May I help?" Lesley asked.

Mrs. Collins answered for Betsy.

" No, you may not. You girls get off with you now. This is your day too—enjoy it. We older ones will manage the food. When we need help we'll holler for it."

Mary and Hannah and Christine rode down to the track together. In the distance Dan and Randolph Baxter were examining the mounts for a group of children—black and white—who were to start off the events.

The girls reined in and sat watching from the distance. Lesley wondered if people felt the waves of feeling that went out to them across the ether. Nothing could have stemmed that welling of tender feeling that rose in her and went out towards Dan. She loved everything about him—the curve of his back as he sat his horse; the long stirrups, with his legs hanging casually yet never once without that hint of nervous strength so inherent in an Australian horseman; his hat pushed a little on the side yet tilted enough over his eyes to keep out the hard morning light; his clean white shirt with the neat blue tie; his long, strong hand on the rein.

Funny that she never felt any of this yesterday! And yet, hadn't she? Disguised and not acknowledged?

Dan turned his horse away from the children and cantered mildly up the track to where the girls were watching him. He raised his hat. Only his half smile was in evidence this morning.

He wheeled his horse so that it came round beside Lesley's. He looked at her and then looked away across the paddock.

"I hope Betsy has made you comfortable," he said slowly.

"Oh, yes, thank you. I'm enjoying myself immensely." His eyes came back to her face as if surprised. Then his attention went back to the children taking their starting places.

"And Alice?"

"Alice seems very happy," Lesley said awkwardly. Please God—let her say the *right* thing the *right* way! Let her mind her words so as not to start a quarrel!

"She seems to be as much wedded to the idea of a poddy station for Coolaroo situated somewhere on the South Downs of England as she is wedded to Randolph."

He was speaking quietly and slowly and without anger, but Lesley felt her heart go cold.

"Was that your idea, or hers?" he asked. Still he did not look at her.

Lesley was silent. It wasn't a bad idea, anyway. She would be a traitor to her own feelings if she denied it now for the sake of pleasing Dan. It was the kind of idea that would take time to take root and germinate. And *blow* Alice for being so importunate.

Lesley sat her horse and said nothing.

"They're off!" said Dan as the horses, with their juvenile mounts, left the starting-post. "Excuse me."

He rode around the track to where two stockmen were watching the finishing line.

Lesley felt exactly like a small child who had had a dream of palaces when she built a house of cards on the hearth-rug before the fire; and someone had come and puffed them over with one careless huff of breath.

For three hours now, ever since she had risen at sun-up, she had been living on heaven's summit. With but a few words Dan had sent her flurrying down like a scurry of snow into a valley of shadow and cold.

The morning's races went off very well. By midday everyone for a hundred miles around had gathered on Alexander and the picnic lunch went forward in great spirit. The trestle tables groaned and when all were replete most took half an hour off for a smoke and a laze under the trees. It was hot and humid.

By half-way through the afternoon the colts, the two-year-olds and the ladies' races had been dealt with. Hannah had a victory, but all the other ladies' events were won by the pretty schoolteacher from the coast who was destined to join the lonely mailman on his overlanding life across the north.

"Where the heck did *she* learn to ride, anyway?" asked Hannah.

The little schoolteacher kept her own confidence. The mailman had first won her heart by teaching her the tricks of bush brumbies and mountain-bred horses.

The last event of that day was the "best turn-out". At last Betsy came into her own.

It was near sundown and Lesley guessed that Betsy had arranged the time-table so that she would not have to come out in the blazing sun with no more than her bowler. Her habit was perfect. The high, spotless stock enhanced the lovely soft contours of her face. Her hair was brushed, silken and gold till it shone, every hair in place. Her boots were polished till they shone like mirrors and her gloved hands were smooth and small and capable. She rode a fine bay gelding and she rode in the manner of championship events in the Royal Show. There was no curved back or long stirrup about Betsy. She could have taken her place without a blush at the Olympic Games.

Of course she won the event. She always did. The applause she received was as genuine and good-natured as the proud population of Alexander could make it. Betsy was their show piece and neither they nor she were going to let the standard down.

Dan, as ring-master for the afternoon's events, led her off the track. When they reached the fence Betsy leaned across, kissed the top of her gloved finger and placed it on the side of Dan's nose. He was off his horse first and gave her a hand as she alighted. He put his arm along her shoulder.

"Well done, old girl," he said with a grin. Brian Baxter brought her a brimming glass from the barrel. Randolph came over with one for Dan and one for himself. This was the first Baxter win of the meeting.

"To ourselves!" said Brian. The crowd gave a burst of cheering which ended in laughter.

Alice, who was standing beside Lesley, watched the Baxters a minute in silence. Then she caught Lesley's eye.

"You see?" she said. "They've forgotten me!"

"They're all in riding togs, Alice," Lesley said gently. "That's the way you should be. If you want to be one of them—you've got to do what they do—the way they do it. Look at Mrs. Collins."

"Would you want me to look like Mrs. Collins in riding clothes?"

"Yes," Lesley said. "I would. She looks jolly and

happy." She turned impatiently away from Alice. If only she had Alice's chance!

"Betsy doesn't go out on the run," Alice said petulantly. "All she's done now is to get herself up in a highly polished rig-out——"

"But she did get herself up in it," Lesley said over her shoulder. "That's the point."

The next three hours on Alexander were one long uproarious picnic. The east and north verandas were polished till they, too, looked like Betsy's boots. To-night would be the dance. Mrs. Collins and the other North-west ladies of her own generation were hard at work on the back veranda cutting up fruit from tins and adding melons, passion-fruit and bananas. Someone whipped up cream and the fruit salads appeared in the end in the white enamel dairy dishes meant for scalding the milk in former days. Creeper was wound round the outside of the dishes and a pineapple set up in the middle to give glory to the luxury of several gallons of fruit salad.

Everyone had to scramble for their own baths, their own supper and their own dressing time. Lesley went happily about doing just that. In her anticipation of the gay time on the verandas later she had momentarily forgotten the chill that had followed her meeting with Dan earlier.

Youth was wonderfully resilient. Lesley was down one minute and up the next! "That's what love is like," she thought. "I'm glad I've lived to love—even if nothing does come of it. It's worth it just to be in love."

It was curious how the past was so irrevocably the past for her. She did not even recollect she had loved before. Or had that former love never been as much love as it had been the desire to have and to be?

Ten days ago she would have been horrified at the idea of being "just one of Dan's fans"; now, so long as it was secretly and privately, she rejoiced in it. The day for heaviness of heart had to come, she knew that, but for the moment her philosophy was "Sufficient unto the day is the evil thereof".

Sundown came and with it the lovely settled silence of the first hour of night. The animals, the birds, the trees themselves stood absolutely still and saluted the glorious quiet night of the tropics.

Betsy blossomed forth in her lovely pink chiffons and with a little bullying managed to find and dispatch a rouseabout to get the string of coloured lights hoisted around the fringes of the garden. When these sprang into a myriad coloured lights and turned the homestead and its gardens into fairyland the girls began to emerge from their rooms and veranda corners like lovely diaphanous moths.

It was enough to bring the concertina players up from the stockmen's camps. Danny McGrew came across the compound playing his fiddle as he walked. Somewhere, already esconced in a pleasing hideout in the garden, the mouth-organist caught up the tune.

> " Waltzing, Matilda, waltzing, Matilda,
> Who'll go a-waltzing, Matilda, with me? "

From dark corners all over the run the menfolk slowly drifted towards the lights and the veranda. From out of their funk hole came the three Baxter men immaculate in their dark trousers, their snowy tropical dinner-jackets and the soft linen shirts with the little conventional black bow tie. The tan of their faces was polished like cedar; their several heads had been washed and soaped and brilliantined until not a hair dared to stray.

Lesley looked out on the glorious night and felt all the happiness a young person can feel who knows that she looks well, feels well and there are at least twice as many charming young men to dance with as there are young women with whom they can dance. No one could fail to enjoy herself on such an occasion.

Now they were all standing poised on the edge of the veranda. On the steps were Dan and Brian Baxter and Bill Daley. Among the shadowed edge of the light were William and Andy Macfarlane, Joe Brennan and two of the jackaroos from Alexander. Farther down were several of the visitors who had come in and, who were camped along the river.

Hannah Brennan, coming out with a swish of taffeta on to the veranda, paused beside Lesley.

" My, oh my! " she said. " The little English rosebud has blossomed with a vengeance. I didn't know you had so much life in you, Lesley."

" It's only the light shining in my eyes," Lesley said. " They're bound to look brighter."

" May the light ever shine in your eyes," said Brian Baxter as he touched Lesley's elbow. " May it always be my luck to wear an English rose—when I lead out the dance."

Lesley looked at him in astonishment. She hadn't thought Brian capable of so many words in one speech, and never dreamed of so charming a compliment to herself. In a flash she realised it was the custom for the host to lead the dance, and everyone waited to see who would be his chief guest. It could have been Alice—or Hannah—or any of the girls. But Brian had singled her out for this honour. Lesley felt as if she danced on air as the concertinas, the mouth-organ and the fiddle struck up.

> " If I had a dream lady
>   That lady would be you . . ."

The men with their shining heads and immaculate white shirts and white coats blended softly and unaccountably with the silken moths on the other side of the veranda. Bill Daley took Christine in his arms; the Macfarlanes danced with the Brennans—and Dan. Yes, Dan danced with Betsy!

The pretty schoolteacher danced with the pilot from the mail-plane, Sarah danced with the Flying Doctor, who had dropped unexpectedly out of the air at sundown. The stockmen found their partners and those who couldn't dance or for whom there were no partners sat under the lighted trees in the fairyland of the garden and watched the laughing faces, the pretty dresses and the handsome heads that promenaded the polished floors of Alexander to the tune of:

" There was a lassie, and her lad . . ."

All went merry as a marriage bell.

Randolph claimed Lesley for the next dance. He was her brother-in-law, dash it all—and her nearest of kin. He had prior claim to Brian surely! Lesley looked up into his sparkling face and ceased to fear for Alice. Sooner or later she would settle down. In spite of her " spoiltness " Alice had one good redeeming feature—she gave in when she knew the odds were too heavily against her. She didn't harbour resentment, nor did she brood on her disappointments. She merely set out for fresh woods and pastures new. If she was beaten on the idea of a permanent home in England she would eventually compromise on an early trip across the world. And who knew? Sooner or later Randolph himself might get one of his " advanced " ideas and persuade Cousin Con to persuade Dan to yield to it.

Yet Lesley could not help loving Dan a little extra for his tenacious hold on the kind of life he loved.

Would Dan dance with her next?

The gallery of would-be dancers, however, intervened on that. When two Baxters had danced with Lesley they thought duty had been nobly done by and they swarmed round Lesley demanding the "next". The biggest and strongest won the day and Bill Daley waltzed Lesley round the dark corner to the less populated east veranda.

"No flirting, Bill," she warned.

"I wasn't even thinking of it," he said, eyebrows raised in pretended indignation. "I just wanted to tell you things are fine and dandy where Christine is concerned."

"Don't I know it. Bill *dear*—don't spoil it! Don't be tempted to smile too wickedly at anyone else. The Mac-farlanes will pit their united strengths against you if they think you're frivolling."

"I won't frivol—I promise," he said, whirling her back to the other veranda.

The night waltzed itself away. Twice Lesley met Dan in a change-your-partner dance wherein when the music stopped the men formed a ring around the girls and danced until yet another tune was played. Then each man danced with the girl opposite whom he had stopped.

Dan was nice, polite, interested in how Lesley had spent the preceding two days—but so far away from her in spirit he might as well have been on the moon. On the second occasion when they met thus Lesley made no attempt at conversation. She would just dance—and close her eyes—and take what little of the good things Fate had to give away on that night!

And Dan said nothing either. She wondered what he felt. He danced well, holding her firmly and yet impersonally. She would have liked to have looked up into his face—just to see—but she didn't dare. Her own feelings might have shone forth.

The supper was taken all over the place. There wasn't room for all along the long trestle tables now cleared of their debris and decorated like wedding cakes themselves. Several barbecues were going in the gardens and by them smaller tables were set up and to these were brought plates and glasses, bowls of salads, towering sponge cakes filled with cream and giving rest to strawberries. Finally, the tropical fruit salad and cream was ladled out into bowls big enough to take the whole feast. No one could encompass one whole helping and Lesley thought sadly of her friends and relatives in England who would have revelled in just half of what she had already eaten.

"You're a wonderful success, Lesley," Mrs. Collins said when bustling round to see that everybody had enough of everything. "Each time I look at you I can only see a cluster of men with a tiny peep of pink lace in between their legs."

"It's wonderful. I've never been at this kind of dance

before—where every girl is courted on every side. I think it's the way God meant girls to be; even the plainest girl is radiant."

"Not all of them, by a long chalk," said Mrs. Collins. "Trouble is, a girl can't dance with the one she wants to—the rest tear her apart."

"But if he wanted to dance with her—he could, couldn't he?"

"Well, he's got to get into the scramble first. Then, if he's one of the owners he's got to play fair by the jackaroos and stockmen, you know. He's got to give them a chance."

Of course! Lesley hadn't thought of that. She had wondered to see the three Baxter men so often standing apart and watching the others dance. It wouldn't be fair to their men to take their partners from them. Was that why Dan hadn't danced with her?

Well, it was a reason she would give herself. She would just pretend. She had only a few more days in which to pretend. With efficient air mails, a letter to and from the Bank would only be a matter of days—and if the Bank thought as much of the Coolaroo Pastoral Company as the company thought of the Bank then a passage would be wriggled for her somehow.

Lesley stood looking thoughtfully into the red coals of the barbecue by which she stood. She hardly noticed Betsy coming towards her.

"What—alone?" Betsy's soft, languid tones allowed themselves to register surprise. "That doesn't happen, you know."

"It's rather a respite, though, isn't it?"

"Have you danced with everyone you want to dance with? Enjoying yourself?"

"Yes, thank you. I think Brian is a perfect host. It was charming of him to ask me for the first dance. I feel very flattered."

"Oh, Brian's very willing," Betsy said. "He does anything I ask him to do."

Lesley felt exactly as if a jug of cold water had been dashed in her face. Brian's lovely compliment had been empty and insincere then. He merely chose the partner Betsy chose for him. So that she could choose her own too? Had she meant Dan to have the first dance with her? And had she meant it that Dan had not danced with her, Lesley, since?

Lesley felt herself stiffen. She sought for words that would be an adequate reply, and yet which would not be an offence. Betsy was her hostess and she was a guest in Betsy's house.

It was Cousin Con who came to the rescue. Across the firelight she saw Lesley's little eager face stiffen and her eyes ose their smile and become dark. She knew Betsy's lazy cruelty of old.

"Dan!" From the "bar" set up under an old tree she called him across to her.

"Bring a drink for Lesley," she said when he came up to her. "Or else take Betsy away. And Dan—you're not being very kind, are you?"

"Kind?" He gazed at her askance. "I'm so kind, Con, those raking beggars out on the run do me down for wasted wages every minute of the day. Why, I'm the kindest man in the North-west. That's what's wrong with me. That's why you aren't a rich woman, old girl."

"I'm not talking about the men on the run. I'm talking about Lesley. Go and rescue her from Betsy."

Dan looked across the fire.

"Does she want rescuing?" he asked, surprised.

"I wish you hadn't grown so tall, Dan. I'd take a stock-whip to you."

"Okay, okay, Con! I know she's the darling of your heart. I'll rescue her."

He went away over to the bar and brought Lesley a drink. She smiled at him, relieved at his appearance, grateful that he remembered she liked lemon flavoured with passion-fruit and a little mint. Betsy looked at Dan coldly.

"I bet you're on Con's errand," she said to Dan. Lesley sipped her drink. Over her head they could fight. She only asked to remain wordless. She didn't want to quarrel with Dan and good manners forbade her to quarrel with Betsy.

"It was Con's idea that I got the drink—but my own idea what to put in it."

Lesley looked up at him, her eyes warm with gratitude. He was fighting her battle for her—and the antagonist was the beloved Betsy.

Dan looked at her and suddenly softened.

"Betsy," he said, "go and look after Brian, will you, like a good scout? I want to look after Lesley—all by myself."

Lesley couldn't believe her ears. Neither could Betsy.

"Really, Dan!" said Betsy. "I think you've been once too often to that barrel."

"So do I," said Dan peaceably. "But I'm awfully glad I picked to-night to do it." He turned to Lesley again. "Promise not to believe a word I say from now till midnight. As someone or other in one of Shakespeare's plays said, 'I am not what I am'."

"That was Iago," Lesley said. "And he was not a nice character at all."

"I'm not a nice character to-night," said Dan. "By the way, can you trust me as far as the garden fence? If we go there we can exchange views on Shakespeare—alone."

Lesley put her glass down on the table and took Dan's arm.

"Lead on, MacDuff!"

Dan kissed the tip of his finger and put it on Betsy's nose.

"So long," he said casually. "See you in the morning."

Lesley couldn't believe she wasn't in a dream as she went down the lovely firefly-lit garden with Dan. If only she could keep on walking like this for ever—and ever—and ever.

Dan put his hand over her hand where it rested on his arm.

"I had to rescue you somehow," he said.

"Dan—is Betsy always like that? Or just to me?"

"On and off, I should say. She's just a little proprietorial—that's all."

"I see." She didn't quite see but she didn't want to force Dan into a discussion of his favourite cousin.

They came to the end of the garden and turning so that their backs rested against the fence looked back on the gaiety all around the homestead.

"It's lovely," Lesley said.

"You like it? You think it's all right? Of course, it's better up here than at Coolaroo. Not so much spinifex and ironstone."

"It's lovely at Coolaroo too—after the sun goes down."

"If you were Alice, would you want to stay?"

"If I was married to Randolph I would—and then after a while I would want to stay for its own sake."

"But you are not Alice."

"No. And I'm not married to Randolph."

They were silent a while.

"Dan——" Lesley's voice was shy.

"Fire ahead," he said. "Get it off your chest, mate. Have I got your return passage booked? Yes, I have. I got it over the air when we came in this evening. You sail from Fremantle on the fourteenth—that's nine days from now. We go back to Coolaroo the day after to-morrow. You spend five days there, one day into Ninety Mile End to catch the mail plane. One day in the plane—and the next day—heigho for England and the white cliffs of Dover!"

Lesley felt shattered. She had brought it all on herself and she had nothing to say.

The silence was so long she knew she had to say something if it was only a thank you. So she said it.

"Don't thank me," said Dan. "Thank the Bank of Sydney."

That's service for you. An hour after they receive a letter they make the booking and radio the reply. And don't ask me why they only got the letter to-day."

"I know why. Cousin Con and Alice wanted me to stay—and you gave in to them. Do you always give in to everyone, Dan?"

"Nearly always—I guess."

"Then one day perhaps you'll give in to Randolph's idea that you could keep up a liaison with British buyers of Coolaroo wool—even though its through the auctions—and Australian buyers of British stud stock. With the promise of much travelling backwards and forwards between England and Australia you will make Alice happy. And a happy Alice will make you all happy."

Dan lit a cigarette.

"Now put up a case for Randolph and his aeroplane."

"Why not? Look how useful Andy Macfarlane's plane—and the mail plane—are being to you."

"You're one of these go-ahead people too, Lesley. You know what? It should have been you that Randolph married. You are go-ahead for the sake of prosperity—Alice is just go-ahead for her own sake."

"You are not quite fair to Alice, you know. She loves Randolph and she'll give him a lot of happiness."

"The sort of man you'd give happiness to, Lesley, would have to be a real hustler, wouldn't he? Aeroplanes—and trips to England! I guess you'd need a helicopter to really keep up with the times."

"Well, why not?" Lesley said with a laugh. But her voice was shaking. She had been quite right to have wanted that walk down the garden path to last for ever. For those few minutes she had walked not on a gravel path but on the very floors of heaven. Now she was back on the cold earth. The lights all around her danced but her own heart was heavy and hurt her as it throbbed. Why did she always say the wrong thing to Dan?

Supposing she told him now that aeroplanes and honeymoons to Adelaide were very good things provided they were for the Alices of the world but for her own taste she would like to do what Dan's parents had done. She would like to ride out into the incredible beauty of the Australian night with a saddle-horse and a pack-horse and that sleeping-bag in which both they and she had slept. Maybe she could round off a honeymoon with a little trip in a pearling lugger up into the Arefura Sea. "By Arefura to the Sunda Sea . . . through the Archipelagos of the Moon . . . by Timor to the China Seas."

How would Dan like it if she told him that she loved him? That the moment he walked—a lone figure—down that long, long jetty on the day they came to Ninety Mile End, something had happened to her. An old wound had healed and Fate had taken a fresh stab at her heart. How would he like it if she told him that every time he smiled something twisted in her heart and though she had pretended to herself, lied to herself—and hid away from herself—deep down she had known with that deep, final, irrefutable knowledge that only a woman confronted suddenly with her ideal man can know— that Dan Baxter, the Master of Coolaroo, was the best thing that had ever happened to her?

She would never forget him.

Lesley said nothing. Fate demands that a woman, if she is modest, wholesome and wise, will remain silent until he whom she loves first utters the words that unlock the heart.

Dan smoked his cigarette in silence.

"I would have liked you to stay—too——" he said at length. The words strained from him as if he were either reluctant to say them or his own intrinsic reserve made it hard for him so to give himself away.

"Thank you, Dan."

What did those words mean? What could they mean? Lesley longed for him to go on, or for herself to have the genius to say the very right thing that would not silence him now.

There were footsteps crashing through the ill-lit undergrowth towards them.

"Ha, ha, my hearties!" It was Bill Daley. Lesley and Dan stood side by side, mute. Lesley could have wept for them both. Some day—before she went back—she would tell Bill Daley she hated him—she must remind herself to do just that.

"What do you know, Dan?" said Bill. "Raking barometer's dropping fast. Radio says a cyclone heading for Darwin. Guess they'll get it in forty-eight hours. We'll get the edge of it."

"I knew it was dropping," said Dan. "We'll get the big race in by eleven o'clock to-morrow, Bill. We'll make the polo match at twelve noon instead of the afternoon and then the planes can get as many out to the coast as possible before it strikes."

Bill danced a mild fandango and shook his hands in the air.

"Rain! Rain! Beautiful rain!"

Lesley found her voice.

"Must we leave?"

"You must," said Dan. "If the rain is heavy the rivers will all come up and the ground will bog—possibly flood. And while that's good news for the Kimberleys it's bad news for itinerant travellers. You've got to get out of here, Lesley, before the air and the ground will be closed to you."

"I see."

"What? Lesley going?" said Bill, pausing in mid air, as it were. "What are you going for, Lesley?"

"Because Dan's got a passage for me," Lesley said in a small voice. "What other reason could there be?"

"There couldn't be someone waiting for you in England?" Bill persisted.

"No. There's no one waiting for me in England."

Dan looked at Lesley suddenly.

"Betsy told me—you were engaged—or something. She must be mistaken——"

Lesley's chin went up.

"She was mistaken," she said. "Shall we go in, Dan? They're dancing again."

"Hey, Lesley!" Bill demanded her attention. "You aren't mad at me?"

She laughed and patted his arm.

"I'm not mad at you, Bill. I only hope you win that race. I've put all my spinsterish hopes on you."

"All your *what*?"

She laughed.

"Never mind, Bill. Like a famous character out of Shakespeare—'I am not what I am.' Are you going to dance with me?"

"You're asking me!" said Bill.

CHAPTER SIXTEEN

The Baxter Marathon was run the next morning an hour earlier than previously arranged. The barometer was well down and scurrying rains were already falling north and west of Alexander. If anything could take the interest from a horse race it was the prospect of rain.

The station was a hive of activity and excitement. Cyclones meant rain and the salvation of the north, but they often brought destruction and sometimes death in their train.

The race itself was the strangest ever run anywhere. Any horse and any horseman could enter. There were no classifications and no bets. The race was to see which was the fastest horse, of any kind, in the North-west. Wildfire, the Coolaroo stallion, ought to win, but the little mare from out-back was an interesting entry. She had been winning out-back races all over the Territory but no one knew for sure what her real calibre was. With Tony Coolaroo on her back she had as good a chance as any other horse.

Twelve horses started but all eyes were on Bill Daley and Tony Coolaroo.

The horses were required to do the course once, leave the course by the stable gate and race to the river bed half a mile away. Thence back to the course and round to the finishing line.

The dingo-shooter's little mare was off like a streak of lightning but Bill Daley was riding beautifully. Everyone knew that it would be on the river course that horsemanship and horse temperament would make the day. At the river Tony Coolaroo was still in front, but Bill Daley was unperturbed and the stallion began to gain ground up the rise. At the gate the mare put both her feet down, brought her back well up in the air, and with a twist like a streak of chain lightning, propped back on both hind legs. Tony Coolaroo was on the ground, and the stallion passed through. Up to that point it had been a grand race and laughter and cheering accompanied Tony's scramble to his feet. The little mare was away to the hills with the mail-man and his mountain brumby full pelt after her. It took the entire station staff of Coolaroo to hold Bill Daley and the stallion.

"What the raking hell!"

Bill was nearly as bewildered as Tony Coolaroo.

"You was ridin' a hoss, boss," one of the rouseabouts said. "The mare had no business ridin' where decent hosses and decent stockmen rides 'em. She's a . . ."

"Ssh! Mind the ladies."

The dingo-shooter was an artist in apology. He was downright sorry, he was. If he'd known the mare was as bad as she was . . .

Bill Daley said if he wasn't taking up all his time and all his strength holding the stallion to the fence he would take a stock-whip to someone. He mentioned no names but looked at the dingo-shooter.

Tony Coolaroo limped round to the stockyards and took a loving caress from Wildfire.

"I plurry well should know better," he said. "You'm fella Wildfire plenty good hoss. That little one was . . ." and he emulated the white stockmen in his language.

Lunch again was taken at any place around the station where a table, a ginger-beer and hop-beer barrel were set up. The polo riders had one hand on their riding breeches and one eye on the barometer. For this occasion the heavy drill working pants and bright cotton shirts were discarded. For polo the men of the north did the honour of wearing a formal dress.

For the first time Lesley saw Dan really ride. On all other occasions she had merely had hints of his prowess in the saddle. On a polo pony he was at his best. His mallet was the surest and his eye the straightest.

"I suppose they get their practice playing with those balls after tea," Lesley said. She would never forget the swiftness of catch and throw at the domestic game of cricket that sometimes took place round the cement paths of Coolaroo at sundown.

Dan was partnered by Tony Coolaroo and if the latter had been deprived of a certain win in the marathon he was now given every opportunity to display his incredible wiry strength and almost mythical skill handling a horse. Together, Dan and Tony made a perfect polo pair. Bill Daley could not compare with them in this game. For his style he needed a big horse and the wide open spaces.

Coolaroo more than acquitted itself and came off with a sizeable victory.

Dan led his team from the field and those who still remained at Alexander gave him a rousing cheer. Dan looked at the scattering parties and deserted camps.

"Seems like that cyclone must be coming in," he said with a grin.

"You boys get bathed and pack up," said Mrs. Collins. "We might find ourselves marooned here for weeks if the river comes up."

"It'll come up," said Brian. "We're not in the main path—according to the radio news—but we'll catch a rub from the whiskers."

Andy Macfarlane, who had not played polo, had his plane ready to take off. He had agreed to fly straight through to Coolaroo with Lesley and Alice and Christine. Joe Brennan was ferrying his sisters and one or two others to the coast where the mail plane would pick them up in the morning. Wire Whiskers was to remain on in Alexander with the horses from Coolaroo. In the first conferences it seemed that Dan was likely to stay too. Lesley felt her heart drop. She only asked one more thing of Fate. One more taste of a somewhat vicarious happiness; that she would not leave Coolaroo without seeing Dan again. In the end Dan made the decision to fly through to Ninety Mile End with the Flying Doctor in the morning. He, too, felt the obligations of host. It was necessary to make the final plans and see to the safe and comfortable departure of a Coolaroo guest.

Four hundred miles as the crow and the aeroplane fly—and they were home at Coolaroo for supper. There would be no sign of Dan until he found his way out from Ninety Mile End the next day. If the rains held off someone could go in for him to the coast.

Lesley felt tired and strangely bewildered. Coming back to Coolaroo was like coming home. She carried her own case up to the homestead, found her own unheralded way to her bedroom; asked for no privileges in the matter of going to the tank-stand and shower. She put on her shorts and took her towel and waited on the bottom rung of the adjacent tank-stand like a veteran of the North-west. Alice was inclined to be irritable.

"They really ought to have bathrooms—and hot water."

"That air-heated water is as hot as I could stand," Lesley said. "And I've got used to the stroll to and from the shower. Anyhow, you've only to ask Randolph to build you a bath-room like Alexander. He will."

Alice pushed the hair back from her brow.

"Thank you for making the rooms so nice, Lesley. Cousin Con told me how much you did." Alice sounded as if she was making a conscious effort to say something cheerful and put a period to fault-finding.

"I'm only sorry we weren't here to do the dusting before you arrived," Lesley said.

They were silent a moment as they sat side by side on the low rung, their bare white knees feeling the soft air that came with sundown.

"I'm glad Betsy didn't come," Alice said at length. "She was awfully nice to me when Randolph and I first arrived at Alexander, but I began to think she was finding it a bit of an effort by to-day."

"You know, I rather like Betsy," Lesley said, after a few minutes.

"I think she's amusing—but I don't like her."

It was Alice's turn for the shower-house for Cousin Con came out, swathed in a cotton housegown and still dripping water down her forehead.

Lesley sat alone and thought of her last half-hour at Alexander. She had been sitting on the veranda, her case beside her waiting for someone—anyone—to tell her where

d when to go. Betsy had come out and despite the fact of
parting guests and a scurry of battening down of outside
beds, kennels and the iron roof of the cook-house and store-
house, had deposited herself on her cane lounge and placed a
cigarette in the long jade holder.

"I guess I'll be seeing you some time," she had drawled.

"If you come to England I'd like you to come to see us,"
Lesley said carefully and politely.

"Well, I'm not likely to do that. You're more likely to
stay here, I should think." She had inhaled deeply and
watched the smoke rings drift gently away.

Lesley looked at Betsy.

"I'm leaving in a few days' time."

"Says who?"

"Dan. He has arranged it."

Betsy blew more smoke rings.

"I'm very fond of Dan——" she said at length. Each word
she pronounced as if it alone deserved a hearing. "But not
the way you think."

Lesley looked surprised but said nothing.

"He's the sort of person who is nearly too good to be
true," Betsy said. "Those sort of people you just love—without
wanting them."

"I can understand that," Lesley said.

"I just wanted you to know," Betsy said. She stubbed
out her cigarette and then took another. She got up slowly.
"I'll have to go and see those fools have got all the garden
furniture and yard tables inside before they're blown away.
The Utility's coming up the track for you, Lesley."

Lesley stood up. She held out her hand towards Betsy.

"Good-bye," she said. "And thank you very much. It
has been a wonderful experience."

"Come again," Betsy said. "We have this kind of a show
every year."

As she shook hands she looked at Lesley appraisingly. A
little thin, but not so very unkind, smile touched her lips.

"I can't see Cousin Con really letting you go," she said.
"I'll bet Dan hasn't been game to tell her."

With that the Utility honked for Lesley and Betsy turned
and went inside. The last Lesley saw of her was a swaying
back, a trail of silk and a cloud of smoke floating above her
head.

Whatever had Betsy really meant?

Lesley, sitting on the tank-stand at Coolaroo, was reliving
the little scene and wondering. Christine came with a jump
of the veranda and ran towards her.

"If it doesn't rain to-morrow I've fixed it we're goir riding."

"Who?" asked Lesley. She looked at Christine wit interest. How cleverly she had worked it that she was tl odd passenger who could take the spare seat in the Ansc and come through to Coolaroo. When Andy had taken off f Hannans Downs Christine had declined to go.

"If Lesley's only going to be a few more days I want stay and see the last of her. The mail plane that takes h south can drop me off at Hannans Downs!"

But Lesley knew it hadn't been herself who was the attra tion. Bill Daley had been sent on by Dan to see how thin; were "on the run".

"Who's going riding?" Lesley asked.

"Me and you and Bill. We're going out to Mars and we' going to pick you a new colt—and Bill's going to show yc how to buck jump it. You can't go back to England witho' buck jumping, Lesley."

Lesley looked at Christine in horror.

"Me buck jump? Not on your life!"

"You only have to learn how to fall. The horse does tl rest."

Alice came out of the shower and Lesley went in.

"What next?" she said to herself. She might fall ar break a leg—or something. If she did she wouldn't be at to take up that booking the Bank of Sydney had made. broken leg had a sudden and unexpected charm for Lesle

True to their threat Bill and Christine took Lesley the ne day to the stock camp at Mars. Mrs. Collins had misgivin in seeing them go. The weather was hot and thunder Away to the north the sky was that opalescent black that w full of electric threat.

"It's well to the east," Bill said. "At the most we'll get wind and thunder-storm. Lesley, do you mind a ducking:

"I can take a thunder-storm, Bill, but I doubt if I could p up with a cyclone."

"The cyclone's well on its way to Darwin. They've hi five inches of rain at Dampier."

So the three of them rode out. The nearer they came Mars the hotter and more humid became the day.

"Do you suppose we're mad coming out in weather li this?" Lesley asked Christine.

"It's worse sitting around the homestead doing nothin That's why we made up our minds to go out to-day. Nothii is worse than an iron-roofed house in thunder-storm weathe

"What's the worst that can happen?"

"Just what I said," said Bill. "A drenching."

"I suppose if you can take that—I can."

At the stockyards the hutter had several horses yarded.

"Just goin' to let 'em go," he said to Bill. "If a storm comes up they'm better in the ranges."

Bill told him to hobble and loose them all except two.

"You'll be all right on Sally Ann," he reassured Lesley. "These two are both experienced cattle horses. We use them for cutting out the cattle. When you turn their heads they come up on their hind legs and turn—that's because they've got to do it in amongst the bullocks."

They tied up their own mounts to the stock-rails.

"I'll get the billy going," said Christine. "You give a demonstration, Bill."

He did. It looked so simple that Lesley ceased to be alarmed and became enthusiastic. With Bill on her back Sally Ann was the perfect lady. In the middle of the stockyard he sat as if posing for a photograph, then gently pulled on the left rein. With perfect composure and grace Sally Ann came up to the perpendicular, turned and dropped back into a standing position. One of the black rouseabouts got up on her and did the same thing.

"Your turn," said Bill. "Or will you have tea first?"

"I'll have one turn first, then I will have earned my tea." Lesley mounted.

"When she comes up press your feet forward on the stirrup iron and stick to your seat. When she comes down rise gently so you don't take the thud. The knack is in timing."

Lesley felt slightly nervous but was confident that Bill wouldn't be having her do something he didn't think she could pull off. She pulled the rein a little too sharply and the first thing she knew was that she was standing up in the stirrups—at the perpendicular and with her nose on Sally Ann's mane. She knew rather than felt the horse spin round and when she came down the jolt set Lesley's teeth rattling.

Lesley shook her head in surprise. It was over, she was safe and Sally Ann was standing perfectly still. There were cheers from the top rail. The hutter sat in moody silence but the black boy grinned from ear to ear and Bill and Christine shouted applause.

"I'm going to do it again."

"Good for you. Do it three times then you'll have got your nerve."

Lesley did it three times. She was no longer nervous when the horse went up in the air, nor when it turned, but each time she jolted when they came down.

"Tea-oh!" said Christine. "After that you've got to learn to throw your feet clear of the stirrups and slide off her back when she's up in the air."

"First lesson in falling off a horse is in sliding off it," said Bill.

They drank their billy tea and ate sandwiches prepared by Mrs. Collins, and Lesley listened to yarns of buck jumping and horse riding that ought to have scared her if she hadn't been feeling jubilant about being able to "turn a horse on sixpence".

The heat had become more intense and would have been unbearable if they hadn't all been so enthralled with their experiments in the yard. Away to the north and east the day rumbled and grumbled.

"I hope they're swamped out," Bill said laconically. "That'll double the price of beef. And I hope to raking hell they've kept Dan's mob alive for the feed. One week of that and he'll get double the price."

Lesley's first slide had not much of dignity or grace but she was full of pride as she sat up in the sand, felt her bones and realised that she was whole—and had kicked her feet clear of the stirrups in good time.

Sally Ann was the perfect instructress. She did exactly what Bill Daley commanded her. After half an hour Lesley had a sore seat and one bruised wrist but otherwise she was an adept at sliding off a rearing horse and scrambling out of the way of descending hoofs.

"Now we'll have Scratch."

Scratch, it seemed, was also a well-trained cattle horse, but . . .

"It's just the same but you've got to be a bit more spry," Bill said. "Scratch is younger and doesn't wait as long in the air as Sally Ann."

He demonstrated and Christine demonstrated and the rouseabout demonstrated. The hutter said nothing except to point to a small cloud miles away over the plain.

"Someone coming," he said.

"Could be Dan," Bill said. "If he could pick up a 'Ute' in Ninety Mile End he'd come this way to see what the feed's like at Mars."

They all shaded their eyes with their hands and looked to the dust cloud.

"He'll be another twenty minutes—whoever it is," Bill said. "Well, Lesley, you going to try?"

Lesley was quite confident about Scratch. She felt she could go on sliding off horses for the rest of her life.

As soon as she was mounted, however, she felt the difference in the horse. Through the taut reins she sensed her nervous tension.

"I don't think she likes me as well as you people," Lesley said.

"Give her a run round the yard," counselled Bill.

Lesley did a trotting exercise for the benefit of the top rail gallery. She brought Scratch into the centre of the yard and sat still for a moment.

"Now!"

She pulled the left-hand rein. She went up but did not clear her foot from the stirrup early enough. Her left foot was free and in the slide she came over the horse's back. She shut her eyes and grabbed the saddle. For a moment it looked as if all would be well. When Scratch came down, however, the jolt threw Lesley's hands up in the air and she fell back, her right foot still caught in the stirrup.

In less time than it takes an ordinary stockman to move Bill Daley was at Scratch's head and he steadied the horse. Christine and the rouseabout freed Lesley's foot but she lay very still, staring blankly at the black sky and not able to believe in pain that was so intolerable.

"Don't touch me. . . ." It was all she could say. Bill Daley straightened her legs and she nearly fainted.

"Nothing's broken there," she heard him say. His firm, hard, brown hands began with the bones of her head and neck. She could see nothing but black sky and Bill Daley's brown dusty shirt.

"Don't touch me—don't touch me."

"Where is it, Lesley?" Christine was asking. "Where mustn't we touch you."

"Don't touch me——"

After that she did faint. When she opened her eyes it was to dizziness and a sickening pain in her chest. When she breathed it hurt. The pain in her right ankle was like a sword but beyond the ankle there was no feeling at all. Vaguely she wondered if her foot had been wrenched from the leg altogether.

She felt as if there were a dozen people round her and they seemed to be doing something on either side of her. There was a brilliant flash of lightning, a thunder of thunder, and several heavy raindrops, like small cups of water in themselves, fell on her face.

"All right! You fellows got it the other side?"

Dan's voice!

Lesley tried to move her head and wrench her eyes open.

When she did, there was nothing on either side of her but wa
of bush rug. Very slowly and very gently she swung in a
then felt herself being carried forward. That's what they ha
been doing on either side of her—sliding a rug under her
which to carry her.

Why couldn't they leave her lying there? It wasn't as
the rain mattered. Bill had said the worst that could happe
would be that she would take a drenching. Her face was w
and clammy with perspiration. She felt she would suffoca

"All right! Steady against the fence. Now hold tight

It was Dan's voice. Miles away Lesley could hear som
thing howling. Wolves? Dingoes? Thousands and thousand
of them! They swept down . . . nearer . . . nearer.

"Now!"

She felt herself, hammocked in the bush rug, pinned fa
to the fence by the pressure of men's bodies. Then the wolv
—a terrific force—hit the fence—herself—the men—with a
impact that made her sick again. She turned her head a litt
to the side. If she was going to be sick, she had better—b
there was only the wall of rug and beyond it the fence.

Again and again the pack of wild animals—screaming an
shrieking—millions of them—hit the fence. Hit them a
Each time a moan of pain escaped her and each time the me
crouched closer, binding her with their bodies against th
fence.

The heavens lit up in one terrific bonfire and then its ro
seemed to crash to the earth. The wolves hit the fence agair
and Lesley fainted again. When she opened her eyes she wa
on a hard floor and someone was wiping the sweat from he
face. Her back ached intolerably. All the horses on Coolaro
were galloping across the iron roof.

"The noise?"

"That's the thunder-storm." It was Dan's voice. "We g
you inside in the middle of it—but the wind nearly took yo
away several times."

She must be in the hutter's cottage. They had put her i
that blanket sling to carry her inside. The wind had bee
the pack of wolves assaulting the fence against which they ha
held her pinned.

Lesley heard Christine saying something to Dan and ove
the noise of the rain on the roof she thought she heard th
sound of a motor engine.

Christine was kneeling at the other side of Lesley. Sh
poured some water into her mouth.

"Listen, Lesley," she said. "Dan is going to give you a
injection. It will lessen the pain. Then Dan and I will hav

176

to examine those ribs. If they can be strapped we can get you out of here up to the homestead. If not, we'll have to stay here till the Flying Doctor gets through. He mightn't be able to land in this deluge for days—even weeks."

Lesley turned her head and looked at Christine.

"I'm all right," she said. "It's my foot——"

"You're foot's all right. Only bruised and sprained. But you've cracked at least two ribs. They'll be all right too—if we can strap them. But we've got to poke round a bit—that's why Dan is giving you the injection. It won't be so painful."

For some reason Lesley couldn't get her head round the other way. She only knew Dan was there because of his voice. She could feel him pushing her shirt sleeve higher and then the sharp, surprising pain of a needle pressed into the forearm.

"Now some tea. Just a spoonful at a time, Christine." Dan again! How quiet and self-assured he sounded. Lesley supposed he dealt with this sort of thing every day. At least she wasn't as much trouble as the lost prospector had been at White Gum Mountain. And Dan hadn't complained about that!

She felt the pain deadening. It was there—but far away. She drank several spoons of warm tea. The pain became something that was miles away. Then she felt strong fingers doing what Bill Daley had been doing out there in the paddock —beginning with the bones in her head and neck and arms and legs—looking for the breaks. She could see Christine's face smiling in a blur.

When they moved her an inch to feel under her she nearly fainted again. This time she started to cry. The tears poured down her cheeks and the sobs almost strangled in her throat.

"I—can't—help it."

"It's the injection," Christine said as if explaining her condition to someone. Was Dan still there?

Lesley tried to stop crying but she couldn't. All the tears she had never wept welled up inside her. Years of little sorrows and unhappy hours burgeoned up inside her. Christine wiped her eyes and blew her nose for her.

"I'll make some more tea," she said. Lesley could feel more than see her go away, and another hand wiped her hair back. Lesley turned her head a little bit. The hand seemed as if it caressed her cheek for a minute.

With an effort Lesley put out her own hand and grasped it. The hand held hers tightly.

Lesley turned her head where she lay on the floor and held

the hand tight to her face. She wept all over it, her cheek and mouth pressed to its strong brown firmness. It's mate went on brushing back her hair from her head and after a minute a large handkerchief wiped her wet face.

But she would not let Dan's hand go. On it she had wept away everything that had ever made her unhappy.

By the time Christine came back with the tea the sobs and the tears had stopped and Lesley had fallen into an exhausted sleep. Dan's hand was still held, much as a little child would hold a parent's hand, against her cheek.

"Poor kid," Dan said over her to Christine.

It was over an hour before Bill Daley got back from the homestead with Mrs. Collins and the big first-aid box. Dan had come across the plain in time to help move Lesley from the horse yard in the teeth of the first blow from the storm.

Lesley was stirring again when Mrs. Collins, a motherly master of the situation, came bustling in. Dan went out and helped Bill bring in the box. Mrs. Collins was on her knees beside Lesley and Christine was explaining the nature of Lesley's injuries.

"What do you think, Dan?" Mrs. Collins lifted her head and consulted the Master of Coolaroo.

"The ribs will have to be strapped. If we wait here and the rain keeps it up the Coolaroo will rise and we'll be marooned. Either here or at the homestead—it's not likely the doctor will get through—for some days anyway."

"That means you and I do it, Dan. And it's got to be a professional job."

"I'm afraid so, Con."

"Right!"

Mrs. Collins was up on her feet again, her raincoat off and her sleeves well up.

"You men can go outside and get something to eat," she said. "When I want you, Dan—I'll call you."

All the time Lesley had said nothing. Every time Dan came into her line of vision she had been watching him anxiously—watching for the look that might register she had made a fool of herself. When they went outside she turned to Cousin Con.

"I cried like a baby. I'm so ashamed. I always thought one had to keep a stiff upper lip in the face of an accident."

"Everyone cries," Mrs. Collins consoled. "It's the hyacine."

"Hyacine? That's what they give women for childbirth."

"And for air sickness. We're always ready for both in the North-west."

Mrs. Collins, with professional tenderness, was rolling up Lesley's shirt and vest and rolling down her jeans as far as the lower abdomen. She wrapped her upper chest in a long white towel.

"You're quite modestly attired," she said consolingly, "so don't worry, will you? Dan and Bill are both professional first-aid men—they have to be in this out-back life—and they'll get the straps round and tightened without any more of your clothes coming off."

Lesley said nothing because the movement had brought on again her tendency to faint. Christine waved a bottle of smelling salts under her nose. After a few minutes Dan and Bill came back.

"I suppose we can't risk lifting her on a table?" Bill asked.

"One of those ribs is broken—the other two just cracked. I'm not advising moving her on to the table until we've strapped her," Dan said. "Okay." They knelt down on the floor one on either side of her. Mrs. Collins handed them the Elastoplast bandages.

With the second wind around her torso she felt relief not only from the pressure on her chest but from the pain. Dan's eyes flickered up from his task and she smiled up at him.

"That better?"

"Mm."

"Thought so. You'll be all right when they're strapped, you know."

They wound her up like an Egyptian mummy. Now she was aware only of the pain in her foot.

"We'll bind that too," said Dan, and having finished with her ribs he presented her with his back while he strapped the ankle. When he turned round Lesley was crying again.

"What's the matter now?" he asked kindly and with pretended surprise.

"I—can't—stop—crying."

"There, there, kid!" said Bill. "They all do that. What Lesley wants is someone to kiss her good night and put her to bed."

"Yes—" then she stopped. How ashamed she would be to-morrow.

Dan was standing up, the backs of his hands on his hips. He looked down at her.

"We'll leave you about a quarter of an hour to get used to that strapping, Lesley," he said. "Then we'll lift you up. If you can manage it we'll get you out of here before the rains really set in."

The wind outside had subsided but the rain kept up a perpetual heavy thrumming on the iron roof.

"I reckon we'll have two inches by nightfall," Bill Daley said. "I don't think the Coolaroo will come up for twenty-four hours but the sooner we're out of here the better."

In the lean-to kitchen someone had been warming up the generator of the pedal wireless and Christine had been conferring with the Flying Doctor base. She was now able to report back that the strapping of the ribs was accomplished and that Lesley was feeling easier.

The "Ute" had been brought in under the iron eaves of the hut and Bill, the rouseabout and the hutter were putting up a tarpaulin tent over the back. Inside they fixed the bush rug as a hammock.

"How about standing up, Lesley?" Dan smiled down at her. He ought to have been a surgeon, she thought. That was his manner. Kind, analytical and yet impersonal.

"I think I'm on the flat of my back for ever," she said ruefully. "How can I move?"

"Plant your good foot against Bill's boot. Press on it hard and keep off the other foot. Right?"

Dan had stooped down and placed his hands under her shoulder blades.

"Now when I lift, stiffen your body so that you come up straight like a plank of wood. Con, you get behind her in case it doesn't work. Get your hands on the small of the back and don't let her sag."

In less than a minute, and without any pain, Lesley was standing upright. One foot wedged against Bill Daley's boot and Dan and Cousin Con holding her.

"Going to faint?"

Christine held the smelling salts under her nose but Lesley shook her head. She felt damp and dishevelled but was too weak to care. They kept her in this position for a few minutes.

"No sharp pain anywhere?"

"In my foot——"

"Blow your foot, old girl. We're worrying about your ribs and your inside. You know we're not supposed to move you at all according to the book of rules. If we don't we'd have to stay here a week. Now how do you feel?"

"All right——" she said.

"Well, who's going to carry you outside? Me or Bill?" He was smiling at her.

Lesley smiled back.

"You," she said. "Bill needs his spare arm for Christine."

Dan had steadied Lesley with one arm along her shoulder. He stooped and placed the other arm below her knees.

"Now keep as straight as you can—and if there's a sharp pain inside anywhere, scream." He looked at her. "And I mean it, young Lesley, that's the only way we know if we've patched up all the damage."

Very slowly and gently he moved her from the upright position until he was carrying her.

"Right?"

She nodded.

"Very right," she said. Then suddenly her eyes filled with tears again. Dan carried her out on to the veranda and had to make a dash for three yards through the downpouring rain.

"As if there isn't enough water outside," he said as he lowered her on to the improvised hammock.

"It's dry enough in here," he said. "I'll get Christine and Bill to ride in here with you. I'll take Cousin Con in the front seat."

Lesley could not lift her eyes to his. She felt immeasurably shy of him. He put his hand under her chin and wiped her eyes.

"It's the hyacine," he said. "Makes you laugh or cry. Sometimes both." His hand pushed back her hair. Lesley turned her face sideways until her cheek was against his hand. She closed her eyes. If only she could stay like that for ever!

Dan bent down and kissed her on the forehead. Lesley's eyes flew open but he was standing up straight again, looking a little impish.

"Thank you," she said. "Now I really feel as if I have been tucked in for the night. And Dan—thank you for the loan of your hand. I suppose that's what patients do to their doctors when they're really up against it."

Dan looked over his shoulder but the others were still waiting under the shelter of the iron roof while he finished his ministrations to the patient. The rain was pouring down on him. He leaned towards Lesley again.

"That was a nice kiss——" he said. "It was nicer than I thought it would be. And I've thought about it for a long time."

"I rather liked it too——"

He leaned down quickly and kissed her on the mouth. It was such a delicate, tender kiss, it was like a moth brushing her lips. They were both so shy. Colour suffused their faces.

"That was nicer still," Dan said.

He straightened up and turned away. He took two steps towards the hut then suddenly turned round and, bending down, put his arms round Lesley.

"I love you—my darling. Could you possibly stand living on Coolaroo?"

"Yes, please. If you'll only ask me——"

There was an urgency in the way Dan kissed her then.

"What in raking hell are you doing?" Bill Daley called. "Something wrong with the sling?"

"Lesley——" Dan said. "Where's my hat?"

"On the back of your head, dear. You said you always kept it there so you couldn't lose it."

Dan put his hand up and touched his hat. There was a look of comical astonishment on his face.

"Couldn't find my hat——" he said to Bill. "You going far?"

"Don't worry about us. The next tram will come along at any time now."

Dan grinned at Lesley.

"See you later," he said.

CHAPTER SEVENTEEN

Lesley's injuries were six weeks mending. Twice the Flying Doctor visited her, but pronounced the ministrations of Cousin Con, Dan and Bill Daley to have been professional.

For three days and nights after the accident it had rained relentlessly. A jubilant Baxter family recorded eight inches of rain. The river was overflowing and there would be feed for the stock for many months. The underground reservoirs of water would be replenished and the watering troughs and tanks all over the property safe for the next year or two.

Christine came on to the veranda on the day of the doctor's second visit.

"I've come to say good-bye, Lesley. Bill is driving me into Ninety Mile End. Andy will pick me up then."

Lesley looked at Christine.

"I'm sorry you're going so suddenly. Why not go with the doctor?"

"No room—and anyway Bill wants to drive me."

"I suppose he does," Lesley said with a smile. "Mind you write to him, Christine—I think you're leaving a cracked heart behind."

Christine said nothing. She looked self-conscious and her eyes would not meet Lesley's.

"I guess I've got to thank you for a lot. I just want to say 'thank you'." She broke off.

She looked confused. She looked at the ring on Lesley's hand.

"Dan's mother's——" she said. "I guess she would have liked that—liked you to have it, I mean."

"Next to Dan himself it's the most precious thing I've ever had. Cousin Con had it, you know. She'd been keeping it for him——"

"You're very lucky, Lesley——"

Was there faint regret in her voice? Lesley wondered if there was some lingering affection for Dan in Christine's rather saddened voice.

When she thought of Dan she imagined what everyone else must suffer because she didn't have him. She still couldn't get over the wonder of being engaged to him—of being married to him in a few weeks.

The thought of it made her feel happy in the kind of way she couldn't quite believe in.

"Well—I'm off," Christine said. "I guess if there's anything in Ninety Mile End off the mail plane for you—Bill will bring it out. Are you in a hurry for anything, Lesley?"

"No——"

"That's good," Christine said. "Well, I'll be seeing you. I'm not going back to Victoria until after your wedding, that's certain."

Christine went back through the house to get her case and follow Bill Daley across the paddock to the Utility which was waiting out by the stables. Lesley thought it was all very strange. Why was Christine going so suddenly? And why wasn't the Utility at the front gate? Where was Cousin Con and why had Christine been relieved that Lesley wasn't in any particular hurry for mail? Bill would be back to-morrow —or the next day!

Dan came out on to the veranda with some tea he had been making in the pantry.

"This is a bad way to begin marriage," he said. "You should be making the tea for me. You know the first thing Australian men do for their women when they get married?"

"No, what?"

"They tell them to go and make the tea."

"That's making it quite clear who's the boss in the first ten minutes, I suppose," she said with a laugh.

"You bet," said Dan. "Nine marks out of ten in any fight to the one who hits first——"

He was smiling down at her.

"Like your tea?"

"It's a lovely cup." Dan looked at her as if he would like to kiss her. He was still shy of her. It was something which, at moments like these at any rate, Lesley regretted. She wanted to be kissed. At other times it was a quality in him she loved. He kissed her so tenderly and always seemed surprised and curiously happy when he did

"It's nice—so very nice," he said.

She knew then it was true what Cousin Con had said. Dan had not loved anyone before—except perhaps Betsy. And with Betsy there had been no demonstration of love between them.

Lesley regretted with all her heart the love she had wasted on Alec. If only she could come to Dan with that surprise and astonishment which are the first attributes of first love. She hadn't told Dan about Alec yet. Some day she would, but at the moment she couldn't bare to spoil the pristine beauty of his love for her.

Coolaroo was to have its second wedding before the season was finished and winter softened the impact of sun and wind on the plains. Mrs. Collins and Lesley conspired together over fashion magazines before they decided on a wedding dress and sent to Sydney by air mail for it to be made. It was to be brought direct by plane by an old family friend of the Baxters who had decided to come to the West for a prolonged stay. The wedding dress was to be a ballerina-length dress of white lace over a full taffeta underskirt. Lesley would wear a large picture hat with roses on it.

"Roses like saucers," Lesley said. "I've always wanted one like that. It wouldn't be any good for anything but a royal garden party or a wedding."

"Who knows? You might have both," Cousin Con said. Someone, could it have been Dan, said that next time a Baxter went to England to look at machinery or buy stud stock they would all go.

Alice was rapturous. The rains had cooled the land down, the green grass shooting had softened the contours of the landscape and Lesley's decision to stay in Australia had reorientated her whole outlook on "out-back" life. She and Randolph were much more obvious lovers—now that all had fallen out so well—than Lesley and Dan. With Lesley and

Dan it was still something to be wondered about. Each in the privacy of his own heart.

Betsy had come through on the radio.

"Thought you'd stay," she had said laconically. "Better to stay for love than because you're marooned. That's what we are up this way. Guess we'll get through for the wedding anyway. Neil says he's going walkabout if we can't fly out. Did you fall off that horse on purpose, Lesley?"

Lesley almost wondered that herself. She had thought how much a broken leg would have helped her and she told the contrite Bill this.

"It wasn't your fault, Bill. I think I was going to do something silly. Fate meant me to. I didn't want to go home, you know, and three cracked ribs and a sprained ankle is a very small price to pay for Dan keeping me."

Bill had been scarcely seen round the homestead this last day or two. And here he was taking Christine into Ninety Mile End without any of the usual to-do that was attached to arrivals and departures at Coolaroo.

While Dan had stood watching Lesley drink her tea his ears had caught the sound of the Utility as it moved away from the stables. He looked puzzled.

"Who's got the 'Ute'?" he wondered. He listened.

"That's Bill. Can always tell the way he revs up the engine and shoots those gears through Where'd he be going now?"

Lesley looked at him in astonishment. Didn't he know Christine had just left?

Cousin Con came round the corner of the veranda with the doctor. They had been down to the natives' quarters to see a sick child.

"Has Bill taken Christine for a drive?" she asked Dan. "I didn't know they were going out on the run?"

Dan shrugged.

"I guess he's found another colt down at Mars he wants her to try. He's spent a solid week taking Christine out to find her a mount."

"If old Macintosh wants to buy a Coolaroo colt for Christine you see you get a good price, Dan. Macintosh never lowered a price for a fellow pastoralist in his life."

Lesley looked from one face to another, bewildered. Didn't they know? Should she tell?

She opened her mouth to speak and then caught the doctor's eye. He gave her a decisive and informative wink. Lesley shut her mouth suddenly and looked in her cup.

"Want some more?" Dan was looking at her and had forgotten Bill and Christine. When the doctor had gone away and Cousin Con had gone inside Dan sat down in his easy-chair and asked Lesley—across the space—how long the doctor had said before they could get married.

"You're too far away to tell," Lesley said.

"It's safe over here," Dan said. "I might hurt those ribs if I put my arms round you—the way I want to put them round you."

Suddenly Lesley knew that he meant it.

"A fortnight," she said quietly.

Dan remained looking out over the garden, and they were silent for quite a long time.

"Does Cousin Con still want to know about your 'going-away dress'?" he asked at length with a smile.

"She does. And Alice is puzzled to the point of indignation. But I'm not telling them."

Dan smiled.

"Do you know," he said at length, "unless my ears deceive me that plane's landed. The Doc must have come down."

"Somewhere near Mars would it be?"

"By the sound of it, it could be. Wonder if he's got engine trouble?"

"I think he's got heart trouble."

"Heart trouble? What do you mean by that?"

"I think he's come down at Mars to pick up Bill and Christine. I guess he'll take them into Ninety Mile End where they'll get married and he'll be the best man."

Dan had shot to his feet.

"What do you mean? He can't do that! They can't do that! That girl's in my care. . . ."

He seemed thunderstruck.

"Sit down, Dan," Lesley said. "I don't know anything, I'm only guessing. You wouldn't have given your permission if they had asked you, would you?"

"A Macintosh marry one of my jackaroos? What are you thinking of, Lesley? Old Macintosh will raise the whole North-west and every pastoralist in Australia on to me."

"I guess that's why they've done it this way. It will be too late to unmarry them, won't it? And anyway, Bill Daley's not really your jackaroo, is he? He's more—a kind of stock manager—or something, isn't he?"

Dan stood gazing at Lesley, partly in anger and partly in astonishment.

"What are you talking about? He's just a raking hire

186

hand, and when Macintosh hears about it there's nothing he'll stop at."

"But you'll be safe. We'll be away on our honeymoon. He won't be able to find us."

"Listen, Lesley. You've got no sense of responsibility about this thing. I'm *in loco parentis* where that girl is concerned. Any girl who stays on my property for that matter."

"Me, too?"

"Of course, you too. What do you think I sit over there in that chair for? Do you think I like sitting half a mile away from you? Do you think I like kissing you three times a day according to the clock and to prescription?"

Lesley started to laugh.

"Oh, Dan!" she said. "I thought it was because you were shy."

"I am shy. I'm not used to kissing people. As for that girl—I'm answerable for her."

"Dan, come here—just a minute."

The fire was dying out of him and he sat on the edge of Lesley's lounge. She put her arms round his neck.

He groaned.

"Did the doctor say a whole fortnight, Lesley?"

"Fourteen days. That's according to the clock and according to doctor's prescription."

She kissed him.

"How do you think they feel, Dan? Just because it's Christine and Bill and not Dan and Lesley it doesn't mean they feel any different."

Dan caught hold of her wrists with one hand.

"I've got to do something about it," he groaned.

"Of course you have," Lesley said softly. "You've got to get in touch with Ninety Mile End and see they're properly married. Then you've got to promote Bill Daley."

"They'll get married all right if the doc's got anything to do with it. He's always doing this sort of thing. I don't know why he doesn't call that raking plane of his a marriage bureau instead of a flying ambulance."

"... and send a telegram to 'old Macintosh'—'CHRISTINE HAPPILY MARRIED TO MY MANAGER TO-DAY. DALEY TAKING OVER COOLAROO DOWNS AS FROM THE FOURTEENTH WHILE I GO ON MY OWN HONEYMOON. RANDOLPH AND WIFE TAKING A SECOND HONEYMOON TO ENGLAND SHORTLY SO DALEY WILL BE FIRST MAN ON COOLAROO FOR A LONG TIME. SIGNED THE MASTER OF COOLAROO. BY ORDER ...'"

Dan looked at Lesley, speechless. But Lesley had a woman's

way of winning now. She put her arms round him and held
him tight.

"Dan . . ."

He said nothing because he couldn't. Lesley's mouth was
pressed on his.

The wedding day broke calm and clear and cool.

Not so many came to Dan's wedding to the English girl
from over the sea, not because they didn't love him so well
but because many were still marooned behind flooding rivers
or beyond bogging landing grounds.

The Brennans and the Macfarlanes were there, however
in full force. Christine and Bill were back, wed and gloriously
happy. Christine's sad moment with Lesley on the veranda
the day she had eloped was now explained away. She had
not been sad because of Dan but because she had hated going
without telling Lesley. Open and sunny by nature, Christine
had not liked to take on—even for a few hours—the character
of deceit.

But rightly, had they waited to inform their friends an
relatives, there would have been no wedding. Old Macintosh
—with a bevy of brothers and cousins, descended on Coolaroo
from the air like an avenging god. He brought a gun an
came up the rise from the plane that had brought him with the
weapon not only loaded but pointed.

Dan, his hat pushed on the back of his head, went calmly
to meet him.

Two hours later when "old Macintosh" had looked at the
account books in the Coolaroo office and some stud sheep an
a crack Coolaroo colt or two in the stables, he consented t
put his gun away.

It was Lesley who had the bright idea of showing him th
rising walls of Dan's house.

"That ought to suit 'em," Dan said. "It'll be a better
house than the homestead. Bill can take the lease of Venus-
that's the poddy station beyond Mars and the ranges—an
run it as an independent station."

"Old Macintosh" had another look at the Coolaroo accoun
books and decided he'd stay for the night—possibly break
fast. Actually he stayed a week. When Bill Daley came
home and Macintosh saw him on horseback his new father-in
law grunted his approval.

"Better'n one of these city blokes," he admitted. "H
knows a sheep from a steer, and, by God, he can ride."

Dan was so tired after these efforts he omitted to kiss Lesley
more than twice a day for two days before their wedding.

"Darling, wait till *our* honeymoon—I'm no good at kissing in a half-hearted way. Are you sure you don't mind living at the homestead?"

"It's where I want to live. Perhaps we could modernise some parts of it—if Cousin Con doesn't mind."

"Cousin Con will love it. She just wants to go on living here with you and me and Alice and Randolph for ever and ever and ever."

"So do I."

"Randolph can do the modernising while we're away."

"Will we be away long?"

"All depends on the cyclones. Do you think you'll mind a cyclone in the Timor Sea?"

"I'd rather just have pearls and coral and flying fish."

They were married just as Randolph and Alice had been married. Dan did not carry Lesley over the steps of Coolaroo. Instead of that, Cousin Con stood at the top and took both her hands and led her over the threshold into the house. She kissed the new member of the Baxter family tenderly.

"I never meant Dan to let you go," she said. "If he hadn't proposed in time, I would have done it myself."

The Brennans, the Macfarlanes, Betsy, Brian, Neil and all the rouseabouts, stockmen and blacks ate inordinate amounts of the beautiful colourful food. Lesley could hardly eat anything at all. Every now and again she would lift up her head and her eyes would find Dan's face. She couldn't believe she was really married to him. He was hers.

"Do you want anything, dear?" he asked.

"Dan—if only the clock would stand still—I want to stay like this."

"Well, I don't," he said with a grin. "I want a honeymoon."

When Lesley went into her room to change, Alice and Mrs. Collins came anxiously in.

"What *are* you going to wear?"

Lesley had her lovely wedding dress over her head and off. She went to the wardrobe and took out a gaily-coloured shirt and new jodhpurs. Out came her leggings and brightly-polished boots.

"All these," she said.

They looked at her astonished.

"Aren't you going with Joe?"

"Not on your life," she said gaily. "Where Dan and I are going there wouldn't be any room for Joe Brennan. That sleeping-bag that belonged to Dan's parents only holds two—at a squeeze."

"Lesley, what are you doing?" wailed Alice. "Where are you going?"

"No aeroplanes or big cities for me," said Lesley as she pulled on one boot. "I'm going for my honeymoon the old-fashioned way. I'm going the way Mrs. Brennan did, and Cousin Con, herself. And Dan's parents. We're going by horseback and our pillows will be our saddles. And when we're tired of it—which will be about Ninety Mile End—there'll be Bill Halidane waiting for us with that pearling lugger he salvaged when he first came through at the time of Alice's wedding. And then——"

"A pearling lugger!" said Alice aghast. "At this time of the year!"

"—by way of a pearling lugger"—Lesley pulled on the other boot—"by Timor to the Arefura and by the Sundra Sea to China. Through the Archipelagos of the Moon to Coral Island—and—right into Heaven!"

Alice sat down on the bed with a flop, but Mrs. Collins stood by the door and watched Lesley's shining face as she recited the way of Dan as he had gone in the wars.

Her own eyes had tears in them.

Thus it was Dan and Lesley rode away towards the end of the day. Long after they had gone down the slope towards the river and Mars, Mrs. Collins stood on the veranda looking to the west.

Randolph put his arm along her shoulder.

"They'll be all right, Con," he said. "Dan loves camping and Lesley's just aching to get ants in her food and mosquitoes under her net."

"I wasn't thinking of them. I was thinking of a day over thirty years ago."

"When the Mater and Pater rode off down there?"

"No. When I rode down there myself."

A mile away towards the river Dan reined in his horse. He sat—his back a little curved, his foot long in the stirrup—the perfect silhouette of an Australian stockman. His hat was tilted a little as he scanned the horizon.

"What is it, Dan?"

"I was looking to see if all was well with the run—a habit, I suppose."

Lesley thought there would always be a will-o'-the-wisp part of Dan that would for ever wander round the boundaries of Coolaroo—watching, waiting, dreaming. He would never be wholly hers.

She wasn't sure she didn't love him more for the wanderer that was in him.

Dan swung his leg over the saddle and dismounted. He took her bridle and looked up at her.

"I don't have to stay so far away from you—now."

"No, Dan."

"Come down off that horse, darling. I want to kiss you."

THE END